AUTHOR'S NOTE

Write about what you know they say. Well there is a great deal of *How to Disappear Completely* that I didn't know about. Or rather didn't know I knew if you catch my drift. Sometimes I wish I could unlearn it all. Other times I'm grateful.

When writing I would often listen to the line "I'm not here, this isn't happening". And though the book is mine – I'm glad that its story isn't. That much I do know.

How To Disappear Completely came about because of happiness, two of the greatest albums of all time and one other person. Having finished this book – made it permanent and then sent it away – I'm thankful they, at least, are still with me.

STEFAN DEMETRIOU

HOWTODISAPPEAR
COMPLETELY

reverb

© Stefan Demetriou 2005

The moral right of the author has been asserted

reverb is an imprint of Osiris Press Ltd

This edition first published 2005 by

Osiris Press Ltd
PO Box 615
Oxford OX1 9AL

www.readreverb.com

A CIP catalogue record for this book is available from the British Library

ISBN 1 905315 06 6

Set in Baskerville 12/14.2pt

Printed in Britain by
Lightning Source, Milton Keynes

For Sarah

I was just guessing
At numbers and figures
Pulling the puzzles apart
Questions of science, science and progress
Do not speak as loud as my heart
Tell me you love me
Come back and haunt me
Oh and I rush to the start
Running in circles, chasing our tails
Coming back as we are

Nobody said it was easy.

– 'The Scientist', Coldplay

PROLOGUE

I have no idea why my wife left me. I wasn't unfaithful, I've never been violent and I'm fairly sure that I wasn't that bad in bed. That sex wasn't always in bed reassures me of this; it suggests spontaneity and passion. Ruth and I definitely had passion. We fucked on a train once.

Of course sex wasn't always so memorable – or rhythmic. Ruth and I had routine and disappointment too; the usual suspects "I'm tired" or even that clichéd line – "Sorry, I have a headache".

We never slept apart though and, overall, things were more than okay.

No, sex wasn't a factor in our separation. I'm certain that Ruth didn't want to see what it could be like with someone else. This was partly due to her character but mostly because, partner-wise, I was her number twelve. I don't mind admitting here that she was (only) my second. And with this bit of information it's immediately apparent that our early sexual careers weren't similar. Not better and not worse, you understand, just different. Not that Ruth was promiscuous and not that I was shy, as such. Purely that she went out, saw opportunities and took them. I stayed in, read books, listened to music and wrote, mostly.

I met Ruth long before we actually got together. We went to the same university though we didn't know each other back then. That would all come much later. At that time our paths rarely crossed. I was English Literature while she was Politics. I was from Essex, she wasn't.

In fact we only spoke once during the whole of my three undergraduate years. I was with some friends in a pub called The Black Griffin, when Ruth, sitting at an adjacent table, leaned over and asked me the time. "8.42" was the uninspired, but accurate, answer I gave. And I shouldn't have bothered with the detail. Ruth only heard the "8". By the time I added the minutes, she was already back to her friends, throwing an all-too-brief "thanks" in my direction. And why would she linger? She didn't know me so there was no need for our conversation to continue. It all happened so quickly, I didn't even have the chance to remove my glasses, let alone think about what I might have done differently.

Of course, there was space for that later – back in the safety of my room. 'Ruth Carmichael asking me the time' became the most significant moment of my romantic career to date. Accordingly I gave it the attention I felt it deserved. Replaying the conversation from every possible angle, endlessly looking for evidence that Ruth was interested in me. It was a welcome distraction from the novels of Charles Dickens.

It was also, to put it simply, a 'result', given Ruth's social standing amongst the first year and her perfect smile. I didn't harbour unrealistic aims of engineering a relationship out of such separateness. And don't go thinking our eventual union was a story of one-sided passion finally requited.

If I'm honest, I hadn't spent the years that had passed infatuated.

If I'm being truthful here – and that's the whole point isn't it? – I had kept Ruth in my life. In a photo taken at our first year Ball back at university. She'd been captured inside a shot aimed at a group of my friends. I got the film developed and there was Ruth, standing to the side, staring off into the distance, no doubt at some rugby-playing suitor from Richmond. Even like that – unposed, unplanned – she looked great, her blonde hair up, wearing a long cream dress that revealed little but suggested more.

The picture's adhesiveness to my life held no great significance, I certainly never allocated it any. That would come much later too. As it contained my friends, the image travelled with me when I graduated, part of a random collection of student memorabilia. One day I realised I'd always loved Ruth, but then, at that time, she wasn't looking at me. The accidental composition makes it abundantly clear. And that was fine. I'd come to terms with it – eventually.

Anyway, during my formative sexual career competing affections lay frequently elsewhere, for example with feelings cultivated for months over a cultivated girl in my Shakespeare class. A girl who said things about Fortinbras that only I agreed with. A girl who almost became my first after a Christmas party, until I threw up in her Santa hat and fled. But she wasn't Ruth.

Subsequently I had a few similar encounters throughout my student days. Everything of potential but nothing of substance. I remained a virgin until I was 21 and a night spent with a woman of a certain age.

And yet by the time Ruth and I got it together, I didn't

overcompensate. Things were not uneven between us. She didn't have the emotional or physical upper hand. We were balanced. I need to make that clear.

It sounds unnecessary to say it, but I'm not bad looking. I'm not boring either. I certainly wasn't nervous. I wanted to be with Ruth for all the right reasons – she made me laugh, I fancied her like mad and I craved her opinion on every subject. Fortunately she liked me too.

So I got the girl and she got me. We got each other.

Imbalance isn't the reason she left me.

There was nothing monumental when fate dealt us another chance four years after our first contact, after we had both been spat out of university and the pressure was on to carve out a place in the world. Ruth and I met again, each defined by the employment we'd found and each bound by a lifestyle we both wanted to achieve. An underpaid local-paper reporter (me) and a struggling PR assistant (her) with the same thing on their minds. Solvency.

Economic disparity is not the reason she left me.

Our relations, once they began, a year after graduation, were always equal too. Twelve months spent sharing a flat, earning the same amount of money, with a similar number of people to meet for a drink. One mutual happiness. Sex became a shared process too, a learning curve for us both. We were quickly able to talk about what we both liked doing. I told her what I wanted. She said the same. We didn't want there to be any room for forced lies or withheld desires; we determined that everything would be open.

I knew from the start that she was the one. We both asserted that if we offered everything to each other we'd definitely last the distance. Ruth talked of visiting Australia and making her own curtains. I was free to imagine grandchildren, several photo-albums of holidays and a garden shed filled with tools.

In all this the only thing neither us planned for was Ruth not being around. But one day she left me.

But it wasn't through frustration, or wanting different things, and it wasn't commitment or lack of. These aren't the reasons she went. I'm convinced that there has to be something else to blame, if not someone. Definitely not someone.

And it wasn't claustrophobia in general that led to her departure.

Our distant hopes of a long marriage and joint retirement were simply that. Distant. True, I saw a long path that stretched out, leading to a final destination. But it wasn't premeditated. It wasn't planned. In our present life I'd attempted romance, wasn't bad at spontaneity and even surprised her with aggression. She'd been thrilled once when I went off at some arsehole who was giving her friends a hard time in the pub.

And not that she left me because I was jealous or over-protective or angry or temperamental.

So why?

If Ruth had actually called that evening, that well-remembered final Friday as I waited for her to come home. If she had called and said "Sorry Ben, you're too close to your brother. I feel shut out. It's just not working for me" I'd probably be okay by now. I would have got over it. If she had called to say, "I'm really sorry Ben, but I've fallen in love with someone else, I'm leaving you" then I almost certainly wouldn't be over it, but at least I would know.

Only she never called.

I stared at my phone, increasingly worried ink scribbles forming on the Yellow Pages and anything else to hand. Violent jagged lines and elliptical shapes that made no sense. And still she didn't arrive.

The time dragged. I swore at the neighbour's cat which had begun to meow constantly. I abused a hapless wrong number. After a while I called all her friends who told me not to worry and then called her parents, who I told not to worry. Knowing that they would and knowing I'd feel better if they were.

Minutes lapsed into hours. But no sign of Ruth. Nothing.

There had been no point getting in the car. I'd already concocted a false-truth that she must have gone with her colleagues from the Pitcher & Piano to some tacky club on Leicester Square. I reasoned that her mobile phone wouldn't be working wherever they'd stumbled to. I'd assumed she'd call me when she got out, contrite and in tears. It would have been out of character but it was my best guess. She was going to call and explain that she'd got too drunk and had literally gone along with everyone else. I distinctly remember phoning my brother who came over immediately but not before I slated Anita, a woman she worked with that I'd always had down as a bad influence. It never occurred to me that she might not come home. Ever.

She never called. She never explained.

And I'd really like to ask Ruth myself but it's an impossibility. I have no opportunity. There's a reason for this, the second significant detail of our separation. Namely, and this is pretty decisive, that I have no idea where she is. I have no way of contacting her, not even through a sympathetic third party; a him or her who has pragmatically kept both names active in an address book. This is not because her friends maliciously picked sides or moved away en masse. No. This is because no one – her friends, colleagues or relatives – has any idea where she is.

My wife is missing. My Ruth is gone and I don't understand anything any more. Everything has changed. I felt terrible that Saturday morning after the longest night of my life when normally immaculate, much-criticised by me, Anita turned up at 8am dressed in a tracksuit and looking like Billy Bremner circa 1972 – with a team of gung-ho volunteers ready to help.

My torment consists of not knowing if my wife still breathes.

And I've got to the stage where I feel I would actually welcome any indictment, however damning, however painful it would be to bear. I was a bastard, I was an embarrassment – anything. I cannot convey how much I need some basic information. In fact when it comes down to it, I no longer even need to understand my wife's decision, but simply require some evidence of the decision itself. A blatant untruth would be fine. She'd feed me some absurd line and it would be enough. Something like "You never took out the rubbish" (I rarely missed a Wednesday night) or "You didn't eat broccoli" (I love it).

I'm being serious. Even if she came back and cited my inability to perform, on that night before the day that she left. The Thursday night when neither of us had felt like intimacy and had slept isolated as a result, barely touching, only breathing, curled up in opposite sides of the duvet, tussling for supremacy. If she declared – "I was worried about your post-pub impotence, it's the beginning of the end" – that too would now be enough. But any reason, like the phone call, like

Ruth herself, like my fucking dick only 24 hours earlier, never came. And two whole years later, it still hasn't.

Nothing makes sense. Nothing stands up.

Perpetual uncertainty. That's what this is. We were in love, we were together – and now, well now we're not. Not together anyway, I'm not sure whether the love part endures.

And so I pray that she did leave because of something terrible I'd done. I pray that it was my fault. That I was boring. That I was a bastard. That I had a limp, useless dick or fuck it, that I left the rubbish piled up. Anything.

And you have to understand that most of all, I pray that Ruth left because she wanted to. That she had a choice.

And now when I look at that university photo I no longer see any of my old friends – only her, staring off into the distance – in a different direction. Sometimes I see the hair first, sometimes the dress – but always Ruth. At least she's always there.

I lost the girl.

Two years of praying. Nothing makes sense. Only that she isn't here. Nothing else adds up.

BOOK I:
DIRECTIONAL

1: TORMENT

It's all part of a process. A formula. An equation even, as my brother might say. Alarm, plus shower, minus aftershave, plus train, plus elevator, plus desk – multiply by smile always equals the start of my day. The same. Every day it begins the same.

And it follows that already, right here in the office, I am out of control. You might think I sound paranoid. And you'd be right. All of you. Right now I'm beyond stability, no longer calm, no longer secure. It's Monday morning and my life is quiet chaos.

It's important to state that I don't enjoy this. This is not how I want things to be. Doubting everyone and everything around me except codified language – the basic materials of my profession. Taking comfort in sentence, syllable and syntax. Words that can be tied down, manipulated – that can be controlled. I like that. I need that. Like ropes tethering a rabid dog they provide safety, they afford distance, space from myself and my surroundings. They are everything to me.

I guess it's why I check words for a living. An ironic phrase that, 'for a living'. In reality it's anything but; at the moment anyway. My name is Ben Carter, I'm 35, live in London and am employed by a magazine titled *Mentor*, subtitled 'direction for life'. A monthly periodical with an editorial remit as relentless and hopelessly twenty-first century as its title – men's lifestyle. Thoughts of life, thoughts of aspiring manhood permeate everything I do. It's all too easy to feel inadequate on a daily basis. At *Mentor* we cover fashion, travel, interiors, arts, sports – the usual suspects. We promote a world of chiselled perfection – edges honed, lines drawn. A current mantra around the office, an office that has been team-built and bonded in all the right ways, consists of exclaiming belief in our readers and most importantly ourselves. Apparently this is necessary. Except I can't. No go. No can do. I need to be excused, thank you very much. I'd like to bring in a note for teacher, or say 'I've forgotten my kit' or maybe just faint right now and be sent home to get better – but it wouldn't make any difference. Not really.

You see my problem is not actually my professional environment; it's more than an inability to join in. At least here, right in the heartland of Gucci and Giorgio, I manage to survive. I find room to hide in the words. Somehow they help me breathe. This is important,

I don't want to sound like one of those disaffected office drones that populate a sizeable portion of the novels published since the close of the last century. No, my job is not my problem.

But even with the comfort of raw copy on my monitor, today is proving more difficult than normal. Today is an anniversary, a reminder that sharpens the pain and screams to be heard. My desk calendar, the Far Side by Gary Larson – a present from my brother – tells me today will be two years. At least it tells me this humorously through a drawing of a dog trying to ensnare a cat with a trap inexpertly marked as 'Cat Fud'.

And it's only five to ten. And there are at least eight hours of pagination, layout and proofing left. I'm not normally this bad, I usually have an emotional strategy in place for the day (and every day after that). A cycle that lasts for each issue and its associated deadlines. Simply to cope, to avoid, to endure. To smile as I scan copy extolling the virtues of Dunhill lighters, Alessi kitchenware and reclaimed surgical wash-basins. But today sitting here, I realise I can't go on like this, or indeed, pretending to like this. Where has the time gone? I feel like something, or someone – most probably me – has got to give.

And of course, I'm useless at giving and even worse at receiving. When Ruth had spent too much on that Bvlgari watch for my thirtieth, I'd simply felt embarrassed.

"People don't give to receive" she'd said by way of justification, folding the carefully considered lilac wrapping paper I'd roughly discarded into a manageable square.

And she'd meant it. She'd really meant it. Ruth was always sincere, always true. And I'd let her out of my sight. Hence my struggle here today. It's a direct link. From one point to another. Straight with inevitable resolution. I'm left isolated, unable to give – and even if I could, what's the point? There'll be no one there to receive me.

You've probably ascertained that for too long now I've been distracted and hopelessly disoriented. My mind wanders. Fuck, my mind wonders. I'll prove it with the next sentence. I can feel my heart always. Sense its insistent purpose in every part of my being. Convinced right now as it demands to be heard in my ears and pleads to be felt in the dull throb of my fingers. I'm certain it is against me.

Take a breath and slow down. Grow up even. Put it out of your mind. But it's in my mind. And still it comes, regular, regular, regular. As does the gentle hum of office banter, reaching my desk in impenetrable form. Until I eventually make out, across the floor, fragments of a discussion ensuing about a programme shown last night on breast reduction.

"Nipples looked like fucking roast potatoes!"

"And that bit with the scab!"

Given my distance from the protagonists (more than simply geographic) plus the significant fact that I missed it, I have no way of contributing. Instead I listen to my heart.

I think about release. A wank. About the logistics involved. I am at work, so it would have to be quick. I can do quick. I'm an expert in quick. I search for the necessary stimuli, rapidly processing assorted images, experiences and vaguely-formed erotic ideas all helpfully stored for just such an occasion. Mentally flipping through a rolodex of impurity. I think about Ruth, about our honeymoon in Florence, the Arno, Il Duomo, her breasts, but the impulses are against me, providing nothing. It doesn't seem appropriate, especially not today, and I am forced to continue my search through my own private neural library of shame. I seize on the image of a woman on the train this morning as she grasped for the handrail and momentarily lost control. And there's something there. It's minimal but enough to get the job done.

Forty seconds to the toilet, left-hand cubicle – the one with the chipped cistern – striding across the brown marble floor. Jason, our Features Editor, is standing in front of the mirror making minute, but doubtless vital, adjustments to his hair. I say "hi". I have no choice. I hate him but he has no idea. Jason is wearing Cerutti. Brown. His fucking belt matches his shoes. He is in control. He actually believes the stuff we print. It's real to him. It's, like I said, lifestyle. Jason is lifestyle. Jason thinks nothing of using the phrases 'diffusion', 'colour-way' and perhaps worst of all – 'hair product'.

We briefly discuss the game last night, playing out a scene with dialogue that is universal and already written. I stare beyond him into the mirror as he speaks, anxious to get going. Get it going.

"Couldn't believe it. 2-0 down as well! Unbelievable goal. 30 yards out!"

Jason uses exclamation marks. I hate that. I think I hate him.

Maybe hate is a bit strong. Let's just say he's not a role model. He's waiting for me to respond. I remember the match last night as a distraction from the corner of the room. I used to be more interested, supported West Ham, going to most games; and now? Now I remember enough to get by.

"Deserved... almost... offside. Good... yeah," I say, dropping words in my rush to complete an adequate response. I do this a lot. People notice. People add this to what they assume. I'm past caring. This isn't the nineties, it's no longer necessary to care. Only to observe accepted social practice. This is commonly believed to be the same thing but it isn't. Jason dries his hands on the drier and leaves with a wink.

And so I wank. It takes longer than normal. See, I have normality in my life. A series of stable benchmarks against which my routine actions and emotions can be measured. However lost I get, I take comfort in the knowledge that I am, in some way, aware of what normality can be. And today, here, sitting in this left-hand cubicle, my wank is taking longer than normal.

I begin with initial thoughts of the Piccadilly Line lurching suddenly into Holborn. A useful image for the job in hand. And then thoughts of the woman carrying her bags from Dickens & Jones, reaching for the handrail. Straining. Yes. Exerting. Yes. This is working. It's definitely working. The train heaves. The woman reaches further, lifting, lifting, lift – shit, someone enters the toilet while I'm in mid... I'm looking for the right word here, what is it? Mid-stroke? Mid-tug? Grasp, I'll go with mid-grasp, it conveys the desperation. Someone enters the toilet in mid-grasp. I pause and feel entirely ridiculous. Sitting there, dick in hand, steadying my breathing, aware of every sound. And conscious of my heart, regular, regular, regular.

This is getting tedious. My neighbour appears to be in for the long-haul, serious movement, not even preparing the ground with toilet paper. He's straight to it, going through the motions. Confidence in his own ability, unashamed, no need for muffling. It suggests a certain type of character. My mind considers this suggestion from all directions, there's nothing else to do. I find supporting evidence in his choice of stall. Surely, given my occupation of the left-hand – of the three available – booths, a reasonable selection would have been the far-right. Leaving space, observing unwritten social etiquette. It's the same principle with urinals. Fuck it, it's the same principle with tube seats, car-parking spaces and stools at a bar. But to choose the middle, the one directly next to mine, cements a theory of character. Arrogant disregard. Suggested balls. Suggested authority. The kind of guy who speaks of Philippe Starck citrus squeezers while he pisses. Or points out a recurrent badminton-induced groin problem in the gym showers. I surmise that it's Lewis and my erection goes down fast. Lewis Franklin, publisher of our title and four others in a corporate stable that includes fashion bible *Tanked* (don't ask) and *Friction* – the widely-praised up-and-coming book cornering a sizeable portion of the luxury car market. Lewis Franklin, all firm handshake, immaculate smile and this season's charcoal Ungaro. My editor's boss. A success story.

So, and get this for pathetic, I tear off some paper, actually pretend to wipe my arse – complete with rustling sound effects – repeat steps 1 to 2, before standing, placing dick (now soft) back in Marks & Spencer's finest, flushing and exiting, past him, as fast as possible. Unsatisfied – a certain type of character.

The rest of the morning evolves with little incident. Playing out the usual. I read and rewrite. I banter with the art girls and study the papers. I scan the proof-copies of upcoming novels that have arrived ready to be reviewed. These routinely manage to make me smile, which is nice – I'm not genetically a miserable git. I also read with interest because I like to monitor the style *du jour* as Wayne, our culinary contributing ed, might say. (Wayne says *du jour* after everything.) At the moment there is a certain style uniformity that's intriguing me. It's as if everyone has been on the same creative-writing programme at some cottage in Devon. The current vogue a George Eliot meets Stephen Fry benevolent, omnipotent, venerable narrator. Like any good unpublished author, I always think I could do better and, even if this isn't true, it's worthwhile taking a moment to imagine how I would portray my own life in this manner. Besides I can't be fucked with work and no one's emailing me.

Ben Carter survived each day by imagining the daylight hours as nothing more than a process. A formula. An equation even. Alarm, plus shower, minus aftershave, plus train, plus handrail, plus elevator, plus desk – multiplied by smile always equalled the start of the day. The same. Everyday it began the same. Such mathematical precision was difficult for Ben who had previously sought a life lived less coldly.

He was not naturally disposed to such behaviour. He hadn't always felt like this, hadn't specifically requested the mistrust that relentlessly arrived each morning at 10.06 when the lift doors spat him out on the 17th floor; a mistrust that unleashed itself and took hold with each "How was your weekend?" and "Would you like a coffee?". In such an environment, and given his situation, a healthy degree of doubt about everyone and everything around him was able to flourish, unchecked by such trivialities as rational thought or what constitutes good manners nowadays.

For Ben everything was uncertain except codified language – the basic materials of his profession. He took comfort in sentence, syllable and syntax. Words that could be tied down and manipulated – that could be controlled. He liked that. He needed that. Like ropes tethering a rabid dog they provided safety, afforded distance, allowed space from himself and his surroundings. They were everything in the midst of so much nothing. Order that yet stimulated – that had the power to keep his soul alive.

You get my drift.

I notice that the clock has reached one and feel liberated to explore the internet – clearly within what could be construed by any observer as lunchtime. My time, as far as it goes. In preparation I tilt the screen away from my nearest colleague, Laura, deep in yet another emotive conversation with her dog's vet. Apparently Samuel, an Airedale, has a limp. Evidently Laura has a problem. But I've shown the right amount of concern when the subject's been raised. And I like Laura, she's sweet. Lonely but sweet. I have every faith in her ability to eventually settle down. She almost managed it once but the guy dumped her on Christmas Eve. She got over it. She bought the dog and never looked back. In fact when Ruth first left me, Laura suggested I take Max, one of Samuel's offspring. I declined. It was hardly a suitable replacement. I briefly wonder whether Laura knows what today is? What it means for me. I doubt it. It's not really an event the office would think to acknowledge. There's no set procedure, not like a birthday or someone leaving – occasions that ensure some peroxide secretary trawls the floor with an oversize Hallmark card; a brown envelope filled with coins and the occasional surprised fiver from someone whose birthday is coming up and perhaps wants to set a philanthropic precedent.

Realising I've been staring at Laura for over a minute, I return to my monitor and the web. The bar creeps along the bottom of the screen, attempting to deliver the required page, until I'm in business, the world at my fingertips or something. I have mixed feelings about the internet. On the one hand it educates, informs and fascinates – on the other it reminds me of the limitations of my current existence, contained as it is within a bloody machine. But I like the words; endless sequential characters on any subject imaginable. And the way it levels the playing field, each user at the same level, anonymous and unfettered. There is no hierarchy that separates a nun surfing in Lesotho to some pimp wannabe masturbating in Leicester – and they can even have a conversation. It won't last though, limits, passwords, access restricted to those with the cash. It's already happening. But for now – for now the possibilities remain endless. The internet is still opportunity. This is all true – but it still won't tell me why I can't stop thinking of a woman retrieving her things from where they lay on the floor of a tube carriage. Items kicked around by commuters eager to depart and interchange with the Central Line – a prospect infinitely easier than interchanging with each other.

My page is delivered. A quick look around and I'm okay. no one's looking. Of course I'm wrong. I'm always wrong. Unwanted interruption is a persistent theme of my current life.

"Coming for a pint fella? Shame to waste the spring rays. Stu and I want to get a couple in before the Miyake launch at The Sanderson."

This piece of dialogue is so absurd, so post new-lad, so utterly lifestyle that I almost laugh. Moreover, I almost choke when I realise it's directed at me. Jason is hovering and waiting with Stu – one of our freelancers – for an answer. By the way, don't worry. I've already clicked the x to make the net, and Gisele, disappear. Like all in this corporate new century I've become expert in this thoroughly modern and *de rigeur* test of dexterity. A finely tuned reaction necessary to exit before anyone glimpses my screen, at least not anyone I can see. But it's okay, I got enough. I saw enough. Christ, I'm 35 and sincerely need a life. Sincere or otherwise – just any kind of life. Anyone's. Please.

Jason's still waiting. Why do I dislike him? Do I need a reason? He's waiting for me to respond. I can't process what I'm supposed to do. This is all outside standard procedure. A deviation. An offer I could refuse. I surprise myself.

"Sure." This from me, remarkably.

I stand quickly. He smiles and shouts to four of the other guys, only two of whom are straight.

"Beer. Now. Then models pouring champagne…"

Grunts of assent fire back. Laura isn't included. She expects this and this is understood by all. Everything is understood by all except me. Anyway she's waiting for her vet to call back while pretending to be engrossed in subbing a piece on sarongs for our Fashion Flashbacks page. I had protested that a retro-piece on Beckham circa '98 hardly qualifies as historic however my sphere of influence here is decidedly un-influential. Don't misunderstand me, I'm no junior – in fact I'm chief sub at *Mentor*, a job-title important but with none of the mainstream cachet of the magazine world. I'm used to such a role. It's a constant reminder of playing football as a kid – endlessly number 12 – carrying the first aid box and the oranges but never making the first team. As I grew I moved from substitute to sub-editing, proofing other people's words. The meaning altered but the inference entirely the same. A valuable, but supporting, player. Stuck on the editorial sidelines.

Five past three and we're still in the bar, newly renamed Olga's – in theme pub terms Ukrainian is apparently the new Irish. Hadn't you heard? It's happening all over. O'Grady's changing to Rasputin's – with the R predictably backwards; Maggie Cassidy's to Dynamo Kiev. In fact the food and drink team at *Mentor*, the aforementioned *du jour*-loving Wayne, are doing a feature for July – 'Back in the USSBAR'. I know. The strapline was Jason's idea. He has many more where that came from.

It's April but the sun's shining so we're sitting out on the street. I check my Nokia for messages – but only 'cause the other guys are. It's something to do. I never have any messages. Ruth certainly doesn't call anymore. This doesn't surprise me. It's hard to leave a text message when you've been gone for two years. I've only had a lager and I feel melancholic but I guess this is one up from my am sense of despair. It's progress, but it won't last. Especially as I have to head back to the office. Before long Jason and Stu grab a cab and 'rock off' (*sic*) to The Sanderson all in the name of business. Which reminds me, I never finished my wank. I never came.

Four o'clock. Coffee. Yawn. Computer crashes. Laura asks to leave early to collect Samuel. She doesn't wait for a response. There's no point. The dog's leg has developed an abscess and they might need to amputate.

I'm tired. Before my life went AWOL I would have spoken to Ruth by now. We'd have had at least one phone call. We'd have discussed red or green pesto. We'd have listened to each other.

I'm desperate to move on. Desperate to avoid things and boredom but the day is dragging. I sit patiently, waiting for redemption in four words that provide solace to so many corporate junkies the world over – 'You Have New Mail'. But that doesn't come either; except for some warning about a new virus from the IT department and a weekly circular advertising a weekend in Helsinki for 99 pounds from last-fucking-minute.com. This makes me laugh. Helsinki has, officially, the highest number of depressed people in the world. I seem to recall my dad's great-grandmother was Finnish. Another piece to the puzzle that helps but the bigger picture is still incomplete. Shit, I haven't even got the edges in place.

The day is almost over. I tick past 6.30pm like the last fucked-off competitor in the London marathon, weary and hoping never to have to do it again; until the next time. I leave, certain that I have accomplished little and strangely elated at having survived. Desk, plus elevator, plus train, minus handrail, plus keys, plus home. This is the sum of my life and it never quite adds up.

My name is Benjamin Carter. I loved my wife. I lost my wife.

*

I get back from Helsinki at one o'clock on Sunday night/Monday morning. I'm exhausted. So much for a cheap weekend deal – last-fucking-minute.com neglected to point out how expensive the city was. Out of principle, I ended up eating in McDonalds listening to John Denver. As an abandoned man uninterested in being sociable, I refuse to pay too much to satisfy my basic needs.

There wasn't much to do in the rest of the city. I drank some beer and took a ferry to the barren island of Suomenlinna, apparently Finland's most popular tourist attraction – a phrase that just screams oxymoron. There was a woman that looked like Ruth walking across a narrow bridge but as she got closer I saw that her eyes were different.

The flight back to Gatwick was delayed, but at least we didn't crash and for this I was glad and reminded of a film I watched repeatedly as a kid. A film about a precocious little brat (Hayley Mills) who could always see the good in a situation, endlessly playing the 'glad-game' when things looked grim. A reason to be thankful even when the shit's hit the fan. And I'd needed the glad-game philosophy as I sat there stagnating on the Helsinki tarmac. Stuck beside a banker from Munich intent on conversation.

My flat, a one-bedroom mess with aspirations (not-mine) at minimalist living, is unwelcoming. I unlock the mortice and feel like a stranger. The Carters no longer live here. Ben and Ruth, as a tangible entity have left little trace, save for the photo of them on the Acropolis shoved hastily into a tacky snowstorm one inspired evening.

I'm back to being Benjamin. It goes like that when people feel sorry for you – in pity they feel compelled to use your full name. Poor Benjamin. One step at a time Benjamin. But when life's going well, when you're part of a couple on some dinner party guest list – you become abbreviated, 'Ben and Ruth'. When one of you goes the lost syllables return.

There are two messages on my answerphone. I press play and wait for someone to enter my flat. It'd be a first for the last couple of months. The message, left on Friday night, begins to unravel. A voice stutters and breaks into… sound, I guess.

"Benjamin? It's Martin."

It's alright. That's my twin brother. Note the three syllables? Ben-ja-min. Martin is a decent guy. He works in the Middle East. Oil. He has a wife, called Alison. Martin definitely has a life. Not sure about the style – but with two kids I don't hold him responsible. Despite the distance, we remain pretty close – though it's slipped a bit lately. We understand each other, except for his mild aversion to words. He's not interested, never has been. He studied maths and then engineering, while I read Donne and Rossetti. Regardless of our academic disciplines, I still look in the mirror and see him first. I believe he does the same.

"Are you there?" he'd said.

No response, as clearly I wasn't.

"I really want to talk to you. Check you're… well I know you're not okay. But just to check I guess."

Martin talks like me. He sounds like me. He looks like me. He's only half an hour older. This meant he got to spend a full 30 minutes on this planet alone. A counsellor I was assigned last year tried to pinpoint this as a key factor in my self's emotional development. That I was left behind in the womb, abandoned. For god's sake, it was my birth. What could I do about it? Fucked before I even started. Martin's still talking. I miss him immeasurably.

"Please call me. I haven't forgotten that it's two years… look, I'll email you on Monday."

I'm annoyed with myself for not telling him about Helsinki. I'd be pissed off too. We don't do this sort of thing, it's not the way we are with each other. Then again the last couple of years have been all about acting in ways I'd never have thought possible. At least they have for me, I believe Martin has remained pretty constant.

His voice disappears and I listen to the next message. I know it'll be mundane. I no longer get that feeling in my gut that it might be Ruth. It's faded. Too many disappointments have removed my capability for hope. And I'm right. It's Laura from work, in tears – calling a friend. That's me, I guess. It was worse than they thought. Samuel had to be put down. I'm incredibly moved. I hear her torment and I can finally cry. For Samuel, I can cry.

2: ADJACENT

Some positioning first. Haifa, a city firmly in the North of Israel, rests squarely amongst the varying levels that constitute Mount Carmel – the base of which lies next to the Mediterranean. This is one of my least favourite places in the world and yet we've remained here for six months. My job takes me abroad. My exact profession is 'stress engineer' though this has nothing to do with counselling or anxiety. At least not directly. Instead I labour under the impression that analysis of oil pipelines and the load they carry is a justifiable method of sustaining a man's lifestyle. My lifestyle such as it is – a pre-occupation I've absorbed from my twin brother Ben, back in London.

I'm driving a Mercedes that pumps air-conditioned... air, I guess, towards my children in the back seats. In return they provide noise and farting. An unhappy trade. It's Sunday afternoon and we've had a day at the beach. It's been hot: 37 degrees.

"Shall we stop and grab a Coke, Martin?" suggests Alison, my wife.

She's pointing towards a shack on the right of the road that is covered in thick dust. Outside, two female soldiers drink from bottles of Fanta, reclining on white plastic chairs embedded in a patchy strip of ryegrass.

The kids seize on their mother's suggestion with their usual noise. They want Daddy to stop the car. Daddy does as he's told. Emily cheers – muttering some deadpan comment about "dying of thirst". Max starts to clap, no doubt provoked by his sister's enthusiasm.

"Okay, okay" I say, shifting the gear. I have no choice.

The wheels grind into the gravel of the lay-by, scaring a lifeless dog that wears a grey bandage around one of its hind-legs. It's quite disgusting. Flies hovering over the poorly covered wound.

I jump out and walk into the dim shadows of the tin building to be greeted by a fridge, a Formica worktop resting on rusty oil drums and a man somewhere in his upper seventies. He invites me to open the cooler. I knock out some rusty Hebrew but there's no need, I simply take what I came for and throw down some shekels. It's a swift transaction and soon I'm outside in the heat.

As I tread wearily back towards the car, I glance sideways at the

Army women dressed uncomfortably in green fatigues. They're rather attractive, early twenties with blonde streaks in their dark hair and thick black eyeliner. As I continue past them they smile and say something intelligible to each other. At first, I think I don't understand but then, then the fucking world stops turning. In their seemingly random patter I suddenly make out what appears to be the word "Ruth". Isolated just like that, clear as anything. My brother's wife.

"Ruth." It's said again. I've stopped dead in my tracks, the hair on my neck standing upright. The usual. Shielding my eyes from the glare of the sun, I stare across intently at them, uncertain and rattled – unsure of my ears.

My reaction offends and the soldiers fix me with bemused looks. A Mexican stand-off without any guns or gangsters but with all of the tension. After what feels like an eternity, I'm eventually aware of Alison opening the driver's side window in front of me, fucking up the air-conditioning and wanting to know what's going on. And I wish I knew, I really do.

"Martin! Come on. What is it?" she's saying. My wife.

I'm going mad. I can feel my heart beating. Regular, regular, regular. By now the soldiers have dismissed me as crazy and resume their dialogue. I reach the car and a family anxious for their chilled caffeine. Coke is distributed to the back seats and we pull away. But not before I check my rear-view mirror at the canine stretched lifelessly in the lay-by. The dog is staring at me. Eyes connecting.

And then we're away. Ally watches me too, all the way home in fact, her seatbelt twisting as she stares at my profile. I'm facing ahead but I sense her curiosity. How can I explain my unease? It's simple. I can't. We drive back up the hillside in silence. Even when Emily says she is going to throw up, I'm determined in my progress. I want to call my brother, Ben, as quickly as possible. I've just realised that I missed the anniversary. Jesus, it's been two years.

We fall into our apartment – the middle of a block in which we are sandwiched between a colleague's family from Oakland, CA above and below by a crone who maintains this building and one across the street. She scares me. Martin Carter is intimidated by an old woman. Let's not dwell on that here.

I grab the phone and hammer out Ben's number. It's his answering machine. I don't want his answering machine. I don't want her voice.

"Ben and Ruth aren't here at the moment." Ruth says.

I wish he'd bloody change the message. I've tried, believe me. Ben simply states that its the truth, Ruth isn't there at the moment and the fact she hasn't been for 24 months has nothing to do with it. I leave my message.

"Benjamin? It's Martin."

It occurs to me he might be screening calls.

"Are you there?"

No response. I blunder on, my eagerness to connect fucking up my words. I do this a lot.

"I really want to talk to you. Check you're… well I know you're not okay. But just to check I guess."

I talk like Ben. I know that. We look the same. There's only 30 minutes between us. I'm older, if you saw us together you'd see it. Everybody sees it.

"Please call me. I haven't forgotten it's been two years…"

I feel incredibly sad. I want to rewrite the message. Wish I could erase what I just said and start again, talk about any old crap instead of having to be so vague.

"Look… I'll email you on Monday," and that's all I say.

My wife is standing behind me. As I replace the receiver she slips her arms around my waist and rests her head on my back.

"I didn't want to remind you Martin." She says. "About the anniversary I mean. You've been so preoccupied lately. What with work and…" her voice trails off as I lean into her, glad to have her there. Glad for everything I have, distinctly aware of how fragile it all is. She gives me a cold Lemonade and I drink quickly, draining the bottle and placing it on the shelf next to the phone. The empty bottle obscures one of those automatic photos taken while on a rollercoaster. We'd just got engaged and look so young – so new. The shot's from the steepest part of the ride, just after the rapid ascent of the track. An image that captures our mad joy, uncertain expectations and genuine, wonderful apprehension at everything before us.

It'd be suitably clichéd to say it was all downhill from then on but I'm afraid ours is not an extreme existence, at least not so far. It may yet turn out to be story of ideals faded but so far we've kept at it, despite everything – despite, significantly, me. So much so that when we've been down, we've always managed to climb back up, always managed to keep the ride going. Unlike Ben – for whom someone simply took the track away.

I suppose we're happy, Alison and I. We've come through a lot. Like Ben and Ruth we met at university, though I managed to get my relationship up and running while we were both still students. Ally had been rushing to a lecture and dropped her books. Callously I'd laughed out loud, don't ask me why. She had glared, snapped a caustic "Fuck you" and that was it, I'd fallen. My response had been 'only if you're really sure' and we were made. Cheesy but that's how it was. For me it was the Berkshire vowels, I was instantly in love with her delicate defiance of upper middle class privilege while pragmatically retaining the trappings that worked for her. Second-hand clothes, Marxist ideals but an innate inability to ever stoop to public transport. And she was beautiful, she still is in fact. A couple of lines around the eyes and the occasional strand of tensile aluminium in her long, auburn hair the only, minor, evidence of having two kids.

Alison has slipped her hand inside my shirt and is stroking my chest. I like this feeling, always have. It usually does the trick, though our lovemaking is fairly infrequent at the moment – has been for the last two years. I fall down onto the white leather sofa that "wasn't a good idea when you've got children" and bring her with me. She smiles and pulls off my glasses and then we're kissing. We're good at kissing. Back on that first day with her books still scattered on the floor, we had joined almost immediately and sealed everything there and then. Now, years later with the kids playing down the hall, my tongue finds hers and I feel my dick stirring. I'm tired but this feels good, really good. If only it could be more. But we're both content just to sprawl here, her hair falling down around my face, our noses touching.

My wife boldly moves her hand into my shorts, her fingers warm and searching, and she's got me. She's holding me.

And what am I thinking?

I'm thinking that Ben no longer has someone. My twin is on his own. And I'm all too aware that blame has not yet been allocated.

About twenty minutes later I've come to take a shower. I hate this bathroom. There's the usual collection of fresh bugs trapped against the mesh screen covering the window. I've hated insects ever since Ben made me eat a beetle for a dare. I did it, reluctantly, and promptly threw up. During the family post mortem my mother said Ben wasn't to blame as "would I eat faeces if he told me to?" She said faeces, she's that sort of woman. Anyway, I didn't have an answer and decided instead it was the insect's fault. Ben didn't stop laughing for weeks, and I've grown to fear the little shits ever since.

The Mediterranean cousins of that half-digested beetle are all around. All the little bastards watching me now. Last week I found a lizard on the avocado bath panel and one on the mirror too, admiring its reflection. Emily and Max love them and will pick anything up. Fortunately Ally is chief creature-catcher in our marriage. She's long since grown tired of my desire to kill anything, however insignificant, that crosses my path; to eradicate without discussion. Though I learnt my lesson a while back, taking two hours to placate Emily after stamping on a spider. I'd told her that it was just like the *Lion King* – all part of the circle of life. She told me something about the *Lion King* being evidence of Disney's "parenting propaganda for avoiding difficult issues" before adding "what about karma?"

"What about karma?" I'd said. I wasn't proud of myself or my tactics. Or my inability to grasp what she was talking about – something that occurs frequently. But at least in here I can close the door and be alone, but not before scanning the floor of course.

I pull off my shorts and t-shirt and step into the separate cubicle. I like the glass bricks. I spend a few moments getting the pressure right on the jets above me. I make sure the water's freezing. The cold water a deliberate move – it's so bloody hot and I want to stand here for eternity, letting it wash over me. Usually I don't like to linger but today is different. I feel dirty.

Eventually I reach for the soap and use my pubic hair to produce a lather. I've always felt this to be the greatest miracle of human evolution. Fuck the voice-box or eyelashes.

I decide to check my testicles, right then left, for anything abnormal. I do this rarely and am not sure why I've been prompted to do it today. Nevertheless, I'm lifting up and rolling around, not exactly sure what normal is – as far as down there is concerned. I'm part-way through the exam when I hear something. A faint but audible speck of noise. It sounds like… "Daddy?"

Eh? I turn around with a start. Nothing. I'm going mad, I really am. Until there it is again.

"Daddy?"

I look down, through the opaque screen. Max, my son, is there on the other side of the glass.

"What are you doing?" is what I think the four-year-old is saying. Innocently. I can't hear properly, I can't be totally sure. I don't want to be having this conversation, especially when I realise I am still grasping myself.

What can I say in effective reply? Nothing evidently. Nothing coherent. And though I'm innocent too I explode at the boy, naturally via his mother who is somewhere else.

"Alison! What the hell have I said about keeping the kids out of the bathroom!"

Max hasn't moved. He was smiling but he's not anymore, rooted to the spot in fear. Tears instantly forming. He looks at me like I am insane. Like he is terrified. I am making a real noise, somehow amplified by the shower.

Alison has her son now, is lifting him out of the way – away from danger, away from me, on whom incessant water keeps on pouring. I can't hear properly. I move out of the inexorable flow. The revised angle of my head now encouraging shampoo to course forward, now running down into my eyes. I roar from unexpected pain, the bass in my voice fucking up the situation further.

My vision returns and its just Alison standing there, Max is gone.

"You bastard," she says, quietly. Alison never shouts. This is a fundamental difference between us.

"You know I hate them seeing me like this," I say, quietly, meaning me naked. She can't be proud either.

We have different ideas about parental nudity too. I'm not repressed, I just believe there are limits.

"I don't care. You scared him. You scared your son. That's not right Martin is it?"

"I'm sorry, okay? I'll make it up to him."

"You'll fix the fucking lock is what you'll do."

And then Alison's gone. She's right though. I do fix the lock, soon after, wearing a towel and using a damp screwdriver. Max helps me by holding the screws. His 13-year-old sister couldn't care less, watching television in the other room.

I finish the job fairly quickly and kiss my son on the top of his head. He smiles gingerly, happily and I wish everything in life could be this easily repaired. Even Alison seems calmed and starts a conversation about something or other.

After dinner we're all sitting quietly in the living room, CNN on in the corner. I have Max asleep on me. Emily is over with her mother practising French verbs. I am trying to be a good father, a good husband. We've played the Junior Scrabble that Ben gave them and that Emily always thrashes me at. Their happiness is my first concern – our security my sole aim. I am driven in my need to look after my family, to protect them. So much so that six months ago I was able to make the decision to leave my brother at home, to put them first. To venture abroad again in search of lucrative overtime and tax-breaks – we needed the money. I had schools to think about. Christ, university even – the rate my daughter's going.

Fortunately I'd been based in London when Ruth first disappeared. There had been a crisis in the oil-industry and I'd just managed to hold onto a staff job in Wembley that paid the bare minimum. Regardless, I took weeks off to be with my brother. I wish it could have been more. It was a terrible time. I felt so impotent, glad when Ben asked me, in desperation, to look after our mother. She'd arrived from Norfolk with a determination to sort the whole mess out. Ally was struggling with her inability to help – busy as she was with a toddler, my son who lies on me now. It was a nightmare. The whole experience was awful – to see my twin cry and not be able to comprehend; to see him so helpless.

So many times I wanted to be the one to say the things that would solve the mystery of Ruth's departure. As his twin brother I felt it was my duty to be the one who would put everything right. I couldn't do it. I didn't have the words; I wish to God I had.

The months followed each other. I had to go back to work. I persuaded Ben to return to Mentor, the magazine he works on and had originally loved. Increasingly I had to follow my priorities, my responsibilities. Eventually I had to follow where the work was. I had to leave him. Israel opened up and there was no choice. Ally and the kids would come with me, though I was against the idea. We had fought but she didn't want to be left. To be abandoned. I countered that I didn't want to drag children to Israel, not when Max was still only four and the world was going crazy. Truthfully I wanted her and the kids to be around to comfort Ben and to be near my mother.

She'd asked if I was making excuses. If really I "just wanted to be alone... like Ben was?"

Maybe I did. Maybe that would have made it easier. Maybe that's what I wanted – to feel some sense of the isolation he was enduring. To suffer too.

It didn't work out how I wanted it though. Things rarely do. Ben waved us all off at the airport, assuring me he was okay. I knew he was lying. I could see the shadows under his eyes. The time had come though, a choice had been made. I said goodbye at departures and cried throughout the whole flight. I haven't seen him for six months.

Ally interrupts my thoughts with a whisper.

"I think we should put this one to bed."

She's talking about Max. I lift up my son and carry him through. I place him beneath the thin blue sheet and leave. It's a silent evening – broken only by the whirr of the fan working overtime from the corner of the room.

What about karma?

3: CLASSIFIED

The sound on the television is down but I'm still watching. My ears are preoccupied, listening to music via my ipod which in turn is linked to the hi-fi. And it's gripping viewing even with the alternative soundtrack bleeding from the speaker. The speaker that rests on the shelf that Ruth said had never been straight, the uneven shelf that was always remarked upon. A shelf that could be termed a conversation piece, an ice-breaker. But not now of course. No, in the last century when Saturday nights meant people. When I would offer wine and tell our guests that I wanted the shelf that way. When Ruth would play her part, rolling her eyes as she came in from the kitchen, offering the same well-rehearsed sentence.

"I keep asking him to fix it but he won't. He's convinced it's straight. He says it's the wall that's not level."

It always happened in the same way. The other women would feel solidarity with my beleaguered wife and begin to empathise, biologically compelled to chime in with similar tales of spousal DIY woe. Their lager-drinking men would shout them down and before long we'd be carrying our glasses to the table. It was all very funny, all good clean fun. That shelf got us through a lot of awkward silences and fractured, fragmented half-sentences about the moreish qualities of Pringles.

I love that shelf but if I'm honest, mostly because it frequently gave me an excuse (as if any was necessary) to use the word askew.

"Ruth!" I'd continue, calling out to where she was busy in the kitchen with dessert or the cafetiere, all the while smiling broadly and winking at our guests around the table, letting them know that I was having a bit of fun. "The damn shelf is not askew!"

I'd never previously been able to use the word, at least not in context. That fake piece of birch from IKEA enabled me. I owe it one.

I realise now that my life before was a constant search to use things, to use matter, in context. In its right place.

"Everything... in its right place"

My eyes drift from the hi-fi speaker back to the television. The Sony Wega 32" digital. It's definitely in its right place, in the corner on a unit bought at the same time as my not- askew shelf. A purchase that went against the advice of a friend who declared widescreen sets the enemy of a healthy and communicative relationship. Sure enough Ruth was gone within six months, but I don't hold the TV responsible. There was a time when I did – last year in fact, during a particularly desperate weekend. I came close to smashing the glass.

Anyway, the TV is still on – there's no sound but I can work out what's happening. Just. It's really not difficult, I can definitely manage this. Esther from Exeter (my guess, she looks like a Devonian) is through to the final round of *Wheel Of Fortune*. Esther's picking five consonants and a vowel and I decide she'll pick "A. I don't say this out loud as there's really no point.

And I don't hear her selection as the stereo is still playing, but the characters flash up on screen and there it is – 'A'. I'm mildly pleased and by now totally inebriated, holding it together for no good reason. But Esther seems calm, her mouth is opening and closing slowly. She's speaking to me, she's saying "I'm not here. This isn't happening" over and over. And then she's not, then she's animatedly guessing Windsor Castle – the 'A' proving somehow decisive. Her husband – her loving, caring, proud and present life-partner – has run onto the stage, taken the keys and jumped into their new Ford. Lights are flashing and they're both waving at me as the credits roll. Lucky Esther. Lucky Esther.

I drain the bottle of Jack Daniel's, the last honeyed drops coating my throat, providing a useless but welcome moment of warmth against the night-time cold. I'm drained too. I contemplate going out to get some food. I know I need to fill the cupboards with something. They're as empty as everything else in this flat and that includes me. I haven't been shopping for over a fortnight, what with my trip to Helsinki last weekend. But I don't think I'm hungry. I don't think food will help. Or maybe it will, maybe that's all I need. Oh fuck it – what's that old joke? "I used to be indecisive but now I'm not so sure."

Why is there no one to show me what to do, to tell me how to feel?

In front of me rests the local newspaper with my 'anniversary' advert ending up exactly where I'd requested it. First entry in the classifieds, like old times. The girl at the paper had remembered me, she'd asked how I was. How had I been coping? Had I heard anything? I didn't mind the concern or her questions. After all, there was a time in the first couple of months when Sharon had been involved as anyone else. I used to call her twice a week. Regular, regular, regular. Desperate for some editorial. Desperate for an article, for coverage, for physical evidence to be displayed to the world of my ongoing search, determined to prove to friends, to Ruth's family and yes, to myself, that I was doing all I could, this wasn't my fault, I really did want to find her.

I'd established a standing order for a recurring ad right at the front of the section. We'd agreed a special rate, a special privilege for a desperate, pathetic man.

"You try the best you can," Sharon would say, when I apologised for my desperation. And I used to wonder if I had. Whether Ruth was watching and waiting to see how much effort I was taking to find her. Whether this was all a test and whether I was failing (her) miserably.

And I had tried, I believe that now – but eventually Sharon and I had to call it off. I sensed she had grown tired of hearing the fear in my voice. There was no need for the standing order to continue. It was my second dissolved relationship in as many months. Ruth wasn't responding. Ruth wasn't coming through.

Not after all the unsatisfactory calls to the police; not after phoning her entire address-book; not after my incessant pleas to everyone in her office. I honestly felt that they were all keeping something from me. I even hit her assistant. He didn't press charges. Said he understood. I said good, would he mind explaining it to me – because I certainly didn't.

I began aimlessly walking the streets, all our old haunts, near the homes of friends and through places like Covent Garden – anywhere where people congregate. Every day becoming more professional in my newly acquired vocation – 'an abandoned relative'. Clutching photocopied sheets and trying to get street vendors to look at a sad picture of just another woman lost in the world. Emboldened enough to start sticking her image to lampposts and giving money to the homeless in exchange for some vague suggestion that a woman matching her description might have been sleeping rough near Waterloo Station last week. Or seen in a coffee-shop in Hammersmith. But nothing. If Ruth was still in London, she wasn't shopping on Oxford Street or frequenting soup kitchens; but then again, why would she? She was, so I believed, the most rational person I knew. Maybe there wasn't violence or energy behind her exit. Maybe she was simply living quietly, in some non-descript town up north, making a new life with a new name – it wouldn't be too hard to do. Maybe she's with a new guy who loves her and asks no questions – maybe that's why she hasn't used our account?

But what if she's not anywhere anymore. What if she's…?

And I still surf the chat-rooms, visit the psychics, make journeys to the shelters and speak to the people that know my name and have promised to get in touch if Ruth appears – but I've given up the daily routine. It came to a halt on the second Christmas Eve after Ruth had gone. I'd gone into a branch of The Gap she used to visit on Regent Street and found myself watching the mad hordes in their scramble to buy the same jumper as everyone else. Walking through the racks on auto-pilot, studying every possible similarity for signs of Ruth without really being aware of what I was doing. And it was all going fine, until 'Deck The Halls' faded from the in-store PA and segued into 'Missing' from Everything But The Girl. With Tracy Thorn, one of Ruth's favourites, singing those words – "Could you be dead? You always were two steps ahead" – and my brain shutting everything out but her voice. And I'd never felt so alone, even when surrounded by three security guards forcibly asking me to leave. Throwing me out into a world that didn't have a clue what had happened to me.

When people disappear completely nobody prepares you for the way in which that world continues. The way in which Ruth's company had advertised her job not long after she had gone. I began to think that if they'd given up, I might as well do the same.

And I began to feel anger. As seasons changed – as the leaves grew and died – it possessed me. Not even a fucking sentence left to explain. No forwarding address, no details, no respect. That I've never found her passport didn't help, neither confirming my fear of premeditated abandonment nor reassuring the police who came calling when my bad dream became a nightmare of violent Crown suspicion. There was no evidence that she had willingly moved on. Why wouldn't they? I hated my wife, hated her for leaving me behind with nothing but a myriad of unspoken accusations. Internal and external. It was easier to deal with the hurt of total rejection than the pain and possibility of Ruth being no longer... well, just no longer.

And so total anger won. I broke several pieces of our Conrad dinner service and tableware, smashing all the wedding presents we'd be saving for our 'grown-up' house. A house that was no longer a viable possibility. Suzie, my second counsellor, said my actions were "cathartic and natural". And I'd respond, "It makes no difference. My anger doesn't go anywhere." Suzie would nod her head sagely and make some note on her laptop.

It was true, nothing made any difference. I hated Ruth and couldn't get enough. Anger, and believe me I took it to some drastic levels, consumed me. But this form of release is only ever temporary, like when you're little and trying to get water out of a hole in the sand that you've inexpertly dug too near the sea – it quickly rushes back in, filling every available space. You're back where you started. No clue how to move forward.

But things did change. Eventually. Long after I'd stopped the counselling. Long after Suzie could say "I told you so" – though she'd never have been so unprofessional. And now I exist in this time after fury where I simply subsist, helpless and confused. A time where someday I can barely move. A series of dulled sensations, of perpetual tiredness, of staring into the mirror at a scratchy ill-formed beard and a smell of the usual. Nothing to do but breathe and sometimes even that seems beyond me. A daily process of sequential events that all lead inexorably to the same conclusion. The equation that always turns out the same. The sleepless nights that lead to another morning without Ruth and another working day of not knowing how to move on. Another day without the answer I need, to the only question I have left.

Why?

The bottle of bourbon is empty. I no longer care about the possibly askew shelf or the fucking TV. Nor about the newspaper or the empty cupboards. I lie down on the sofa and it's late and cold. I can't be bothered to turn off the light. Or pick up the duvet from where it rests on the floor. I wonder if placing my hand over my face will block out the glare from the bare bulb dangling above me (I'd smashed the glass shade long ago). I try but it's useless, the light still gets through. No matter. I keep my palm on my mouth and feel my wedding ring against my nose – the only solid reminder of my old life. Everything else has become this abstract… drift. The room starts to rotate. I'm in control. Just.

*

I am in the gym that's next door to work. I don't know why. It's only my fifth time since I joined the company. We all get subsidised membership, what the fuck happened to luncheon vouchers? Instead we have this. A windowless basement touted as a key employment benefit for the staff of *Mentor* and all our sister titles.

My hangover was bad this morning. I woke up to find the TV still on and the music continuing via the iPod on permanent recharge. The shuffle function doing its job to infinity. My neighbour gave me a withering look as I stumbled out of the flat. I almost told her to fuck herself but instead apologised profusely. I've sensed recently that my socially acceptable grief period has come to an end. My tormented behaviour will very soon, no longer be tolerated. Arbitrary or not – my days of grace are drawing to a close. It's almost time to move on Benjamin.

How?

I have a headache and my stomach is on spin-cycle. I don't like the smell down here at the best of times. A mixture of sweat and stale air that surely can't be good for you. At least there aren't many people, the intimidating machines sit unused along the walls like dormant medieval torture devices.

I notice a woman from our marketing department, the cover-mount specialist, smiling up at me. She's lying on a mat doing something to her abdomen that doesn't look natural. I nod a hello down in return. We've never properly spoken but I remember we once performed as Elton John and Kiki Dee at a Christmas karaoke party, not long after I'd first joined *Mentor*. Back when I'd felt like joining in.

Ellen, that's it, that's what I think her name is. It's actually a favourite of mine. Ellen's breasts look fantastic in lycra but her face

41

looks as if it is about to explode. She's really suffering. I want to tell her to stop this madness. To come for a pint and a bacon sandwich but she'd think I was insane. We're all fucked. I find this incredible.

Nevertheless, in a bid to get away from my desk, someone's tuna sandwiches and Laura's constant use of me as a shoulder to cry on for dear, departed Samuel – I've come here too, hung my clothes on the peg with the rest of them willing to search for the holy grail of modern times. The six-pack. The perfect body shape. Conditioned body-conditioning. Which also happens to be the subject of the article I'm subbing at the moment, you could say I felt inspired. It'd be wrong but you could say it.

Oh fuck.

Jason is on the shoulder press halfway through a set. He's grunting and making all the right noises, doing all the right moves. And, of course, he's wearing a matching outfit – pristine Nike Air trainers, short shorts and a fuchsia vest for chrissakes. His muscles on display for whoever wants to look. Which is pretty much just Jason as far as I can tell. He keeps checking his reflection, no doubt for evidence of improvement to his deltoids and pecs and whatever else it is we're all supposed to have nowadays. I can't believe nobody else thinks he's a prick.

I stand in front of the bank of mirrors along one wall and stare at my ragged 6ft frame and the tiny flecks of silver in my black hair. I used to look alright, didn't I? I used to look alive. Anyway, by way of contrast to Jason, I'm co-ordinating grey tennis shorts with faded *Taxi Driver* t-shirt I bought in my last year at university. My legs and arms appear sallow under the harsh spotlights in the ceiling – my face three different shades of green, my blue eyes distinctly bloodshot red.

Ruth once told me that when she was eleven she would whisper the word colourful to her sister because it looked like she was saying "I love you".

I am no longer the man my wife fell in love with.

I'm not sure what I'm supposed to do first, but as far as I'm concerned, this is one area of my life where I don't need direction. There's no instructor on duty and I'm glad. The last thing I want is some overenthusiastic moron appraising my extra body fat and lack of technique in the spirit of misguided motivation. And then I realise

Jason is padding over to me, wiping his forehead with a Hilfiger towel.

"About time we saw you down here Ben." "We," he said. Inside I'm screaming.

With the mohican De Niro on my t-shirt I really want to say "You talking to me?" but I don't.

"Really?" I offer instead.

"Yeah… it's not just about keeping fit. It's good for the mind."

"What is?"

"Working out… keeps you positive."

What is he doing? As he's talking, he's grabbing his left elbow and forcing one arm down behind his head towards his back, like an over-developed ape. Is this for my benefit?

"What are you doing tomorrow night?"

He doesn't wait for me to answer. This is good as I don't have one.

"Only Annabel and I thought you might like to come over. We're having a bit of a dinner party. We need another guy."

He swaps arms, holding my gaze in the mirror but still not letting me speak.

"Don't worry. It isn't all couples… not that you wouldn't be invi…"

His face flushes red, I'm not sure whether from over exertion or a realisation that he might be putting his foot in it, hitting a nerve or something. He's finally silent.

"No thank you." I say.

"Right. Maybe another time then?"

And then his hands are on his hips, thrusting out, one leg forward, one leg behind and admiring his reflected torso. I turn away, climb on an exercise bike and begin to pedal.

I wonder why I said no about tomorrow night, I'm not going anywhere.

4: SHAFT

My office has a great view. Mount Carmel is without question a beautiful part of the world. Everything seems serene up here when fact it's not far north to The Lebanon and to the south is an ongoing war zone that's destined never to calm down. Out of sight, out of mind? A rule I've lived my life by, certainly for these last two years. But there's always a threat in the invisible distance; a presence that never lets you forget it is there.

Yet as long as I can see foliage and sense the water far below, I can see enough to make me believe that all is actually okay. This helps ensure I'm only mildly pissed off with Ally – furiously playing the glad-game (I'll explain another time) to get me through.

Maybe I'm overreacting? I've just put the phone down from my wife after she called from an exclusive spa she visits with some of the other partners; a typical ex-pat group that hang out uselessly together while their partners work. They meet for lunch after a morning of tennis or a session with a spiritual guide called Noah who's no doubt raking it in, and all this before collecting the kids. A group of varying ages, operations and sizes that progressively includes Brad, the resplendent Yank house-husband of one of my colleagues, a ruddy but wiry Lancashire woman called Christine. Times really have changed. Brad purports to work from home as a novelist and Chrissy brings home the bacon. Or the beef – this is Israel after all.

Chrissy is from Stockport, bright ginger hair and a bloody good engineer, an expert in petro-chemicals. We started our careers together in Aberdeen well over a decade ago, away from our loved ones and wondering how we'd ended up in Scotland when our peers were landing posts in the Middle East or Canada. The dreams of college drifting into an 8am to 7pm-plus overtime reality.

Alison had stayed south, in Gerrard's Cross with Emily and my in-laws. We'd had Emily fairly young, only a few months after Ben met Ruth again and they'd finally got it together. We weren't prepared for parenthood, at 22 we felt like we could barely look after each other. We were always crap with condoms though I'm not normally an irresponsible person. Anyway back then it was easier for Ally to stay with her family; we were saving for a deposit, relocation was unnecessary. I came back on weekends and that was enough to keep us going. Our life had a pleasing mathematical symmetry. We'd have most-likely seen Ben and Ruth on the Saturday, listening to tales of their exciting, if virtually destitute, London life that all seemed incredibly glamorous. I remember the four of us would take the baby – Emily – to the park and Ben I would reconnect, realign ourselves; it never took long. Then, on Sunday, Ally would stroke my chest and we'd make love, leaving time for food, arguments and parents. A routine that worked for us. Culminating late on Sunday night when I'd travel back alone, crossing the border up to the granite city and a landlord from hell.

The weeks were sparse; Aberdeen is hardly Sydney, but Chrissy likes football so we'd go from work to the occasional midweek football match at Pittodrie and eat meat pies. The time became manageable and through our work, and the passing years, we've cemented a friendship that's had time to develop – amicably, reassuringly even, but always at a safe, manageable distance. And over the last decade our lives have overlapped at different periods, meeting in The Hague, Grimsby or Oslo and now the Middle East. Where we've caught up on our shared history and reintroduced our families (including new arrival Brad).

Chrissy gets on well with Alison, they're always civil and as such I've felt duty bound to return the favour and welcome her long line of new men. This has never been a problem. Until now that is. Brad, from Miami, is different. From the beginning, my wife expressed an interest in spending time with him, an interest that has troubled me. I shouldn't have any issue with this. What do they call it, give and take? But I'm crap at giving. And if you love and trust your wife, giving in this way shouldn't be unusual behaviour.

Ally was laughing on the phone and I'm positive I heard Brad request, in his lazy drawl, another two cocktails. Some health spa. And just two cocktails? Where are the other wives?

You know the more I think about it, the more the view outside seems less pretty. In fact I hate it. I realise I am insanely jealous, jealous of the pair of them lazing in the pool while my day consists of studying numbers on a screen, broken only by intermittent periods when Chrissy, who I've never found remotely attractive, asks if I want to go out onto the fire escape for an unhealthy Marlboro Light. She's about to suggest this now. I look at the clock. Jesus – it's only midday. I decide to share my burden and begin summarising the details of my phone conversation, in the vain hope she too might resent our partners self-indulgence.

"Ally's just called, they're all at the spa. In the jacuzzi."

"Bastards. Brad's supposed to be finishing a chapter."

But I can see from her face that she's not really bothered. I speculate, as I have done for many years, that Brad and Chrissy have an open relationship. The type I used to read about in those woman's weeklies with the crunchy paper as I waited for the doctor to prescribe me some more propananol. I'm sure they're all 'car keys in the bowl' types, happily swinging for Anglo-American relations and proud of it.

I know Alison, I trust Alison, but composure is required. Chrissy's indifference isn't helping.

"I know what you mean." I continue, trying to provoke a reaction. "It's bloody typical. Ally had promised she'd go to the supermarket. Instead she's in a bikini while we've got nothing in the fridge… it's a tough life for them, isn't it?"

But as I said, Chrissy's not really listening, instead she's anxiously trawling through her gargantuan designer bag in search of her fags. Muttered swear-words leaking from her thin mouth as she sends tampons and tissues flying. Silenced, I watch this woman, a woman about whom I suddenly realise I know nothing and everything. That odd grey area that exists between the sociable colleagues we somehow wind up spending the majority of our lives with, becoming familiar but never intimate.

Chrissy's holding her bag upside down now, shaking it furiously. A bag that suggests wealth and a total lack of style. I don't need to mention that Chrissy and I earn shedloads plundering the world of its non-renewables.

"Everything's good while it lasts," Ben said to me once, when as 18 year olds we were arguing over nothing, as usual. Justifying our career choices, trying to gain the upper ground. He'd continued with some comment about my proposed profession "… being finite, mercilessly exploiting a limited aberration of geological development".

Typical Benjamin, clever-clever words when one or two will do. He didn't give a damn about the environment back then, he just liked turning the phrase, making the statement. And then, when fully warmed to his theme he'd be in a position to issue his verdict.

"Profiting from those that came before. It won't last, it can't last." Then it had been my turn. In one swift sentence I'd expressed a similarly negative view about his proposed career in journalism: "You waste time writing about total shits." And that was that, the pair of us laughing at each other and immediately forgetting all about our feud. Even through all the professional and academic differences as our careers developed, we've always found reasons that support our genetic bond, that unite rather than separate us.

Now I see that Ben was right and I wonder what type of industry will profit in fifty million years from my remains – while their partners sun themselves recreationally. And I'm back to Alison. I wonder if Brad is sunning her recreationally. I wonder how he would do this.

"Thank fuck for that!" Chrissy's finally found a fag but is still loitering at my desk, situated as it is nearest to the exit. Like a restarted record, she resumes her earlier theme of Brad's dedication (or lack of) to his novel. But I note that, unlike me, she's still smiling. She's not really pissed off.

"I've given up on him finishing that bloody book, but as long as he cooks and fucks me with that cock of his, I really can't complain."

With this sign-off she's gone, lighting up before she's even left the room. My face flushes red. I automatically look around to see if anyone else heard – I certainly hadn't needed to hear it. Chrissy's mouth – sod it, her entire being – belongs in the gutter sometimes. She's always thought nothing of describing her intimate moments to me, or indeed my wife. So much so that I know that that 'cock of his' is 8.5 inches when erect and curves slightly to the left. He has a six-pack stomach and is an acrobat in bed. I pray that Alison never shares in this way. Jesus, what am I worried about? There's nothing to share. We kiss, we're great at kissing in fact, and we sometimes make love, I'd even say we were still in love – but there's nothing to share. Not on that level anyway. I really can't compete; not with Brad who sounds like he belongs in a circus.

I remember that Brad is sitting in a hot-tub with my wife. He's probably wearing those ridiculous black trunks, that he calls his 'European bathing-suit', that cost more than my golf-clubs. A grin on his face like the Cheshire-cat that got the sodding cream, except that Brad would sound the second syllable of Cheshire to rhyme with mire. This is the kind of thing Ben notices.

The view out of my window no longer has any chance whatsoever of controlling my mood. This desk no longer seems like a viable place to spend the day. My work-station with its large monitor blinking, with its multi-coloured windows hurtling towards me from some computer-generated vision of outer space, anathema to every part of my being. The symbols closing my world around me rather than implying any opportunity for escape and a life beyond.

I'm really bothered, pulling my tie loose from my collar and craving a drink. Alison has said many times how good looking Brad is, how well he dresses. Apparently he exfoliates and moisturises. I'm still not completely sure what exfoliating is. When I let slip once, over drinks at their immaculate apartment, that my brother Ben works for *Mentor*, he was very impressed. He's got an international subscription and keeps all the back issues. But I knew this before he even told me. It doesn't take a genius. It never does.

Why am I bothered? I can't be the only one who feels this way. More to the point, do I have any right? And then I look up from the screen and notice Chrissy still hovering out in the corridor, fag in her mouth and, somehow, furiously biting the nails on her right hand. Just when I think she cannot possibly multi-task further, she brings her Blackberry up to her face, with her left hand, and manages to hammer out a number with rapid-fire thumb as if her life depended on it.

*

Returning home early, crossing the hallway, I stumble into our bedroom. The kids are nowhere to be seen. The curtains are drawn even though it's the middle of the afternoon. A thin crack has been left between the heavy material, allowing a shaft of light into the room and making dancing dust particles visible in its luminous column. But there, following the beam from the window to the bed is Brad, shagging my wife right in front of me. Giving it to her in a way I can't.

Arse in the air, hands in her hair. I can't see her face but I can hear her moan. He's got that cock of his (8.5 inches, slight curve to the left) sliding into her, no doubt, big fucking grin on his face. Regular, regular, regular. She's loving it – asking for more, desperate for more. When I've really, and I mean really, had quite enough.

"Erm... hello?" (this from me)

My wife's face appears from underneath him – except suddenly it's not her. It's not Alison. It's Ruth. What is Ruth doing here? This doesn't make sense. Not to say it would make sense if it was Alison, but this, this is not good.

And now I only see Ruth. Fuck it, even Brad's disappeared and it's just Ruth.

Ruth crying. Like she was the last time I saw her. Ruth naked, covering her breasts. Like she was the last time I saw her.

"Martin... Martin…" she repeats softly.

Alison is waking me up, saying my name slowly. I'm aware of tears. Mine not hers. She's asking me what's wrong. Telling me I'm safe. After an eternity I speak, only one question on my mind.

"Alison," I say, quietly.

"Yes. What is it Martin?" soothing concern in her voice.

"Do you want more?" I ask.

I study her as she listens to my question.

"Do you really want more?" I repeat.

She doesn't answer. Emily is screaming with 13-year-old vocal cords for her mother from the bathroom and demands to be heard. I surmise that she's somehow locked in. 'Trapped' is the word she's using. My recent repair job is evidently unsatisfactory. Evidently ineffective. Clearly not up to the job.

*

Out of sight, out of mind? A rule I've lived my life by, certainly for these last two years. But there's always a threat in the invisible distance; a presence that never lets you forget it's there.

5: ONE THING LEADS TO ANOTHER

I'm sitting here with Maggie about to go over some old photographs she's found. She thought I might like to look at them. I'm not yet sure if she's right.

Maggie is Ruth's younger sister, they don't look much alike but occasionally there's a smile or an expression that catches me off guard. Maggie lives here in London, studying Art History, a career decision taken solely to be nearer to where Ruth was. Her parents, my in-laws, have stayed away. They live in Cheltenham and make fewer and fewer visits up to town, they say it's too hard and of course I don't blame them. This arrangement is easier for me too. I prefer not having to deal with endless reminiscing about their favourite girl, which in itself is preferable to those initial, aggressive, accusations levelled at me when Ruth first didn't come home. All the unsaid familial opinions about who or what or why might have taken her away.

Distance is easier for everyone concerned. Ruth's dad, Cecil, and I get on fine, but Stella, my mother-in-law, needs someone to blame. As such I am no longer in the sun as far as she's concerned. I don't mind that her damaged subconscious has returned a verdict that points vaguely in my direction. I know that this helps her. Stella is a beautiful woman, ageing gracefully and Ruth was her world. That she will always mistrust me is something I am powerless to prevent. But I won't protest. I won't complain. It makes a change to be able to help someone, even if it is by being an object of suspicion.

Ruth's parents justify their ongoing inactivity through a maintained belief that if their daughter does ever come back, it will be to them, to the rural family nest she grew up in. While I don't believe that she will, if I'm perfectly honest, I am glad the bases are covered. We have a tacit understanding, though it's never been discussed, that that there is no question of anyone moving until we know what's happened to her. The thought of Ruth returning home to either location, only to find strangers is too impossible to contemplate. We have no choice, we're trapped.

How can anyone be expected to move on emotionally when they're physically not allowed to? How am I supposed to find a way out when everywhere there are signs that point back to my wife?

Maggie is cupping her mug of coffee with both hands just like they do in commercials or twenty-something dramas about young urban professionals.

"Is work getting to you again?" she queries.

"I feel like I don't belong any more," I reply. "I don't have the same concerns as my co-workers."

"I don't know why you don't leave?" she spits. "They're all twats from the sound of it."

Maggie's heard all the stories and it occurs to me that she probably has an unfair view of the people at *Mentor*. However ridiculously I view our product, maybe I should have been fairer. Or maybe not – I recall that it was Jason's birthday today, that he bought cakes for everyone only to then refuse to eat one himself. Complex carbohydrates – no way his abs could take it.

"I can't… change. I like the work itself," I continue weakly, prodded somewhere inside by a nagging sense of shame about my almost endless ability to speak so aimlessly. Maggie meanwhile nods that she's heard, if not quite understood.

To be honest, Maggie and I never delve too far into 'how we are feeling'. Always interested, never too emotional; we discuss broad memories together but keep our theories to ourselves. Maggie doesn't demand any process of healing, has never told me to pull myself together and never encouraged me to meet new people. In this she is unwittingly part of the pressure I feel to try and keep things as they were. I guess in a perverse way she doesn't want to accept that her sister might entirely disappear. I sense it in the way she ensures I am holding the pack of photos firmly, not relinquishing them until she's satisfied I've got them – as if she's literally determined to ensure I hang on to the past, and to the life her sister and I had together.

But I know she's struggled to understand what kind of life it was. The sisters weren't close, they weren't… connected. I'm sure guilt was the catalyst for her decision to move to London, over-riding her avowed hatred of the capital and its 'poncey' inhabitants. If truth be told I guess in some way she has a better relationship with Ruth now than before, a wider, more tolerant view of my wife's married lifestyle such as it was. And I'm certain the realisation of this increasingly affects Maggie, especially as her sister slips further into the realm of memory.

51

Ruth rarely receives junk mail anymore – an important indication of no longer occupying a place in the modern world.

I see Maggie a lot. She usually comes and meets me for lunch. We have a sandwich and a coffee while she informs me about bastard boyfriends, lacklustre lecturers before listening to me moan about the standard of freelancers. I am her surrogate sibling. In a way she is now mine too.

This evening, as I've mentioned, we are in my flat and I can tell she's only mildly disgusted by the state of the kitchen and the takeaway boxes that litter the lounge like a bachelor cliché. She however makes no clichéd attempt to add order to my dishevelled surroundings; there is no prospect of her rolling up her sleeves to add a woman's touch and help this poor man out. Maggie, with her Chrissie Hynde meets English student hair, is about as far from 1950s woman as you can get. Instead she pushes away some books lying on the coffee table and spreads out the newly retrieved photos of her sister – my wife.

A deep preparatory breath. And then I'm poring over them, scanning the whole collection at the same time – drinking them all in like some pathetic junkie taking a methadone fix. I haven't really seen Ruth for ages, apart from the one shot from university that's a permanent fixture on my bedside table (but in that she's not looking at me). I'd long ago put away all of our photo-albums in the airing cupboard, the sight of them too painful to bear. I found a space for them where the china wedding presents had been, before I'd attacked those 18 months ago. Life helps out like that sometimes. I'd kept the snowstorm out from the Acropolis – left it on the phone-table in the hall.

These are pictures of when I'd first got together with Ruth. Our first proper Christmas. We were spending New Year's Eve at the country pub near her parent's home in Cheltenham. It was snowing and I remember everything had seemed so pure.

"I can't believe I wore that then. Me in a dress!"

Maggie is pointing at a borrowed black number she's wearing. I hadn't noticed it – all I can see is my Ruth grinning and raising her glass to the camera. She's smiling – she looks fucking gorgeous – wearing a piece of silver tinsel in her hair. My brother Martin is standing next to her, he's got his arm round her shoulder, holding a pint of beer. Martin used to drink loads, almost an alcoholic, in fact he was sick that night, throwing up in the road as we all trudged back to the house, spoiling the crisp whiteness, crying and feeling entirely sorry for himself. Alison – who was pregnant at the time – was far from amused. She'd already had to be persuaded to spend the holiday with her brother-in-law's new girlfriend's family, hardly the close surroundings she'd have chosen at that time of year. I couldn't blame her for not being full of festive spirit.

But I've always found Ally to be the most tolerant and certainly compassionate of human beings – she was certainly a great help when Ruth went, even though she had my nephew Max to contend with.

"She's so beautiful." I murmur, wishing I could go all the way back to that evening. To my wife. To have my arm around her welcoming in the New Year – like Martin is in the photo.

"Isn't she? I used to be so jealous." Maggie retorts. "She always said she'd rather be me. Bitch – I never believed her."

It's strange but looking at these pictures doesn't heighten my sadness, there's no sense of melancholy at our separation. Instead I'm smiling, grinning at the memories and mesmerised by my wife's beauty. I used to say something to Ruth I saw in 'The Age Of Innocence' – it's never been more true at this moment.

"Every time you happen to me all over again," I say under my breath.

And she is. Happening to me. Ruth is alive and I'm looking at her now. Smiling and remembering why.

Maybe I can keep going?

After we finish looking at the pictures, twenty out-of-focus, poorly-lit images lasting an hour, I open the bottle of wine Maggie bought and we contemplate watching a video. She's staying with lager, pouring it expertly into a glass. I'm glad of the company and don't mind her hanging around. In fact she used to stay quite a bit, virtually moved in when she first came to the city about three months after Ruth's departure. Gradually she came round less and less as she inevitably built up a new circle of friends at college, all of whom I disapproved of simply because I believed that's the line Ruth would have taken.

"I feel like watching a movie," Maggie announces, so that's what we decide to do. She crawls in front of the cabinet underneath the television. I can't see her face but I'd lay money she is unsatisfied at my collection of cassettes. I haven't upgraded to DVD. The format took off after my wife left.

After a short period Maggie speaks, tentatively, without turning to face me. "What about the wedding video?"

"No," I say bluntly.

She moves on quickly but the damage is done. The spectacle that was mine and Ruth's union has been conjured in both our minds. The wedding. A big deal. A big, happy party with Dean Martin songs, champagne and 260 people dancing on the tables. There's absolutely no question of me watching it, I tried about six months ago on the miserable evening after I'd waved Martin, Ally and their kids off at the airport. In a tidal-wave of self-pity I'd come home ready to wallow in the past. But I couldn't do it. The day was just too perfect. I barely saw the opening shots of my wife getting ready, preparing to meet me. I'd pressed the stop button but it didn't matter, my tears made further viewing impossible. And I never used to cry about anything.

And I was never more aware that family isn't a permanent thing. It can still run away from you. Is only ever loosely contained. The adage that blood is thicker than water isn't evidence of permanence. After all, blood is still just a liquid. It's still fluid. It moves. Becomes diluted.

So I'm sure the wedding video would destroy me, the vows, the first dance, the kiss. And I'm sure that Maggie's glad I declined too, she would have been unable to watch it either. Perhaps she mentioned it only as part of a painful self-test she gets a bit further along with on each attempt.

"Jesus, you've got a lot of shit."

Maggie is now at the back of the cabinet, pulling out movies and blank cassettes – never-watched episodes of *Frasier* and late-night showings of Almodovar – discarding each one after a cursory glance. A pile amasses quickly behind her. She's almost cleaned the unit out when she strikes gold.

"A-ha!… *Grease*."

She hates it but it was, is, Ruth's favourite film. My lack of protest means the tape is inserted and volume increased. Maggie stays in front of the screen, kneeling but upright, instantly singing along with Rizzo who is ridiculing Sandy during the sleep-over at Frenchy's house. I realise this must be where Ruth had left the tape, I certainly haven't watched it since then.

"Won't go to bed, till I'm legally wed…"

I've finished my glass and contemplate moving back to the kitchen for more – resolving to save time by bringing the bottle with me on my return – when the doorbell rings. This is outside standard procedure. Maggie looks as shocked as I am.

I stand up and pace out to the hallway preparing my defences, wondering if Mrs Benson downstairs is about to give me hell about my speakers again.

I swing the door open. It's not Mrs Benson.

Laura – from *Mentor* – my colleague – is standing there. Her own bottle of wine clutched tightly like some kind of modern passport into other people's lives. She's wearing make-up and there's a weird Hermès-type scarf tied round her neck, sticking out comically as if she's in a sketch about WWI fighter pilots. Laura's gone glam. For me? I'm not sure.

"Laura," I say, wishing I had something better to offer.

"Hello Benjamin." Her tone is light and pleasant. Check the syllables.

"Had we arranged something? I'm sorry I…"

"No," she cuts in quickly "I just thought. I mean if you're busy?"

She's heard the television. Olivia Newton John belting out 'Hopelessly Devoted To You' and she's puzzled, trying to work out if it's on 'normal telly' or I've chosen to watch this. I suspect the former might have curtailed any prospect of her bold appearance here tonight.

"No, no… come in."

I hold the door even wider to allow her entry. She steps into the flat, playing nervously with the folds of her raincoat. For one horrible moment, I think she's wearing nothing underneath – it's that kind of coat – and this is a clumsy attempt to seduce a lonely man. But as she slips it off I see she's wearing the chaste black polo neck that always gets her comments in the office.

"You look very nice," I say, because she does.

"Thank you," she says.

I take her mac and hang it on the stand we have in the corner. My leather coat and denim jacket are abandoned on the floor, around the base, next to my trainers, but I think it's important to make this effort. I haven't entirely forgotten how to behave. Laura smoothes her skirt with both palms; smiling at me all the time.

And then it hits me. Laura reeks – there is no other suitable word for it, reeks of Givenchy's Organza. I hate this fragrance, I hate that I know the name. Goes with the territory in our line of work. To my eternal frustration I can tell the difference between any number of scents, unlike my brother Martin who couldn't pick out Chanel No 5 from a line-up of our closest relatives. I edge away from Laura and lead her through into the living room, my nostrils grateful for the respite.

"Um, Maggie, my sister-in-law, is here," I say breezily, though somehow this comes out like a warning, Laura registers the information with a palpable flinch. She hadn't expected Maggie. She knows something about my current lifestyle. She knows this isn't three years ago, when there were always people. But if she's disappointed she recovers quickly.

"Oh, right – she used to live here didn't she?"

Laura says this innocently but I know she's bothered that I'm not alone. And to be honest, there's a part of me this interests. Why has she come round? I'm quite intrigued to let this situation develop.

I make the introductions and then Laura perches herself precariously on the edge of an empty armchair – Ruth's favourite armchair. Sure enough Maggie is instantly aggressive, and though the seat isn't fully occupied, it's evident this apparent pretender to her sister's throne is making all kinds of trouble. We sit silent for a few moments, the three of us – watching Danny Zuko place menus all around the table so his mates don't catch him with plain Sandy.

Laura has realised how her late night appearance must look.

"I work with Benjamin," is the olive branch offered to Maggie, as if it's normal to turn up at 10.30pm simply to talk about life at the UK's number one men's magazine.

My sister-in-law snaps it in half.

"Oh. You're one of them. Ben's told me all about you lot," Maggie says, drumming her fingers on the elbows of her fortress of folded arms.

Whoa, time-out. I'm on my feet in seconds.

"Who'd like a drink?"

Maggie waves her clearly full pint of beer as if I must be blind while Laura looks distinctly uncomfortable. I feel sorry for her, coming to see me of all people, making this effort – perhaps she just wanted to talk about her deceased canine. Though she's attractive and funny, I suddenly decide that Laura can't have many friends either.

"Would you like some wine? I've opened a bottle of red," I grab the glass I'd bought in for Maggie.

I can see she's grateful for the diversion.

"That'll be nice, thank you."

As I pour, I kick some debris away with my right foot, suddenly ashamed of the way I live.

"Sorry about the mess. I haven't had guests in quite a while."

'It's fine. It's a beautiful flat. I love the way you've decorated." Laura offers nervously.

"My sister has excellent taste." No prizes for guessing where this came from.

"She does" Laura agrees sensibly, and Maggie is momentarily quietened.

"So, is everything okay?" I ask, just in case there might be a real reason for Laura's social call.

"Fine. I just thought you might like some company." I'm not convinced, and she continues "… to be honest, I couldn't bear to be at home any longer. It's so lonely now that Sam has gone."

I can see this statement gets Maggie's attention. She understands what it's like to be left behind. For chrissakes she even went on one of those daytime talk shows to share her experience on the subject.

The movie is no longer entertaining for Maggie, Laura is far more diverting. She kicks into action. Before I know it they're connecting and talking and, crucially, listening to each other.

"Ben – go and get me a glass," she barks without looking up. I do as I'm told.

"I want him to come back so much," Laura continues. "I can't believe he's not there when I come home. That'll he never be there again."

I hear them from the kitchen. Laura is stuttering about the funeral. Shit, I remember that it was today. Only a dog's funeral but I'm not a bastard. I know this must be hard for her. I return with the glass. Maggie takes it, again without acknowledging me. Instead she's too busy empathising.

"You keep searching for him, even though it's pointless… can't get him out of your head?" she pushes on erratically, drunkenly, like Sally Jessy Raphael on speed.

"Exactly… yes!" Laura agrees, animatedly. Her eyes are striking when she's animated – an infrequent occurrence in the *Mentor* office, where she adopts a sedentary and anonymous role.

"… You go over everything, wondering if it's your fault? … If there was something you could have done differently?" Maggie says.

Her interrogative tone makes me want to contribute "… take two bottles into the shower?" but I don't. They're now ignoring me completely anyway.

Laura slides down into Ruth's seat, responding well to this interest in her plight.

"But I know there was nothing I did that could have changed what happened."

"But it doesn't help," Maggie pauses here for effect "I'm right, aren't I?" As she speaks, Maggie's turning the volume down on Grease, her body language increasingly sympathetic.

But, I decide, this is alright, they're getting on. It doesn't matter that I am invisible. It makes a change not to be the focus of sympathetic attention. I'm just glad that disaster has been averted and I almost don't want to explain that the deceased in question – Samuel – was a dog, when Laura explains -

"I had Sammy from a puppy."

And then, terrifyingly, I think Laura is going to cry but she doesn't, she carries on. And then, even worse, I think Maggie is going to laugh but she doesn't, she starts making this weird clucking noise and comes over to comfort my colleague, who is now sniffling away into her silk scarf. A scarf that is now slightly askew. Like Ruth had always insisted the shelf above her head was.

"It affects you, it really does. People say they're just pets but they don't understand. I know I must seem so selfish. My God, how pathetic; what with you and your poor sister, your terrible loss..."

I'm watching Maggie – waiting for her scorn but she's surprising me by continuing to make all the right noises. Saying all the things that people have no doubt said to her over the past two years. Saying things she's never expressed to me, of course there was no need – I had what felt like half the western world covering it.

"It'll get easier, you'll get through it. But for now you have a right to be sad…"

Laura's in floods. I return my gaze to *Grease* – we're at the drive-in, Danny's on his own. Stranded. I can't hear him but I feel his pain.

I don't want to go back into the office tomorrow. I really don't.

*

Laura has phoned in sick. I didn't speak to her, but apparently it's woman's stuff. In a virtually all-male office, we never question menstruation. We once had an assistant picture editor with period pains every Friday for three months before it was tentatively queried.

She left with Maggie last night. I finished watching the movie, while they'd finished my wine. They shared a cab, chatting like they'd known each other all their lives. New friends. I think they arranged to have lunch next week. I think I don't mind.

Anyway, there's no time to worry about how my private and public life might be merging, however slightly. I'm well behind on work – and people are starting to notice. I've been given a lengthy buy-in from an American title that needs Anglicising – pretty mundane, pants to trousers, cookies to biscuits, favor to favour – the usual. But it's diverting stuff and I need to be diverted. I'm following instructions, making all the right noises, observing directions.

6: CLEAN

It's evening. Ally is out with Brad (again) helping him buy a present for Chrissy – and I'm looking after the kids with the help of a Chinese takeaway. Emily is reading.

"Is it good?" I ask my daughter, who is currently in the middle of an extended period of sanctions, manifested as silence, towards me. We're talking days here. For no reason other than the inevitable clash between adolescent hormones and a "desperately pathetic old man".

"*Oliver Twist* I mean. Any good?"

She raises an eyebrow in my direction, utters a brief snort and concludes her response by turning even deeper into the back of the armchair in which she has sat hunched for the past two hours.

"Emily?" I say. "I asked you a question."

She rolls her eyes.

"Yes dad. It's good. Okay?"

"Maybe I'll borrow it after you." I say, with no intention of doing so. Ben hates Charles Dickens, and now I do too. She sees through this and doesn't comment. Instead she lifts the next page and adjusts her cushion more comfortably.

I realise she's 13, I realise she's female and thus indecipherable. I realise many things but each rejection bothers me immensely. She's my daughter – I want us to get along. I want her to understand how much we have in common.

"Finc," is all I say and head out of the room.

The Mediterranean sun is descending behind the trees, bathing the interior walls of the apartment through an orange filter. Long shadows are cast down through the hallway. I'm trying to keep my mind empty, thinking random meaningless thoughts. Like why it is in movies that no one ever has the same name? I know three Toms and two Richards – but it never happens on the big screen.

I flick on the radio in the kitchen. An Israeli station in English. There has been a suicide bomber in Tel Aviv. Twelve people dead. I flick it off and study the shopping list Ally has on the worktop. She has her house in order.

7: FOCUS

"There's no room for error people. We've got to be focused."

Lewis Franklin, he of the confident toilet technique, is preparing to command the office, offering everyone the same pep talk. A call to arms. Invoking that collective cry of belief I mentioned before, the belief in our readers and ourselves. There's a reason for this. It's no secret – to Lewis or the editorial in today's *Guardian* – that there's been a seismic shift in the reading taste of the UK male. Or to put it another way, the latest circulation stats have been released and *Mentor* is being chased by *Fraternity*, an American mag that has aimed squarely at our territory and is catching up fast.

I want to feel motivated. I want to feel renewed like some faithful disciple inspired by the careless consonants of Lewis. I want to feel something. I know we've been here before. I warned you that everyday I feel the same. Always the same.

"Let's reconnect with our core reader. Let him speak for himself."

Despite my persistent disinterest, I had predicted, only to myself of course, that something like this would happen. Though highly aware of its imminent UK launch, *Mentor*'s publishing director had dismissed our newest rival as too young. As unlikely to connect with the mature segment of the market. He was, to put it bluntly, wrong. It further transpires that our localised emphasis on Euro-style (at the expense of 'global life', whatever that means), was also wrong. Which all explains why we're sitting here hearing how we need to focus on 'who we are' as 'international citizens'. I feel sick, I really do. At least he's not using his fucking fingers as quotation marks. At least I have that.

With Rick Hatcham, our editor, only able to watch helplessly, Lewis changes tack, preferring to now address his captive audience with a series of penetrating questions. Questions that form the next step in his quest for us all to 'seek and own our new identity'. To not only understand but be in a position to shape our new direction.

"If *Mentor* were a car what would it be?"

I sigh, remembering it's only Wednesday. Despite my time off in Helsinki I'm still knackered. Are there really two more days till the weekend? I want to lie in bed and watch Japanese cartoons.

Someone shouts Alfa Romeo Spider and Lewis nods assent.

"What movie?" he thunders.

I contemplate shouting "Titanic" but our acne-ridden work experience beats me to it, squeaking "*Jerry Maguire!*"

"Explain," Lewis barks.

"Cool, handsome, romantic, sporty – emotional responsibility but with an emphasis on career achievement."

Lewis smiles a broad smile that reminds me of my weird uncle Trevor. The work experience has only been here a bloody week and already he's one of them. I'm feeling distinctly uneasy.

"If *Mentor* were a city which one would it be?" – this one aimed squarely at golden boy Jason, decked out today in simple Hugo. I want to blurt out "Helsinki" or perhaps "Aberdeen" before he can respond, but the challenge is immediately met. Returned via a graceful volley with only a hint of top-spin.

"Sydney."

"Why? Tell me why? Come on let's focus people. Go narrower. Go deeper."

"The old and new world," Jason drawls in his best West London mockney, regardless of his Surrey origins, choosing to elaborate further, "a synergy of sport, style, sex and the synthetic," before finishing with a flourish, "the ultimate urban creation."

This statement strikes a nerve with Lewis. Yet it is evidently the right thing to have said. Clearly the focus Lewis is looking for, he claps his hands in predictable delight.

"Jason's hit it right on the head!"

I briefly envision hitting Jason right on the head.

"Sydney says it all about where we want to be, and how we want to be perceived…"

Oh god, Lewis is going with this in a big way. He moves to the window and faces the glass, his back to us. I notice a damp vertical mark down the spine of his pristine shirt, maybe he isn't so calm and assured? Maybe he's weak too? Then again, I realise it is fucking hot in here – feels like 37 degrees – nah… the bastard's enjoying every excruciating second.

"We need to position ourselves anew. We need to be the Sydney of magazines."

He's actually saying this. I'm not making it up. Even worse, people are buying it. Normally disinterested Laura has temporarily stopped sniffing for her departed canine. She swivels her chair around to get a better view, away from her desk where I notice my Finnish postcard stuck to the bottom of her Mac. For a moment I'm touched, I only sent it because there was nothing else to do, but yes, I'm pleased she's kept it. Since her recent visit to my flat Laura and I have spent some time lately talking, having lunch and sharing stories. She and Maggie, my sister-in-law, now get to be lifelong friends and have so much fun. There've been emails back and forth and trips to the cinema – so much so that it's Laura who now lets me know if Maggie's going to be coming round.

The upside however is that she has mentioned her dead dog a lot less frequently.

The rally is continuing from Lewis. Everyone is immobile, watching their leader speak. All activity has ceased – screensavers have begun to kick in on monitors around the floor. I look around and everyone's smiling. And Lewis is still going. Changing letter from Jason's 'S' but delivering alliteration like nobody's business.

"Refresh. Regroup. And we have to be ruthless."

And then I don't hear anything else. Lewis is still ranting but I hear nothing else. Except for that last word, ruthless, which spirals around my brain at a rate of knots. Ruth less. Without Ruth. I'm standing here listening to this crap and I'm without the woman I thought I'd have forever. And I don't know how it happened. It's staggering. I'm terrified all over again. I need to get out.

I stand up. Lewis has stopped talking, everyone is looking. At me.

Ruthless. It's still reverberating. Laura has wheeled over and is gently tugging my arm, my sudden quest for absence causing a considerable stir, but this is no longer an issue. The latest issue is no longer an issue. Not to me anyway. I pull away from her, oblivious to her concern and leave the office. I walk right past Lewis, past them all, and leave the office.

Desk, plus elevator, plus train and divide by everything else. There is no correct answer. I don't do mathematics or science – that's Martin's territory. I know that every action has its equal and opposite reaction. Furthermore, I'm convinced that nothing equals nothing.

Later I would realise that Lewis had succeeded where everyone else had failed – he'd even achieved his own aims. Out of everyone I'd encountered over the last 24 months – the in-laws, the police, the 'people who'd been there', the homeless, the shelters, the friends – Lewis, the slimy bastard, had provided me with focus. A realisation of an incontrovertible fact. I have to be ruthless. There is no other way. She is gone. Jesus, I already am ruthless. Might as well start acting like it.

She may never come back. I may never see her again. But I might find out why. Or I might not. That's not the point.

The point is I can challenge this. Myself included. Up to now, I've explored constantly the reasons why Ruth wouldn't have left but never remotely touched on the reasons she couldn't stay.

I can deal with the truth both of her departure and the reality of my current situation. I can be ruthless in both hurting and also in protecting myself, I need to be. I can use this in anyway I need to. I can do whatever it takes.

If it comes to it I can accept that she might have been killed. Murdered, maybe even painfully, terribly, horrifically – by someone or something. I can do even this.

I need to be ruthless. In moving on, in ignoring wankers, in finding some happiness – something for myself.

I can be ruthless. I am ruthless. I have two years of practice.

*

Before I know it I'm on the tube. It's empty – this is unusual. It's 2.46 in the afternoon and it feels liberating to not be at my desk thinking up captions for an article about naturism in California. Though "Mind the gap" springs into view. This too is not part of the routine. I enter my flat in a hurry, find a bag, change my t-shirt and am back out the door in seconds. I notice the answerphone is flashing; I tell it to fuck off.

I have my keys and walk to where the car has lain dormant for several months. Inactivity caused through having had nowhere to go. I used to really like driving but only when Ruth was with me to point out the way. I'm useless at navigation. Anyway, it's a nice car. A Renault Clio Sport, three years old; a compromise between Ruth's demands for a small, safe vehicle and my determination to integrate at *Mentor*; in short, my early leanings towards men's lifestyle. I hadn't a fucking clue what 'Sport seats' or 'Sports dash' actually entailed – they just sounded cool. What a fool.

We called our car Albatross. This was not some wanky reference to the Coleridge poem but instead a giddy romantic gesture, the name of the club we met in – the place that brought us back together.

It's a memorable story, our reacquaintance after university. I was the barman, working weekend nights to supplement my paltry income on a local paper; Ruth was struggling on a minimum wage in PR, trying to find a way through debt. Party invites, product launches and free bars were no good at clearing the thousands exhausted at college, so Ruth had sought an alternative source of funds. And thus my future bride was the stripper sent one evening to perform at Albatross, earning herself a supplementary 60 quid in the process. Her nipples went in opposite directions, like the pair that humiliated Katherine Ross in *The Graduate*. Anyway, I took a towel to where she was getting changed in the women's toilets and we joined not long after.

Okay, I'm lying. It's not true. She was just having a drink with a group of friends but I was the barman. And there was a regular stripper but hardly anyone ever noticed her – which was a shame, she was very sweet. And her nipples did go clockwise and anti-clockwise at the same time.

I went through a phase of telling people that lie about Ruth as an exotic dancer; about her shimmying back into my life once more. I'd grown bored of hearing others talk of their worthy chat-up lines and instant animal attraction. People always used to treat my story of three years of silent, unknowing admiration with the absence of passion it deserved. I wanted to shock them, so began to paint a picture of salaciousness. Ruth never minded. It only used to bother her when they would respond with "Wow, that is so cool!" as they looked my wife up and down in a new light; as if she would be capable of such a profession. I don't blame them though. It was a pretty convincing tale, you just have to add details. The cementing factor in this instance being my assertion that my wife's stage name was 'Babe Ruth'. The story couldn't fail.

*

I'm driving along the A13 – the tarmac corridor that leads out of London to my family home. The home that's not there anymore. But it doesn't matter, the drive is helping, the drive is all. I don't need a map. I know the way.

It's a good road – a new road – that bypasses much – that takes you straight there.

Suzie, my counsellor, used to encourage me, whenever I felt stranded, to try and retrace my origins. To "reconnect my unattached soul to the foundations of my life" or some such garbage. I never actually believed her. But here I am, doing it. I realise that she probably meant for me to retrace my steps metaphorically – verbally – on the couch, not to take her literally. Not to get in the car and drive, but this is better, this is working, and I actually feel like I am about to go back to before. Perhaps there is merit in literally starting from the beginning? Returning to a life before Ruth, to a time shared only with Martin. To be ruthless in getting back to me.

Let's be realistic, I'm not sure what all this will achieve, whether I will find anything to help, anything to explain. Whether things will become clearer or remain out of focus. But I do feel nearer and this makes a welcome change from the distance I've felt to everything – and everyone – recently.

Nearer to what is unclear.

So, I'm heading in an easterly direction. I've switched off my phone – fed up of the incessant messages from the office about walking out on Lewis. Jason's was the most recent – stating that he'd "done a bit of damage control", told them all it was a "difficult time, what with the anniversary and all" and that Rick, the boss has already said "not to hurry back in; to take my time". I'm not sure what I'm more surprised about – not being fired on the spot for my dramatic exit or the fact that Jason, of all people, had actually remembered it's been two years since Ruth's departure.

In the sessions with Suzie, I'd talked of this road and what it represents for me. The A13 that runs from the city to Southend. My territory. Essex, the county that begins with the suburban fallout of East London and doesn't stop until it reaches the sea. A much-maligned but self-made region, whose inhabitants are frowned upon by their metropolitan neighbours and indeed the rest of the country.

For no good reason save a misguided negativity towards populist taste and slack consonants. Your New Jersey to your New York if you will.

I've always loved Essex, loved its self-belief, its unabashed provincial pride. Essex is the most American of English counties – a meritocracy of hard work – an ambitious mix of tawdry glamour with the threat of real violence. Essex schools regularly top the national tables, unemployment is low and our economic classes mix side by side in a manner unheard of in Berkshire. In short it has a lot going for it.

I've arrived in my hometown – Grays. A perfect name I've always believed for this unapologetic, industrial and honest heartland. And now I'm driving along our road, barrelling way too fast down the moderate incline I know so well. This will always be our road; Martin's and mine, we claimed it back in 1971 when as babies our parents realised they needed more space and upgraded from a large but anonymous flat to an outspoken four-bedroom Victorian semi-detached with a garden. Our house was surrounded by identical dwellings, all inhabited by couples of a certain maturity whose own children had long flown the nest. My parents' arrival was treated with great interest. It was the perfect environment. From an early age we were paraded up and down the hill in identical prams by our proud parents. The twins. The ones everyone stopped to look at, compare and remark upon.

As the years inevitably fell away our impact increased yet further – "Stand them back to back – see who's the tallest!" – the pair of us nurtured by our protective street like cuttings in a climate-controlled hothouse. People would queue to baby-sit, or encourage us to play with their visiting grandchildren. These holidaying contemporaries of ours were always grateful outsiders – escaping the adults – and relied on us for all the best places to hide, the best way to have fun in the street.

My mother has said that we always seemed so calm and content. I shared this with Suzie who said that this was inevitable given the reassurance that comes from having a permanent best-friend – there was never any need to try and impress or fit in with anyone else. We didn't need them. We had a ready-made gang. If Martin and I were together, everybody wanted to be part of it.

We gained our own reputation that preceded us into school. Good grades but with cheekiness, implied through the presence of a doppelganger, without ever actually having to exploit it – was enough to ensure we weren't ostracised by either the school rebels or the teachers. We achieved novelty without saturation. Don't get me wrong, this isn't arrogance. Just how it was. I'm certainly not claiming we were cool, or fancied by all the girls, or great at football – we weren't, we were just 'the twins' and that was all we needed to stand out. We never had to forge links with the smokers or try to be the class comedians. We didn't have to have the latest trainers or know all about sex. Ours was an already defined, unshakeable clique that no one else could break.

I guess given our grades and all-round luck, looking back it's a wonder we weren't hated. But it can go like that with twins. If you play it right you end up being 'in' with everyone. Though there were a few occasions when people would get irritated and make it be known. I was a coward; fortunately Martin wasn't.

The only times our combined strength was ever jeopardised came during those random periods when Martin and I fell out, usually triggered by one of us daring to become close mates with another. Leaving the other behind; and coming up with private jokes that shattered the previously invincible code of twin conduct, prising a wedge between us. It never used to last very long. Normal service resumed fairly quickly but it's telling that the feelings evoked have never really left me; I can remember all too easily the sense of isolation and incompleteness as I watched Martin be close to another. Like when we were eight and he went through a winter collecting football cards with Brian Adler from school. I hated Brian Adler. Eventually Martin did too.

I park the car and stand outside the building that used to be ours. It no longer contains two semi-detached homes. Neither ours nor the Harrisons. Instead it has been divided into flats. Opened up and re-configured from within. The external aspect remains the same but inside everything is different. Priorities have shifted, viewpoints have been altered, space reallocated.

I feel as if I have only half my powers. I need Martin to be here. Together we were strong. Back then we were untouchable, indivisible. Things are different now. Life has got in the way. Externally my

brother and I are still as we were. The framework remains. Inside...
well I'm not so sure.

Here on this pavement I recall throwing stones to the opposite
kerb for no discernible reason; somewhere behind that fence there I
can see Martin breaking the shed roof; over on that path, I'm hearing
our incessant whining for Mr Harrison to return our football.

I think about who I was then. About who he was. That I was
Martin and he was me. That we were the same.

All this was before everything else. Before Ruth appeared in my
university photo or asked me the time. Before Martin laughed at Ally
dropping her books. Before my niece and nephew were born. Before
my mother moved away.

Before Dad died.

"Benjamin? Or is it Martin?"

The question throws me. Not least as it jolts me abruptly from the
past but mostly because, at this precise moment, I'm not sure of the
answer. I turn around and it's Patricia – a friend of my mother's. A
woman who, like her own house down the street, has remained
resolutely here. A living reminder, a permanent fixture – importantly
somebody aware of who I was before.

"It's Ben," I say.

"Ah yes. I see that now."

I don't ask how – not wanting to know what the deciding
difference might be. I don't want to feel separate from Martin. Not
here, not when I've been remembering how united we once were.

"How are you Pat?" I say with genuine warmth, studying her
sympathetic features.

"I'm very fit," she says, and I can see she is. Somewhere in her
sixties, Pat is the kind of person that is never ill and never complains.
Martin and I always liked her. Everyone likes her.

Pat carries on briskly, like a woman with an agenda that's already
behind schedule.

"I had a letter from your mother the other day. She said that you
were well."

"I am," I say, truthfully.

"It must be so hard. With no news."

"It's been over two years now." I find myself offering this

voluntarily, the words escaping without any new pain. Pat seems pleased by my matter-of-factness. "She'll be back," she says in a display of positivity that I haven't heard from anyone in a long time. Her eyes twinkle almost mischievously, at odds with the seriousness of her tone.

I've just remembered that Patricia is an amateur psychic. I even visited her with my mum when it all happened. I sat as she took both my hands and closed her eyes, there in the Anaglypta back room that she used for readings. It didn't last very long. The ground didn't shake; however hard my mother had willed for it to happen.

Pat didn't give me much but of Ruth's return, she was certain. Adamant that my wife was alive and in control. I was a desperate fool and allowed myself to get carried away by her confidence. After that session my mother had been highly excited. Pointing to Pat's achievement the previous summer in telling some neighbour where their rabbit, Teddy, had got to. I remember Martin had told her to shut up. He'd refused to come with us. Didn't even want to know what Pat had said.

"I wish I still had your faith," I tell her. "I'm resigned to never knowing."

"It's enough that I have it." Pat asserts briskly. "Anyway, still going to all those parties, meeting any pop stars?"

Her conversational *non sequitur* doesn't surprise me. I'm certain that my mother has filled the remainder of her correspondence with tales of the high-life I'm apparently living in London. This is partly my fault. It's simpler to tell a concerned parent about glamorous work-related stories, however tenuous, than risk upsetting her with news of my ongoing desolation and never-ending heartache. No contest really.

"You and the high-life eh? Not like us out here where nothing ever changes."

"Things have changed," I say, pointing to the flats that used to be my home.

"The real things stay the same," she says enigmatically.

"Yeah, I guess they do," I say, picking up on the intrigue in her eyes that has been there as long as I can remember.

"Anyway, I'd best be going. Got an appointment with a man." She gives a throaty cackle before kissing me on the cheek and one final quick question.

"How's your brother doing?"

And I realise I'm not totally sure. I lie and say. "Martin's great, really happy."

"Right, right," Pat says flatly, before waving goodbye and continuing on her way. I get the sense that she doesn't believe me. But before I can ask why, she's gone. There's nothing more to be said. Had I met anyone else, had it been any other of my parents' old friends I could have expected them to cling to our meeting, to ask me in for a cup of tea and a trip down memory lane – but I guess Pat's never been that sort of woman. She had several affairs when we were growing up – even moved in with us once, until her equally philandering husband pleaded for her to come back. She did. Only when he bought her a new Hoover. Pat has always done her own thing.

Her lack of conviction about Martin stays with me. Once again I am thrown back into the past, adamant that it wasn't always like this. That there was a time when I always knew what he was thinking or how he was. And how I was as a result.

I climb into my car and give a final look towards the house through the windscreen. Recalling the first time I was aware that I might actually be distinct from my brother. When for once it wasn't possible to realign ourselves with a few conciliatory words.

A day I pinpointed with Suzie as the beginning of his ability to lapse into remoteness; the start of his other pressures; of his drink problem even. A defining moment in both our lives. A possible cause that led to a major effect and a time when even I would be unsure of what he might be thinking for days on end. Not like those childhood periods of separation I've mentioned, not even confrontation, but instead my growing inability to know what was in his head or his heart.

A day when I had brought Ruth home, here, for the first time. My memory alights on the moments before I took her inside to meet my parents. Ruth and I waiting outside, steeling ourselves, me preparing the ground. Sitting in a car, Ruth's old car, just like this and staring at the house – just as I am now. Thirteen years ago. Twenty-two years old. Hardly old enough to look after myself – let alone a prospective life-term partner.

Ruth had been terrified of meeting my mother. She didn't say as much but she had been silent throughout the whole trip. I knew something was up of course. Normally she sang 'Live To Tell' by Madonna at the top of her voice. But that day she was quiet. All the way down the A13, the old version of the road that wound interminably through Dagenham, back when the Ford plant was fully functioning, not the modern, fast-lane equivalent that brought me here today.

I hadn't helped matters by telling her for the first time that my mother was very posh. That she was distant aristocracy, that in her head, she didn't live in Essex – but that she loved my father, who did, above all else. Her heart may have resided with a man in Grays, but her character, her breeding, her resolve, was resolutely Norfolk and there it would always remain.

I remember I got out of the car and made Ruth carry the flowers she'd bought. She wanted to run.

My father had answered the door. I was glad. My Dad liked everyone. Everyone liked my Dad. He was wearing a suit, he hated wearing a suit. This choice of outfit had my mother's instruction stamped all over it. Ruth noticed his cricket tie straight away and said how nice it was. My Dad beamed. He tried to catch my eye as he was gathering our coats, as if to say she's lovely Ben. She's lovely.

In the next instant my mother arrived in the hall, a restrained kiss on my cheek and quick up-down appraisal of Ruth.

"Ruth. A pleasure. What lovely flowers. Thank you so much. Now can you give me a hand dear? I've got Yorkshires in the oven and the gravy needs stirring."

And that was that – Ruth was off to the kitchen before she knew what was happening. My mother always expected women to help. It's always been her way. Even if the kitchen had been on fire, she wouldn't have asked her men to get involved. Unless the joint needed carving.

I was left holding the bouquet until Dad called me into the front room.

"It's a good sign," he'd said when I arrived "It was the same with Alison"

"She's insane." But I was definitely relieved.

Suddenly there was a peal of laughter from the kitchen. I looked through the hatch that my parents put in sometime during the seventies. Ruth was wearing my Dad's apron – the one with a French maid outfit on. She was grinning; literally getting her hands dirty with the gravy. Ruth was crap in the kitchen.

I'd tried to catch her eye. Make sure she was alright. There was no need – I could see she was.

"She knows what she's doing, your mother," Dad said behind me, as he restored the volume on the snooker final.

"Shame Ruth doesn't." I said grinning.

And I realised my Dad was right, my mother did know what she was doing. Getting her involved was the quickest way to make Ruth feel part of the family, as if she belonged. My parents knew all about my long-term awareness of Ruth, that we'd met again and that I was determined to marry her. I'd avowed to them that she was the one. It was only later Dad told me that, as a result, my mother was as nervous as I was. Wanting desperately to like her other son's choice and to know I too was going to be happy.

"Where's Martin and Alison?" I'd said, after a while.

"Alison's not coming. She's not well," Dad said.

"Where's Martin then?"

"Up in your room."

I was surprised I hadn't even realised he was already here.

I took the stairs three at a time, like I'd been able to since we were 11. I pushed opened the door that had our names carved into it. Martin was at the window. Looking down into the garden. I didn't see him when I first entered, too taken aback by the sameness of our room. It never failed to direct me immediately back to childhood. The way that we had decorated the skirting boards with lists of football results charting a whole season. The claret and blue curtains which pledged our allegiance to West Ham. The fact that there were two spare bedrooms in the house yet Martin and I insisted on sharing. We weren't stupid, we used the other two rooms, one each, allowing us time alone but always slept in the same space.

Martin turned around. Something was up. His eyes were funny for a start.

"Ruth's here," I remember saying, breathlessly.

"Oh right." Unenthusiastic, uncaring even.

"What's wrong Mart?" This was a question I'd never previously asked him. How strange is that? I guess I always knew the answer without having to enquire.

As I said, I remember it as a day of firsts.

"Nothing Ben. Okay?"

"Is Ally alright? You're getting on ok, aren't you?" I'd figured that he must have been finding it hard travelling up to Aberdeen every week. With only his new mate Chrissy for company.

No response. I was nervous. This was a first too. "How are the wedding plans?" I continued bravely.

"Look she's fine, Ben. The wedding's fine. Can't wait for the bloody thing to be over."

"It's a shame she couldn't come. I can't wait for her to meet Ruth." I sat down on my old bed. "Dad said she's not feeling well?"

"Something like that." He said, still non-committally.

Martin wasn't responding. He wasn't coming through.

"I'd better go back and see if Ruth's okay."

Actually I wanted to speak to my Dad, see if he knew what was up with my brother. More than anything, I was angry. This was my day. This was supposed to be about me bringing Ruth into the fold. Martin wasn't allowed to do this.

"You coming down?" I tried, one last time, genuinely unsure of his response.

That strange look in his eyes that I didn't recognise.

"Yeah."

At the door, I turned back.

"It's Ruth!" I said, passionately. "You remember – as in 'Ruth Carmichael asking me the time'? You know how much she means to me Martin."

And with that he slowly stood up.

He did. I know he did. He'd heard all about her when he used to come and stay with me at my university. Heard my constant retelling of our only conversation; my reference to the photo of her in that dress. But I guess maybe he hadn't picked up how much she had really meant to me. Martin certainly didn't visit as much as I would have liked. He'd met Alison by then and things were progressing swiftly.

The times he did come down I'd take him to the student bars with my mates, show him my pissed-up life especially aware that his own was firmly set within a relationship. A proper relationship.

It wasn't strange that he'd started down this path, that he had another confidante in Ally. This wasn't a point of difference. I didn't feel left behind. Occasionally perhaps when I daydreamed about a girl who may or may not have been a viable possibility, I had the sense of feeling slightly inferior but not often. Not with Martin. He didn't read desperation into the picture I had of Ruth on my wall. Maybe he hadn't read anything. By the time we got to us standing there, in our old bedroom, four years had passed since it was taken. And now I wondered if he even remembered the shot.

The dinner table had been laid by the time we went downstairs, for a laugh I wanted Martin to race down like we used to, but he trudged down slowly, feet meeting each step. I sat down next to Ruth who was back to being nervous. She had a glass of sherry so things had been going fairly well – my Dad never offered his sherry to just anyone. But I could still she was trembling.

"Martin. This is Ruth,' I'd said.

"Hi," he said, and then offered his hand. It was too formal. She paused, uncertain, before shaking it, across the roast beef, having to stand up to connect. Accidentally knocking table legs – making the gravy boat lose liquid overboard.

The subsequent meal was torture. Martin resolutely avoided conversation with Ruth at every turn, however hard my parents tried. I felt terrible. She had already said it was going to be difficult meeting him. That I was to understand how bizarre it would be. He was, *is*, a carbon copy of me after all. I'd joked on the way that she better not fancy him and she hit me, hard.

And there we were, the dinner turning into a total nightmare. Made worse in that I couldn't imagine what was bothering him and could only watch as he worked his way through drink after drink. The atmosphere was appalling. A typical exchange went like this.

"Isn't it funny that I spoke to Ruth back then? That we lived no more than half a mile from each other for three whole years." Me trying to lighten the mood.

Ruth smiled a wan smile that said she's heard me tell people this before. My father grinned too and said, "Maybe you just weren't ready for each other then. Fate has a funny way of organising things."

My mother didn't comment, content to let me continue as she served Martin extra potatoes with focused precision from a lifetime of practise. Dad stepped once more into the breach.

"A lovely story. Isn't it a lovely story Martin?"

And of course Martin still wasn't listening or even acknowledging the extra food on his plate. He was pouring himself another glass of wine.

"Yeah," Martin repeated absently, for the fifteenth time that day.

When the meal was over, my mother decided to tackle my brother head on.

"Martin. You and Ruth do the washing up, I want to show Ben the sunflowers that your father's grown."

It had been an unexpected suggestion. I protested immediately, stammering something about her being a guest – this was no time to leave her alone with Martin. Not when he was acting so unlike him. And by now so pissed. Ruth looked horrified but naturally couldn't protest. It was all left to Martin who strode off purposefully into the kitchen. She had no choice but to follow. I'd looked at my father incredulously. He'd shrugged. "She knows what she's doing."

And incredibly, it worked. They came out of the kitchen half-an-hour later talking animatedly, laughing at the pictures of twins hermetically sealed to the fridge. The magnetic pull of a decade. I couldn't believe it but wasn't about to start questioning 'why?' or 'how?'. Unfortunately Martin had obviously carried on drinking, but I didn't care. I was grateful that his mood had softened. That his normally impeccable manners had returned and given Ruth a chance to see what he was really like.

I took an opportunity to pull him aside when it became Ruth's turn to see the sunflowers. We were alone in the living room.

"So? What do you think?" I asked quickly. "She's great isn't she?"

"Yes. She's great... great," he iterated, also quickly.

I wanted more detail. This wasn't good enough for me. He obliged, going further in his praise.

"I mean it. She's lovely Ben."

Not enough.

"You're acting funny Martin. You never act funny."

"Ben. I like her. What do you want me to say?"

"It's not about what you're saying. Something is wrong. Something you're not telling me."

Our eyes connected. His breath stank of alcohol and the inebriation showed in his lack of focus. Somewhere behind them I could see he was struggling; desperately trying to pull it together. After an age, they sharpened momentarily and I caught a glimpse.

"Look Ben, I have to tell you something. Alison and I are..."

And that was that. I knew my brother, my twin brother, was going to be a Dad. I sat down straight away. Shit! They weren't even married. And immediately I knew that he was terrified and uncertain about the future. I remembered that Ally's family were Catholic and an abortion would never be countenanced.

He was about to finish the monumental sentence, when Ruth returned with my parents and launched into conversation straight away, as if determined to keep the hard-won momentum going.

"You two really do look alike!" she exclaimed, apropos of nothing.

But all I was thinking was that Martin was going to have a kid. And I knew he wasn't ready. I knew this because I wasn't ready, and such an event would inevitably affect me, well, if not equally then pretty damn close. I was already afraid of resenting the baby, what it would further do to mine and his already unequal lives. Not selfishly you understand, I knew things change, I understood that. But a baby was different. It wasn't on either of our horizons. But I simply had to react – I had no control over the timing of this shift, the words he'd just spoken or the inevitable events that would follow over the months and indeed years. It was how it was going to be. I just had to get on with it.

From that time on I experienced a sense of real difference from my brother. Not just in his new responsibilities but in my awareness that I was absolutely no longer his 'other half'. And also in his evident need to find solace in alcohol.

Later, with Suzie, I was able to trace much to that time. To – of all days – the day he met my Ruth.

Yet Ruth and I went from strength to strength. And there didn't seem to be any real damage to Martin and me. We grew close again as he navigated the wedding, the birth of Emily and an increasingly lucrative career.

The situation was helped by Ruth and Ally becoming friends. Everything became normal, became stable. It seemed that as twins we realigned once more, each with our own new position but, crucially, the same space between us. Or so I believed.

Perhaps only now do I sense that we were never completely the same. That there was more going on than I understood. And maybe that's not how it had to be, maybe it wasn't inevitable.

That day then – there, in our old house, stands out in my memory. It was a day of firsts.

I start the car and head back to the city. Back to my flat.

8: LOYALTY

Chrissy is quiet today. It's such a rare occurrence that everyone has noticed. Three of the guys have tried to get her to go out for a fag and she has declined each time. Instead she has opted to spend the morning sorting through the drawings that clutter the floor around her chair. There's been a few muttered, relatively chaste, swear words but that's about it. No cackle, no jokes, no Chrissy. And I am moderately concerned. I've known her long enough to know that this means something's up. Despite my total disinterest in her, frankly embarrassing, relationship with Brad, I don't want her to be unhappy. In saying that however, at least musing over Chrissy's problems allows me to take my mind off events at home and ghosts from the past that may or may not have reappeared.

I've eaten lunch at my desk – a salad, some fruit – I have no real appetite at the moment. Chrissy has remained silent. She knows I keep staring but is resolutely not responding. Her body language like some school kid hiding an exam paper from classmates, hunched over the desk with squat forearms flat on melamine surface. I paused at her computer on my way to and from the toilet five minutes ago, but it made no difference. She didn't acknowledge my presence. I'd tried tempting her with chocolate and a can of coke from the machine but she didn't acknowledge those either. Not even to look up.

Boy wonder Brad hasn't called either – which is strange. I'm sure the two non-events are related. At the very least, and at this relatively late time of day, he's usually phoned by now with an 'awesome killer sentence' or 'phat phrase' just conjured and no doubt certain to make his masterpiece a best-seller. And if this were a normal day Chrissy would then recite the passage out loud, thrilled by the exciting prospect that her boyfriend might actually be the next Sidney Sheldon. I hate it when this happens. It's so humiliating for all concerned. I cringe every time it happens. I have an almost total aversion to anything self-proclaiming itself as art, yet remain confident in my belief that Brad can't write, at least not in a manner that might give Salman Rushdie reason to lie awake at night. And yet, and I hate myself for this, I always pretend to be amazed by his prowess, his linguistic dexterity. I have to – no-other ex-pat in the office gives a damn and Chrissy, being the only woman, already feels isolated enough. As for the Germans and Scandinavians here, well they pretend not to understand, even though their English is probably better than mine. Me? I pretend to care and in doing so, guess that on some level I really do.

Things are different when Chrissy announces that her man has fashioned a hot new sex scene. Then the lads ask for it to be emailed and I am torn between revulsion at their shallow interest and happiness that Chrissy momentarily feels like she belongs – that she is pleased with their attention. Sure enough, with immediate and inevitable resolution the latest passage will arrive a few moments later. It is retrieved by a gleeful Chrissy with the relish of a schoolgirl temporarily allowed to hang out with the cool crowd. We all listen as she holds forth with the tawdry details – a litany of crass passages populated by terms such as 'gash' and 'pork'. She invariably gets a superficial round of applause.

Once I glanced at a printed email and noticed Brad had typed 'Copyright. All rights reserved' protectively across the top of the page – as if there were some likelihood of plagiarism. There's about as much chance of catching the Queen doing a stand-up routine. "One wonders if there is anyone in from Balmoral?"

Ben, my brother, is always trying to get me to recognise the brilliance of Fitzgerald or McInerney when all I need from books is escapism, an airport novel that's preferably about an airport. A siege crisis from which only a maverick CIA agent can save the day. I don't do words for words sake; I do hackneyed plots with Scud missiles and megalomaniacs – full of thrills and danger but ending with nice tidy resolutions.

Talking of words, today isn't just all quiet on the Chrissy front, Ben isn't responding to my careful emails either, he's not coming through. His out of office message set to bounce back each time. I can tell it wasn't written by him. For a start it says Benjamin but for the most part, I can just tell. I have a dull sensation somewhere inside (My gut? My head?) that he is consumed by something new. A vague unformed notion that he is preoccupied. Something has changed lately, why do I feel like the wind is changing for both of us? Shit, I sound like Mary fucking Poppins.

Chrissy's continuing mood and the silence from London are unsettling to say the least.

*

Evening. We have come out for something to eat. We are with a couple we know quite well from the golf club. They live in Brighton ("Hove, actually. Just outside. Have you heard of it?"). They are older and have 16-year-old daughter who is babysitting our two back home. To Ally this teenager is just a child. Only three years older than Emily. It took a full 15 minutes to persuade her to leave our kids in Debbie's care. Fifteen minutes of written instructions and mobile-phone numbers for every conceivable scenario. We won't be late but it doesn't matter. My wife is a good mother but sometimes she needs to let go.

Anyway, we've managed to get out for a couple of hours and the couple, whose names are not important just yet, are reminiscing about England in a way that is making Ally misty-eyed and boring the fuck out of me. I have a strong suspicion that three gin and tonics are contributing to Ally's teary melancholy but as I'm on orange juice I have no way of ascertaining whether this amount of alcohol and mixer would produce a similar effect on me, or, specifically, my lack of enthusiasm for mindless chatter that ensues about "Desmond Lynam – A Brighton and Hove supporter, you know?" and the "unspoilt quality of Windermere through all four seasons".

The sun has gone down but the air is so warm. I am wearing a short-sleeved shirt that Ally bought in every colour. She knows I hate shopping so whenever I profess the slightest preference towards anything, rest assured she'll exploit the opportunity. Ally is wearing a long white cotton dress that shows off her tanned arms beautifully, she wears little jewellery – just the two platinum bands on her ring finger and the thin bracelet on her right wrist. A present from Ben's wife Ruth; given expertly, for a reason that I cannot remember.

The restaurant is called La Trattoria, situated on a tiny palm-decked square that could almost be Italy. Terracotta pots, taped mandolin and a strong smell of pizza adds to the illusion. I have eaten fettuccini, Ally had spaghetti bolognese like the rest of our party. "Spag Bol" is what they actually ordered. We bought the kids here when we first arrived. Max had embarrassed us all by asking for brown balls – when he really meant profiteroles.

I'm bored with our conversation and scan the surrounding area, examining the couples interested in each other's lives and the party groups ordering more and more wine. I would like a drink. 'Like' is an understatement. An understatement that doesn't imply the twitch in my eye or the dry sensation that hogs my throat like sandpaper.

My roving eyes come to a halt on a darkened window in an apartment above and to the right of the restaurant. I get the uneasy sensation that I am being scrutinised. Somewhere behind the impenetrable mask of the glass I'm sure someone is watching me. A figure is there. An outline that doesn't alter, even when I squint to get a closer look. Why are they watching me? I cannot make out details, only form. The vagueness of all this is incredibly unsettling. I lean forward to rectify the situation, my aluminium chair scraping noisily on the stone floor of the terrace. When Ally nudges me violently.

"Martin? Are you with us? Karen was just saying that Howard can get tickets for Wimbledon fortnight."

Karen and Howard – that's their names.

"Best seats in the house at that," Karen's husband, Howard, underlines proudly.

My manners take over and I rejoin the conversation, refilling everyone's glasses and gesturing politely to the waiter that another bottle might be in order. I almost ask for a fourth glass to be brought.

"I've never been. Always fancied it. Haven't I Ally? Always fancied it?"

"He has. Always saying he'd fancy it."

What's happening to us? I feel like we're two guest stars on that old sitcom about couples who fuck up each others lives on holiday. *Duty Free*, I think it was called.

"We must go together. We'll do it when we're all back in Blighty."

Karen said Blighty. She actually did. And this is so depressing that I return to my window, certain that I'm still being watched.

My wife takes up the slack.

"We'd love to come," Ally says, "But why do the women have to grunt so much? It's positively disgusting."

I hear it but Ally's comment bothers me. She's playing a role here, and I'm not quite sure for whose benefit or more worryingly, if she's even aware. Whatever, Karen laughs, clapping her bony hands in agreement. I can only half-concentrate on the window and silhouette above.

"I know! It's ghastly…" and then she leans forward, whispering "It's always the Germans. No idea of the spirit of the game."

Jesus. I push my plate to the centre of the table, dragging the tablecloth into uneven folds. I've had enough, in more ways than one. I gaze at Howard and Karen across the table. Vapid, vacant faces with less depth than the shallow-end in Max's paddling pool. They've lost me again. I look back towards my window but this time for some respite. The unease it may deliver actually preferable to participating in this farce any longer. But there's no one there. I must be imagining things. I'm annoyed by myself and this takes over. Bile rising.

"What spirit is that Karen?" I interject, a tad aggressively. "British reserve doesn't win Grand Slams does it? Which I always thought was rather the point of competition?"

I notice Karen's husband bristle visibly at my attack, harumphing away under his moustache. Ally's mouth falls open at the rudeness of it all – but maybe there's a smile in her eyes? I can't really tell for sure.

We round up proceedings pretty quickly after that. I pay the whole bill out of a sense of atonement. Ally certainly expects me to, her body language is quite clear on the matter. We vacate the premises saying goodnight (only I attempt the Hebrew) to the waiter – he's a nice guy, God knows what he thinks of us. As we leave Karen thanks me graciously while hubby only manages a reluctant grunt. He does! I almost tell him he sounds like Martina Hingis.

We stroll the quarter of a mile back to our apartment side by side (in relative harmony). Ally takes my hand and it's nice to be walking. We fit so well together. I like the smell of her perfume. It's strange, I never like it at the start of an evening – it always seems too sensual, inappropriate even. By the end of the night it has mixed with her own fragrance and become something else entirely. Not that I know much about these things – I don't even know what it's called. Wouldn't know where to buy it for her.

In front of us, Karen tries to get her husband to hold her hand. He doesn't, instead he's pointing out stars. A small child runs up gabbling in American English for a dollar, he gets nothing – they ignore him completely.

As we are following several paces behind, we soon become the boy's target. Ally digs in her purse and finds a shekel or two – thrusting it in his hand. The kindness in my wife's eyes is manifest. As the boy runs off, I take her hand even more tightly.

The Israeli boy returns almost immediately with three squawking friends, and suddenly it's like being in Jerusalem. We don't normally get this up in Haifa, at least not in this area. But times are strange. The North is meeting the South. Ally's eyes harden and her hand stiffens in my grasp – she's unable to deal with this inevitable circumstance. It's no big deal but she feels threatened. I wave the boys away and we continue undisturbed. Ahead of us, Karen looks back and shakes her head in our direction, no doubt thinking we have a lot to learn. And we do... just not the things she and her husband have to teach.

As we cross the square, a man steps out of the shadows holding what I immediately determine is the Bible. He is wearing a thick green sweater despite the humid temperature. On his right arm is a gold pin in the shape of a cross. It is a simple decoration but somehow screams 'nutter'. I move silently around my wife, positioning myself between her and our imminent, unwanted, companion. I can see he wants to talk to us, is preparing to share his vision. And now I just want to get home.

"Sir. The Bible was written for you," he asserts directly – in my direction.

"It wasn't," I reply categorically. Ally keeps quiet, save for the noise of her heels clattering on the pavement. She's religious but I can tell such a man doesn't correspond with her idea of faith, on any level.

"You have a choice to make," his voice is insidious, creeping under my skin.

"No thank you," I say, with all the Englishness I can muster, Karen and Howard would be proud, if they hadn't continued ahead that is. Not wanting to get involved, no doubt.

The man is not listening. He's keeping pace, matching us step by step.

"Do you know what love is?"

"Yes. Thank you."

Ally wants him to go away, I sense she might snap and swear, but for now she holds her tongue. The guy is close – I can see hundreds of blackheads littering his greasy nose, he stinks of body odour.

"Who do you love?"

"I love my family, my wife," I snap. Why am I bothering to answer? I can tell that Ally is angry with me, that I have made this contact.

"Don't leave them. Don't leave your family," he says.

"Martin, come on. Howard and Karen are waiting. Don't pay him any attention."

Her rudeness doesn't trouble the nutter in the slightest, underlining my belief that his words are aimed at me. Not her, not us.

"In Jesus. There is a lesson for us all. For you. About commitment."

He's rambling now and it's easier to dismiss him.

"Right. Thanks for that. I'll keep it in mind," but in a way I'm almost daring him to carry on. Confident that I have the upper hand.

Ally curses and stalks off, leaving me to my conversation – for that is what our exchange has somehow become.

The man smiles a wide tooth-decayed smile and taps his bible gently. Irises kaleidoscope into focus. He has flecks of grey in his green eyes.

"As Ruth said, 'Don't urge me to leave you or to turn back from you. Where you go I will go, and where you stay I will stay.'"

He is no longer smiling.

"As Ruth said…"

I resist the pressure to vomit. Telling myself to calm down, he's a bible freak and this is Israel. You don't have to go too far into the tourist areas to have a psalm or teaching thrown at you. But it's more than hearing the sound of her name. It's the words. The words that land like arrows. The words attributed to *her*.

He's persisting, finishing me off with Ruth and her words. Words that wound.

"'Where you die I will die, and there I will be buried. May the Lord deal with me, be it ever so severely, if anything but death separates you and me.'"

With that he's gone. There's no further drama. No clap of thunder, no burning bush. But they're all there alright, only in my head.

I somehow manage to move on, manage to rejoin our group, a group I now feel even less of a part of. I'm sweating and hoping they don't notice – it's warm – they won't notice I tell myself. Feels like 37 degrees. As I get close, a Hampshire accent drifts towards me, intoning "that Orion is the greatest of all constellations". I arrive to see Karen rapt at her husband's stellar knowledge. Ally is gamely trying to join in, nodding enthusiastically, but I can see she's pissed off I carried on talking back there.

She didn't hear the nutter mention Ruth did she? Fuck, why the hell did I linger? I brought all this on myself. Of that, I'm more certain than ever.

No further reference is made about our Christian suitor. And I don't want to be the one, but I am desperate to articulate *something*. I can't, of course. Ally, troubled by the turn of events and the new direction the evening has taken, resolutely studies the floor as we begin to navigate the streets home. It's time to move on. She is anxious to collect our kids and return safely home. I'm inclined to agree with her.

As we cross the road near Howard and Karen's apartment, Ally makes some comment about biting insects and begins to scratch her elbow furiously. Karen leaps to the rescue, rummaging in her bag for some cream. Howard offers advice about application. I keep quiet, grateful now for their animated chatter about the civilised lack of mosquitoes back in England. And I have to agree with them.

*

The ring begins instantly, I'm constantly amazed by the power of telecommunications, by the speed and clarity with which I'm connected to other human beings on other parts of the planet. There is click and life appears on the end of the line. I imagine a thin, elegantly manicured hand removing a pearl earring – my mother has always dressed like a tame Raine Spencer – even though my father was an Essex man – she remains resolutely House of Windsor – Sandringham, Norfolk to be more precise.

"Mum. It's Martin," I say, fiddling with the mouse on my desk as I talk.

"Martin? What's wrong? The children?"

My mum never gets me mixed up with Ben, everyone else does.

"No – they're fine. I'll send you some pictures," I say on autopilot, knowing I'll forget. 'No, it's nothing like that. Work is slow today, I just wanted to chat… ."

The "Sorry. Benjamin Carter is out of the office" email that was waiting in my in-box again this morning has propelled me into action. I had a terrible night's sleep. More bad dreams. I dreamt that Ruth was calling to me from the window above the restaurant, that she was up there laughing alongside that bloke with the bible. I'm unshaven and irritable. I ignored Ally's small-talk and avoided the kids' demands to umpire an argument over the tv remote this morning. I arrived at the office to find Chrissy still preoccupied. I was hoping that at least she would provide a sense of the usual, I was even prepared to listen to an account of the fantastic oral sex she and Brad performed on each other last night, if it meant I'd get a degree of normality back. No such luck. Everything seems to be falling apart. I'm desperately trying to hold it together.

Until, that is, I saw that my most recent email to Ben had gone un-answered yet again. I have no further information, save the opportunity to contact someone called Laura if it was urgent. I briefly thought about doing just that. But who's Laura? Why don't I know who Laura is? I know who Jason is, Rick, Stu and Rebecca – I even know Ruth's old friends like Anita. So, instead I called my mother. And here she is, waiting for her eldest son to continue.

"I was on my garden kneeler – the one Ally sent me. It's wonderful."

Ally is great with my mum, always gets it right. She sent my mum this bloody kneeler five years ago and she still gets complimented. Apparently I made a good match. We both did.

"I thought you had a man come in and do the garden for you these days?" I say, momentarily troubled by the vision of my 65-year-old, arthritis-ridden mother keeling over in her herbaceous border.

"Mr Dwight? He still comes once a fortnight, but I like to get things tidy for him, pull out the weeds and what have you…"

I can't be bothered to tell her she's insane and missing the point of having a gardener. She's obviously happy with the arrangement.

"Mum. Have you spoken to Ben lately?" I say as lightly as possible, which obviously isn't enough as she falls silent at this point. She is desperately worried for my brother.

"Mum?"

"I haven't Martin. Not directly, not for a while. It was the anniversary…"

"I know," I say.

She sighs and I wish I hadn't called. My mum has a quiet life now. She doesn't need this. She's quite happy living her routine social existence in Old Hunstanton up in Norfolk, in the cottage she and Dad were going to retire in before he inconveniently died on her. To her credit, and, if I'm honest, mine and Ben's relief, she pressed ahead with their dream, using his sensible life assurance policies to transplant her life wholesale from Essex back to the county of her roots. She believed that her two sons were happy with their lot and able to push on with their lives. She's kept very busy – and even took part in one of those naked charity calendars for the WI. I asked her not to send me a copy. She was determined to spend her retirement painting. My mother is a fantastic artist – some distant relative of Dora Carrington or someone from the Bloomsbury group or whatever it is. As far I understand the line is 'removed' somewhere. Ben would know, it's the sort thing he retains.

"Pat's seen him," she offers.

"I'm sorry?" I splutter, thinking I've misheard her. She did say "not directly".

"Patricia. Remember? From Grays, she saw him outside our old house yesterday. She called me to say he's fine. Said she 'was supposed to tell me' in that way she does."

My mother pauses to scold Ferdy her cat. When I really need her full attention.

I remember that Pat is a fucking psychic or whatever they're called. That she gets feelings about things.

"What was he doing at the house?" I don't understand. "What was Ben doing?"

"Pat said he was sorting things out."

"Sorting what out?" This is making me feel worse.

"Making sense of things," is all my mother says.

I think back to our house, the house that's no longer there. I think of my brother sitting in his car outside. Staring at it. The image is so strong. I am bothered by my mother's assertion that Ben is making sense of things. What things?

She's still talking. "He's going to be alright. Pat said he'll be in touch with me soon."

"He's not dead mum." When I really want to say "What about me?"

"Of course not. Don't be silly," my mother says bluntly. "She asked after you too."

"Who did?"

"Pat. Asked how you were. I said you were very well. You are very well Martin. Aren't you?"

"Why, what did Pat say?"

"Nothing, why would Pat say anything?"

I'm getting worse. I don't know what this conversation is for. I look up from the desk, desperately seeking fresh air, uncontaminated by talk of Pat and Ben outside our house. Chrissy is making a poor job at pretending she's not listening. I sense a breakthrough in office relations, I decide that this is an area to concentrate on. My mother is unnerving me with her words and I choose not to deal with this now.

"Mum. I'd better go."

"Okay Martin. I love you." She never used to say that. Not that she was cold, far from it, in fact she regularly expressed her feelings but always through tactile gestures. That we now communicate mostly by phone has meant she's grown accustomed to saying what was previously unnecessary. And I appreciate hearing it. It calms me.

I hang up and Chrissy instantly bricks up her wall. It's not even worth trying. There's no opportunity for me to forget the image of Ben outside our house 'making sense of things'. I'm there with him. I can see everything he's seen.

I used to love that house. Now it only reminds me of the end, of the last years when everything changed. I think of them carrying my father's body out and then later of handing the keys over to the estate agent, while my mother sobbed in the car.

I think also of the day when Ruth was first introduced.

Alison had had morning sickness; she couldn't go five minutes in the car without throwing up. We'd argued. I'd needed her with me but knew that she wasn't up to the drive from Gerrards Cross. I was knackered too having flown down from my new job in Aberdeen. But there was no backing out, Ben had arranged the dinner for weeks. To meet Ruth.

Ruth who I'd already met. Ruth who was already more to me than a photo on Ben's wall.

9: FEATURE

Coming back into the office feels strange. I haven't had time off between Monday and Friday for quite a while. When there's no one to spend it with holiday is pretty easy to accumulate, in fact I must have around seven weeks due.

I feel more confident. The morning started like all the rest but I'm getting on with it. I have been civil to most people and raised my eyebrows on passing Lewis in the corridor, a universal gesture that says 'Alright?' without any need for dialogue. I reached my desk, deep in thought on providing a cover line for our main feature this issue – an Armani tribute from a plethora of famous actors, statesmen and fashionistas. I have logged in and seen there are several emails waiting patiently from my brother. I was about to read them, to see how he is and more importantly, reply. I definitely need to reply. But Rick, my editor has had an idea and is sitting here on the edge of my desk trying to get me to understand 'where he's coming from'. Trying to interest me in a concept. Trying to get me to buy into his vision, 'to own it for myself' no doubt. This novelty is making me forget all about titles for Armani articles and replying to Martin. And I am listening intently for no other reason than it makes a change from the usual distractions and mostly that I do consider Rick, my boss, to be the most sincere person here.

He's had what people always call a meteoric career but in his case really mean it; moving out to Italy, working his way through the usual fashion bible suspects before being called back to London to take the reins here at *Mentor*. Somehow managing to stay well-respected and by all accounts enjoy a moderately normal family life. He even brings his kids into the office, where they invariably end up with Laura. Shit, I must speak to Laura today. But I must also keep listening to Rick who's flicking his prematurely silver hair – which does actually make him look distinguished and somehow younger than me – and still trying to broach a subject I'm not sure I'm going to like, despite my new-found focus. He's loosened the thin knot on his tie – Rick, like Jason, always wears a suit though this is far from compulsory. Thank god.

He's definitely skirting something.

"You used to do some writing Ben?"

"Not for a while. But yeah, when I started on my local paper," I say defensively.

It's true I had. Went the proper journalism route, all that training and reporting of local garden fetes and cats that survive weeks in abandoned washing machines. Back when my dreams were to write for *Vanity Fair*, *The New Yorker* and the West Ham United matchday programme.

"Great, great."

Rick often repeats words, it gives him time to think.

"Why do you ask?" I cut in, trying to sound as disinterested as possible. I have an aloof reputation to uphold.

"We…" I look around, wondering who 'we' might be, Rick corrects himself. "… or rather I, have been thinking about a possible feature for the magazine – but I want you to say no if you're not up to it."

I nearly say 'no' immediately but I have to admit, I'm mildly curious. See, things are changing. I haven't even checked the clock for the last forty-two minutes. Too late, it's 10.15.

"What kind of feature?"

"As you know I've been trying to steer us in the direction of real life, integrity issues. We have the new *Mentor* Torment section…"

I should explain. Apparently consumer research has shown that our readers are responding to features which share real-life experience, which encourage empathy, which give them something to take away with them. We might not be able to change the past, but we can learn from it. I'm quoting verbatim from the recommendations our marketing team derived from their questionnaire two months ago – the clumsily titled MentorMen 'Reader Survey'. Apparently the big thing is magazine-reader interaction. Mutual support. Two-way journalism. In both directions.

And I do understand the reasoning behind this, support is a valid concept. Our world has to some extent relearnt compassion, certainly on a domestic scale. So far we've done bereavement, rejection and unemployment and they've worked. no one used to write into magazines, not really, not in their thousands – now? Now they're involved. It is after all, their magazine.

I'm inclined to believe the lunatics have taken over the asylum; nevertheless in principle the idea is possibly worthwhile.

He wants me to write my story.

And I do get it; mostly. Hadn't I'd felt marginally less alone when talking to others who had 'lost' people? Even when talking to Suzie. But a whole feature? No; not when it's my torment. I'm not ready. Don't they understand? I can be ruthless, but at my own pace. That's the whole point. I control it now.

Rick's hands are at his temple, massaging them with his index fingers, his gaze averted to the flat grey carpet that covers our entire office like newly laid tarmac. I'm way ahead of him, he hasn't even asked yet and already I've decided on my answer.

"… and it occurred to us, to me, that it might be worthwhile asking you to…"

I feel myself needing to swallow. I may be ready to deal with me but I'm far from dealing with it for other people.

"… your story is one that needs to be told Ben. I think it would help our readers and most importantly yourself."

Beyond Rick I see Jason, biting his nails anxiously and trying not to observe what's happening and I'm certain that this was his idea.

And I don't want to be rude to Rick, he's a decent guy but I can't help it. I feel myself sliding into the abyss. Losing my grip. Forgetting all about Armani. About my brother Martin waiting to hear from me.

I spit, pure venom issuing forth, "With all due respect Rick, fuck off."

And to the poor bloke's credit – after all he could easily pull rank – he does. He puts his hands in the air, palms facing me, and backs away without protest. No further pressure, not even a "won't you think about it?", not even a "but". As he trudges off, I can see he's genuinely sorry. Upset that he might have offended and I feel bad. Maybe it would have helped?

At least Rick realised I wasn't ready. That he'd crossed the line. And of course, to provide perfect counterpoint here comes Jason ready to take a running leap over it, both feet firmly in the air. God, he's a twat.

"I know it might sound like exploitation Benjy," he volunteers breathlessly. Benjy!

"It sounds like a waste of time," I snarl. "I knew this was your idea. Come on Jason, there's not even a junket you can link this into? Or let me guess, you want to link it to the new Manic Street Preachers album? The anniversary of their missing guitarist?"

He hadn't thought of this. I can see him imagining new angles instantly. It never hurts to be able to tie in a celebrity connection, especially when amidst the dour territory of real-life human experience – in this case losing a loved one to thin air.

And then he does something I don't expect. He says: "Why don't you just snap out of it you miserable bastard?"

For a moment I think he's joking. Trying reverse psychology or something. I'm wrong, he's merely warming to a theme.

"You sit here everyday – acting like we're all scum, as if we've done this to you. Jesus Christ, you're not the first person whose life has gone a bit pear-shaped."

This is the first time anyone has described losing Ruth as just one of those things that happen. But he's right. I'm not the first person, I do understand this now. But this is Jason, Mr Vacuous. Mr Plastic. I don't want to acknowledge anything he says. Just because. Okay?

"How dare you?" I say, like some outraged pensioner. "What do you know about my life? What do you know about anything except whether St Tropez is still an 'in' destination or if white socks can ever be justified?"

Somebody laughs – I realise people are listening.

His face goes all red, like when he's in the gym. He's very pissed off, normally I'd be amused, instead I'm slightly scared that he might have a heart attack. I may have gone too far. I may have some way to go in reevaluating how I relate to my colleagues. I want to apologise but I can't escape the overriding view that this is none of his business. Jason's eyes seem odd – his voice reaches a strangulated falsetto.

"I've tried to help. To listen. To support but you just sit here and refuse to even help yourself. You're pathetic. I feel sorry for you, we all do – but I won't pity you. Life's too fucking short."

I check to see whether he has this all written on the back of his hand and momentarily think about asking him. The possibility that he is actually being sincere is not getting through. At least not until he picks up my computer monitor, violently wrenches it from the base and throws it out of the window, or at least tries to – toughened glass is a remarkable thing. Nevertheless the noise is immense and his anger is well and truly evident for everyone – especially the unsuspecting window cleaner on a gurney outside.

What's going on? I don't know what just happened. His display of passion leads me to think he might be about to declare how much he loves me. I'm not sure what to say or do next. Jason is heaving violently, invading my space, not forming words but saying loads. Placate or run?

I can't run again. I can be ruthless. I am ruthless.

Rick rushes over, pushing his protégé out of the way.

"What the fuck?" he yells. A justified, and refreshingly precise, query given the circumstances.

Jason, who is now hyperventilating, is helped away by colleagues. A point has been made, his seriousness underlined and finally I'm quiet. And embarrassed. He leaves me standing there without anything suitable to say. I can see Rick expects me to try. I opt to report a factual version of events without mentioning any possible provocation.

"I... I... e... he just freaked out."

"Jason doesn't freak out," is all Rick suggests. "Not without reason."

"I guess I'm the reason then."

We move to Rick's office. As I enter he circumnavigates the room, pausing to stand at each pane of glass, dropping the blinds and switching them shut. As the last section of slats fall I catch Laura watching me nervously, chewing her emery board. I smile weakly in her direction and this helps her – she waves briefly, playfully and then, almost as quickly, is back facing her screen and typing.

Rick's office is a testament to his success, Italian magazine covers and articles in frames – snapshots of children and beautiful wife – Journalism awards and a signed image of him with Sophia Loren. He points me towards the sofa in the corner and I'm reassured that this is likely to be a sympathetic chat, despite the seriousness of what's occurred. If he had taken the large chair behind his desk, I could have expected to see a side of his personality only ever rumoured about since his Milan days. A one-off cocaine 'incident' saw an entire fashion department receiving the sack but not before he first tipped off the carabineri.

"I'm sorry," I offer.

"Sorry is not what this is about."

"It would have been if that monitor had gone through the window," I say.

"It didn't. Thank God." He's not smiling. I realise he has other, bigger, priorities.

"I think the window-cleaner is on his knees to our heavenly father right now," I say.

Rick looks like he might laugh but I know this is far from likely.

"Ben. What the fuck is going on?"

I note that he didn't add syllables to my name. This is important.

"I don't know," I say.

"It's time to deal with this. I've let it go on too long."

"Sack me," I say, hoping he won't.

"Don't be ridiculous," he snaps. "I'd have a bloody good case though. I very nearly had no choice after your performance last week in front of Lewis."

"Can you blame me – the guy's a power-hungry twat."

"A power-hungry twat who happens to run this magazine."

If nothing else, it is nice to have my suspicion confirmed that Rick views Lewis as being somewhat less than perfect.

"Look, I am sorry." I repeat. My penitence is genuine. "But I've thought about many things, about what I want."

"You can't just satisfy yourself." Rick says. "You need to think about your relationships at *Mentor*. Yes, I'm concerned for you – but to be honest I'm trying to run a magazine, and that takes precedence. For the hours you're here, watching the clock – don't protest, I've seen you – work is more important. And as the editor of this magazine I believe your behaviour isn't helping everyone else."

"The team," I say, sneering at such a long-winded and obviously managerial comment.

"Yes. The team," he asserts, annoyed I'm not listening. "The good of the team must be my priority."

"I didn't ask for attention, I don't ask Jason to interfere," I say, angry now – after all my work-rate hasn't suffered, my productivity is good, in fact I know it's shit-hot. Okay, shit-tepid, but certainly not shit.

"I asked Jason to interfere," he asserts.

This is news.

"I'm sorry?"

"I, as Jason's boss, asked if he would keep an eye out. I know he's always respected you and was genuinely moved by your… situation."

I need a glass of water. I think about upending the pencil vase that holds a brace of orchids and taking a swig.

"And before you accuse him of acting sycophantically to please me or whatever other cynical thoughts run freely through your thick skull… when your wife disap…"

"Ruth," I interject, just like that, and I'm fine saying it. Not even bothered by the past tense.

"… Ruth, Ruth," Rick repeats. "When Ruth – disappeared – Jason actually asked if he could move desks to be near yours. Because he gave a shit and because he wanted to try, when nobody else dared. Wanted to try and work out what to say, rather than just say nothing. And for what? Two years of silent hatred and a broken pc."

I feel terrible, recalling my impatience, my inability to connect.

"I don't hate the guy," I say but I know he's right. I have hated him. Hated all of them in fact. Hated the ease with which they've seemed to process days, social engagements and the aspirational lifestyles we continued to peddle. And hated for myself for my inability to do the same – my inability to reconcile understandable, but now tedious, grief with the life and lives that are going on around me. Hated myself.

"I know Jason can be irritating, I know he buys into all this stuff and be a bit obsessed at times."

Rick says this while waving a hand dismissively beyond the wall-mounted evidence of his career and towards the general direction of the office out beyond the closed aluminium strips.

"But I also know he is a decent guy. With problems of his own. Like the rest of us here – but we get on with each other and we get on with making the magazine."

I rest my head in my hands, hunched forward on the sofa and remember that someone in Features' wife had had a second miscarriage (a second? Christ!) last month; I recall that Laura misses her dog every waking moment and even recall the red-eyes of the eager work experience we had to let go merely because Lewis didn't believe his acne was right for the title's internal image. The fact that my editor is saying all this softly, compassionately, is making me feel worse. I'd have preferred him to swear loudly. I know he's slipping into stuff learnt on his management course – but whatever, he's right. And I've been wrong.

I start to cry. In public. This is a development as far as Rick as concerned. For my part it's bloody frightening. Don't worry. I haven't seen the light or anything, I haven't been reborn – the ice-caps are still melting and I'm pretty sure that Jason will still be irritating even when all is said and done. When my apology is said and done. Nevertheless, like some terminal prisoner on death-row, I'm thinking that it might yet be worth opening my eyes and facing each new day. There might a point.

Though I'm still captive, I'm hearing the morning bell. And I'm definitely waking up.

*

Jason and I are having lunch together. He made a big show of turning off his Blackberry. Placing it there on the table so I could see. I appreciated this, I understood the gesture, entirely 21st century in its process and import.

The staff of *Mentor* pretended not to notice my exit from Rick's office moments after I'd agreed to try harder. They kept their eyes on their screens, on the contact sheets, on the next issue. All except Laura who came running over, placed a soothing arm around me and asked if I was okay. I told her I was.

"Jason's down in the Lion," she said, uninvited, and returned to her desk. My orders were clear. I noticed that she smelt great, having dumped the Organza, maybe Maggie had had a word? She's wearing something I don't recognise – I have been slipping. I think of Martin's unanswered emails and decide he can wait.

I entered the Lion & Unicorn about five minutes later. Everyone comes here from *Mentor* – it's where we have most of our leaving drinks. Leaving drinks – a funny phrase, a very British institution. Everyone you've never really spoken to gathers round in a large ill-formed circle of "is anyone sitting here?" borrowed stools before proceeding to ignore the honouree, instead choosing to sit in small groups chatting about the annoying printer in the office. All the while the leaver sits in the middle and gets bought an anaemic drink or two. Then maybe your line-manager (its always about lines) says a public goodbye, people promise to remember your new, non-employment related email address, and you leave at 11.17pm wondering what all their names were again. The Lion & Unicorn is normally a place for exits – it's not one of Jason's usual haunts but is the nearest place that serves alcohol. I expected to find him surrounded by the Fashion guys, but he was alone, nursing a Guinness and clearly still in a state.

"You on your own?" I'd said, when it was clear he was.

"I told everyone to fuck off. Seems to work for you."

I'd laughed and this triggered his own outburst; Jason laughs like Ray Liotta in *Goodfellas* – loud yaks that make his mouth look like a puppeteer's dummy.

And here we are, still in the pub eating lasagne and chips. Jason is eating chips. We're just talking. I haven't yet apologised for anything. For any behaviour.

"How's Annabel?" I ask, secretly amazed that I remembered her name. Jason's fiancée is a former model turned photographer. Though she's the width of a piece of spaghetti, 6ft 1 and blonde, she does do pretty worthy stuff – cover-images of *Newsweek* and *Time* that kind of thing. Almost got herself killed in Chechnya. I've never admitted to Jason that I'm a fan.

"She's great. It's all good." He says this like he's not sure. I'm actually intrigued and challenge him.

"What is it?"

"I'd rather not talk about this Ben."

"Fine," I say. Sorry."

This slips out so easily, I almost don't realise it's the first time I've ever really apologised to Jason. It certainly isn't lost on him, he leaps on it like Gordon Banks against Brazil.

"Sorry for what?"

"Oh," I say, caught off guard but finally seeing that I have to deal with the reason he's down here and not at his desk.

I veer off desperately "The lasagne's not bad."

I'm a wimp, I really am. Why can't I just admit I've behaved like an arsehole? I examine the beer-mat under my pint, its edges soggy. My glass is empty.

"Do you want another?" Jason says, helping me out.

"Yeah. Thanks. That'd be cool."

I watch him slide out from the bench opposite and make his way to the bar. It's weird that it's not weird to be in a pub with Jason. It's also weird that there isn't anyone else here cracking jokes about the tits on women in accounts or boasting about their six per cent body fat.

Jason returns with two pints of Guinness. He places one before me before sitting down. Automatically we both say 'cheers' as we begin to drink. I take a long draught before steadying the pint back on its sodden base and it suddenly seems like time. The right time. A barmaid collects our plates, she's wearing more chains round her neck than Mr T. One of them says 'Mum'. She looks about 95.

Time to put things right that are askew.

"Jason. I am truly sorry," I say, contritely.

"Ben. Don't. I understand. You don't have to mate," Jason says softly.

The waitress drops cutlery on the floor, the noise jarring into our conversation. I retrieve a knife from where it has fallen and hand it back to her.

"But that's just it," I plead. "We're not mates. We don't have anything in common. I don't even like you. But I am really sorry for the way I have behaved."

"Whatever then, I'm past caring."

The waitress finally leaves.

"I don't know who I've become. I see the worst in everybody," I explain.

"Don't bullshit. You could be a rude bastard even before she went."

Jason refers to Ruth in a way no one else does. So off-handedly.

"You're right, I could. But I am aware, and ashamed that I've dismissed everything you've tried to do."

"I don't want to sound pathetic, but I was only trying to help mate."

This is getting into territory that isn't natural for us – even with Jason's predilection for new-man dialogue ever since he did that story about a male-bonding camp in Utah.

I think about what I can say to steer us away. I no longer need Jason to try and explain his actions and I sense he wouldn't appreciate a grovelling apology. But I decide I must tell him this.

"The one thing I appreciate – more than anything – is that with you Ruth came second." Reminded of the way some people in the office tried to help by offering reasons on why she might have gone or tips on where she could be. Or shared similar stories of female abandonment.

"How could it be any other way? I didn't know her." He says. "But I do know you."

"You don't know me," I point out.

"You're lonely, constantly tired, probably sexually frustrated, think you're a better writer than me and therefore resent the magazine and everyone else. You support a crap football team, you like Radiohead – especially Kid A – are a bit too anal about words, oh and Laura has a crush on you the size of Birmingham." He isn't smiling as he says this. He isn't finished either. "… And you probably watch too many shite game shows on tv each night."

I down my pint in two quick gulps.

Did I ever tell you I hate Jason? If so, I didn't mean it. I've changed my mind. In more ways than one – as I then say, really surprising myself this time – "I'll do the article."

I don't give him the chance to respond; opting to continue instead with the serious stuff as I'm genuinely curious.

"So, what's this about Laura fancying me?" just as our waitress comes back to retrieve our newly empty glasses.

Jason laughs.

"Everyone can see it, everyone's seen it for months," he confirms.

"Seen what?"

"The woman will do anything for you. And it ain't pity – she's in lust. You must have realised? Any opportunity she can get she's next to you."

I think about Laura arriving with a bottle of wine at my flat; about her showing me how to use the photocopier when I haven't asked; about getting me peppermint tea when I complain of stomach cramps; about wearing a pink Farhi top repeatedly ever since I said she looks nice in it.

"And everyone discusses this?"

"Don't go getting paranoid again Ben, God you're a nightmare. But what do you expect? Everyone discusses everything, especially who fancies who. Human nature mate. It's not always about you."

All this time and I've been involved – it's perversely gratifying to know I've been discussed in a capacity other than having a missing wife. It's also rather disconcerting to see that Jason, who I've always dismissed as vanity personified, thinks I have an ego problem.

"She wants you bad."

Jason's firmly in lad territory but I don't mind. He brings back two more pints.

"No she doesn't," I say, petulantly, when he sits down, firmly in adolescent teenager mode.

"Does too."

"I don't think I could."

"Just take her out, how hard can it be mate? She's got great tits. Nice arse as well."

I find myself agreeing. Laura wouldn't mind. She'd be glad I was contributing. Maggie would kill me, saying something about being chauvinistic. But Laura *has* got nice tits. I allow myself to think it.

I want to change the subject now. We've done enough. I go back to Annabel. Suddenly wanting to know more. I don't say anything about Jason's wife's tits though. There are limits.

"So, what's Annabel up to at the moment? On assignment?"

"You could call it that," he shrugs.

"Don't follow." I'm confused.

"No I don't either. Not really," he mutters into his pint glass.

I begin to wish I hadn't asked. Not wanting to drag us down from our new found happy heights. But getting on with people is about give and take. I'm tired of being useless at both. I take the plunge and urge him on.

"We're having a trial separation," is his response.

"Oh." Pause. "What happened?" I say, genuinely concerned, genuinely surprised.

"She slept with someone."

I'm shocked and want to ask who but that's not the next question so I continue in a more appropriate manner.

"I'm so sorry."

"That's just it. She was too, which makes it worse. Still moved out though, didn't she? Remember that dinner party we had, the one I invited you to in the gym? She did it then. Walked out while I was doing drinks. In front of everyone. Said she couldn't handle it anymore – what she'd done to me, to us. How does that work eh? She cheats and then suddenly I feel crap because she feels so terrible about it."

"I'm not sure."

I think about Jason inviting me along. I'm still glad I didn't go, but now for a different reason.

"Anyway. She's at her parents and, yes, I want her back. But I'm worried that I'll resent not being able to be angry. She's taken that away from me."

"Jesus. I'm sorry mate," I say.

"It's alright. It'll work out somehow," he shrugs, draining more liquid.

"Look on the bright side – at least you know where she is." I said that. Me – being flippant about my missing wife. I can't believe I said it. And I can't believe I can laugh while saying it too.

"Yep. There is that," Jason concurs, smiling.

We head back up to the office, conversation moving to the planned photo-shoot taking place at *Mentor* that afternoon. Pictures to support a 'how to deal with women in the workplace' feature. Publisher and general twat Lewis thought it would be great to use our actual offices – get a load of models in, stage some scenarios, knock out some blurb about the different 'types': the flirt, the strategist, the mother figure, the boss etc etc. Laura went mad – not at the stereotyping, bimbos in glasses with pens in mouths – but because when raised in the ideas meeting, the phrase 'deal with' was used as the strapline. It's going to be changed.

Swaying slightly, we arrive back to find it all underway. A thousand stares at a line of bored models in lipstick and A-cup Wonderbras. One of them is on my desk, holding a clipboard and, for reasons I cannot fathom, wearing a hard hat. A light-meter thing is being thrust in her direction. She's pretty enough but extremely ambivalent about her surroundings and the endless proposition of "coffee or anything stronger?" offered by my leering colleagues. Sebastian, one of the staff writers mutters "I could turn for that Imogen, I really could."

But in truth, the models are not that beautiful and most of them look tired. Bored and tired – like they would rather be anywhere else but here.

I march up to Laura who is resisting this parade by busying herself with the flatplan for the next issue. She turns to face me as I draw near.

"All sorted?" she enquires sweetly, meaning Jason and me.

"Yes," is all I need to say.

"Good."

I notice the whiteboard beside the next issue's flat-plan layout. A screen of mocked up pages and tacked photos. In the listing of features is the *Mentor* Torment subject matter – its still blank. I turn around and shout to Rick who is standing in the doorway of his office watching the photographer climb up a stepladder for an aerial shot. I know Rick is thinking insurance claims – he's like that. Always sensible. "careful, careful" I hear him repeat.

"Rick," I shout above the cacophony. It's the loudest my voice has ever been here.

He looks around, sees it's me. "I'll do it," I shout. Meaning the article. He hears and gives a McCartney thumbs-up in return. That's all. And that's all I need. I look round for Jason but he hasn't acknowledged the exchange, he's got straight on the phone – is hunched over his desk, ignoring the models with their fantastic figures. He's talking quietly and I can guess who to. I move back to Laura who's standing patiently – I realise she's retouched her make-up in the interim – during my trip to the pub – and say: "Would you like to go for dinner tomorrow night Laura?"

"That would be nice," she says. "I'll have to call Maggie – we sort of had plans, but nothing that can't be moved."

"She won't mind," I say, somehow knowing that she won't.

So that's that then. I've got a date on Saturday night.

I realise I've still got to finish subbing the Armani. I slide into my seat with purpose and see that one of the models has used my keyboard as an ashtray. Emails from Martin blink expectantly but I have a feature to write too and a restaurant to book.

But guilt sets in. I open one of his messages.

```
To: Ben:@mentormag.co.uk
From: Martin.Carter@Midaret.com
Subject: Anybody there?
Ben
Whr r u?. All ok?
M.
```

That's all he's written. It does feel like ages since we've been in touch. I wish he wouldn't streamline. He's like a 15 year old texting his mates.

```
To: Martin.Carter@Midaret.com
From: Ben@mentormag.co.uk
Subject: I'm here.
Sorry Martin.
Things are good but so much is going on. I'll try and call
on the weekend.
By the way — I'm learning to be ruthless. I'll explain when
we speak.
Love; Ben
```

I hit send.

10: CONNECTION

At weekends I always make sure I turn off the seven alarms on my wristwatch. Ally insists upon it, determined to make sure there's every chance for us to sleep in. And sometimes it works, sometimes I manage to get to 9 o'clock before the kids make too much noise or a car backfires outside. But today, although it is Saturday and the locals are religiously doing nothing, I am awake before 6 am. I've opened my eyes and taken a few moments to realise the phone is ringing violently – the staccato sound sprawling digitally around the flat. I leap out of bed, naked, and dash to the kitchen careful not to disturb Ally. I'm not that worried, Ally can sleep through anything, on planes, in cars, even during labour.

My feet recoil from contact with the cold kitchen floor. The air-conditioning has been working overtime all night. My thoughts are of Ben back in London and I imagine him waiting expectantly on the line. It's about time. He emailed yesterday to say he'd call soon.

It doesn't feel weird that I have no clothes on. I have exactly the same body as my brother. At least the same raw material. I snatch up the receiver.

"Hello?"

But there's nothing in return, nothing but silence. Everything but noise.

I'm used to Ben calling at odd hours. It doesn't feel strange to be standing here, doing this. It is unusual, however, to receive silence.

I try again, speaking clearly into the mouthpiece of the phone.

"Ben?" Hoping that it is him. That his voice, my voice, will sound back at me. And that my irrational fear that something is up is just that. His email yesterday didn't help at all. 'So much going on' he'd written. And that line about being ruthless. It just seemed so aggressive. I feel nervous, stomach on spin cycle.

Still nothing. All I can hear is my wife moving about in our bedroom, woken by the interruption as well. I push the phone tighter against my ear, sensing that someone is there, there is someone listening to me. I grasp the handset yet harder with two sweaty palms and repeat my brother's name, but he's not coming through. I stay like that for a few more seconds, my brain now entirely awake and searching for an explanation of whom, if not Ben, the caller could be. Listening to the space. Willing them to speak.

And so I try a different approach. For some unknown reason I try…

"Ruth?"

And there's an intake of air; a breath somewhere in the void. Disembodied, distant but somehow connected to my phone – to me. The hairs on my arms and, curiously, my balls, stand up. Until I hear a woman, a familiar voice say –

"Martin?"

And it's pure voltage down my spine. But then I realise this has come from Ally. From behind me. She's made it to the kitchen and is simultaneously tying her dressing gown, smoothing her hair and opening our retro chrome fridge all in one multi-tasked second. What is it with women and multi-tasking? I'm anxious that she might have heard me say 'Ruth?' but there was no suggestion of this in her half-asleep tone.

I don't answer my wife, remaining intent on the silence in my right ear. I'm waiting for confirmation before going any further. My heart is racing. Meanwhile Alison is not prepared to be so patient.

"Who is it Martin?" she repeats, from inside the fridge.

Her voice is louder and I try to minimise the chance of it being picked up by the phone, moving my left-hand to muffle the handset. There's no point, I hear a click and dead air. Monotone phone-tone. I've lost whoever it was.

I reluctantly return the phone onto its efficient wall-mount. My wife is now managing to unscrew orange juice while throwing away out-of-date eggs.

"Ben, huh?" she knows he's supposed to call today. She, too, is used to unorthodox hours calls and the poor connection we usually get between the UK and Israel.

"I'm not sure."

"Why? Couldn't you hear each other again?"

It's a reasonable question. I give a reasonable answer.

"You know what the lines are like sometimes." I say, moving over to the kitchen window, opening the blind with my right hand, levering the slats upwards before continuing "… he'll probably call back in a

105

minute. Maybe he was trying from his mobile." I'm staring at the darkness outside, at the silhouette of palm trees above parked cars and nearer, the white perimeter fence. I hear Ally leave the kitchen, suitably satisfied – and turn to watch her slip out of her robe at the bedroom door – a glimpse of her back and she's gone. "Come back to bed," I hear her say quietly from inside. But she knows that I am eager to speak to my brother and though I haven't articulated the distance I've been feeling – I guess that she knows I won't follow her.

I'm wide awake. I look down and realise I have the beginnings of erection. I move quickly to hide my modesty, retrieving a hand-towel hanging half out of the washing machine, wondering if Alison noticed. I decide that she must have, she never misses anything. This realisation unsettles me, I don't want to dwell on what, exactly, she might have surmised over the years.

There was a definitely a breath. A response to my "Ruth?"

I won't be able to get back to sleep. Instead I need to think. I decide not to follow Ally but to go for a run instead. I haven't done this for ages, normally I hate doing it, but I am desperate to get out. To make up some ground.

*

Jesus, it's hot. I'm really not designed for this country.

I run for half a mile. Downhill towards the park, my feet working while my considerably faster thoughts run energetically around my brain. I cannot escape them, cannot leave them behind, however much I try. Eventually I reach the intersection before the grass begins. Over the road, the water sprinklers are already watering. The turf slick with spray. I leave the concrete to take advantage of the softer terrain only to feel my foot slip and realise I've stepped in some dogshit. I'm grateful for the excuse to catch my breath, to pause and return to the pavement. I'm calming down. I feel better. Thoughts of the phone call recede.

I'm scraping my trainer against the kerb when I hear a familiar voice on the other side of the street, loud Lancashire and swearing for England. It can only be Chrissy.

"Supposed to be lucky that is!" she calls off screen, like some stagey bit-part in an end-of-pier revue.

Looking across I see her and Brad, both up early and, alarmingly, wearing co-ordinating tracksuits. She has a sweatband on a la Bjorn Borg, unsuccessfully keeping her matted orange curls off her forehead and out of her eyes. To put it bluntly she looks awful. Brad, being Brad, appears to have hardly broken a sweat. As they come over to say hello, he simply flashes a 'winning smile'. I sense the pair of them won't help my mood but resign myself to this unexpected meeting. I watch them bounce over, confident and comfortable. He scratches his balls as they cross the road, while she adjusts her size 16 knickers through the fabric of her blue Adidas tracksuit bottoms, prising them out of her arse with a probing finger.

I don't know why I am surprised to see the odd-couple, as Alison charitably terms their relationship. They live only a block down from us and I guess it's not that much of a co-incidence. Nevertheless, the fact that it is 6.00 am lends our exchange a novel, amused air – at least on their part. They know I'm a lazy fucker and both seem rather too pleased to see me. Evidently the lack of communication between my colleague and I over the last couple of days has been forgotten, consigned to the past. I hate that Chrissy has decided normal service can resume whenever she feels like it, that there is no longer any issue between us.

"What are you two doing out of bed?" I offer lamely, instantly wishing I hadn't drawn attention to their second home.

"I've worked out a get-fit routine for Chris," Brad drawls.

"Really?"

"Yep – light weights twice a week and the rest is all cardio-vascular."

"Cardio-vascular?"

"Important to get the heart-rate up for at least 20 minutes. Aerobic exercise. You know, jogging, swimming at the spa or even sex. Sex is perfect."

Of course. He grins at me, waiting for a repressed English reply. Chrissy hits him playfully. I keep quiet for fear that I might produce bile.

"Bastard done me first thing this morning. Still saddle-sore. What is it you called it again love?"

"Callisthenics," Brad replies, and she claps her hands in delight. He kisses her wet bull terrier nose.

I knew this topic was coming, I start to jog again on the spot as if ready to move off. I'm afraid of what I might do if forced to endure this any longer.

"Well, better head back, want to be home before Ally gets up."

But Brad hasn't finished with me. He takes his hand off Chrissy and offers a final piece of advice while resetting the stopwatch hanging professionally around his neck.

"You wanna get Ally into this sort of programme, not that she needs it."

Total arsehole. Brad always compliments my wife. I wish Chrissy would get offended but she doesn't, instead she says: "Us girls always need it, lover-boy." And there's that cackle again. I'm lost for words, simply unable to endure these two talking at me any longer.

"And you too," Brad continues, prodding my chest with his index finger "there's a great article in *Mentor* this month – surely you've seen it? Fab Abs?"

I've had enough and make abrupt excuses to leave, like some tabloid reporter who's undercover sleaze assignment is getting a little too close for comfort.

"Better go. Sorry. Bye."

And I'm off, running away. I try to put them out of my mind. It's all too easy, as the early-morning phone call quickly demands my attention again. Brad and Chrissy have shattered my hard-won calm moments before. The memory of the earlier silence steals in – "Ruth?" – spreading malice.

There was definite recognition. I mentioned Ruth's name and someone responded.

It can't be her. Why would she? After all this time?

And yet, I've been almost expecting her to appear. The signs have been there. Real or not; imagined or otherwise. Unbidden, Ruth's presence is resurfacing in my life and I am powerless to stop the tide. And I'm not sure which is more frightening, the prospect of her wilfully haunting me or the notion that my mind might be playing tricks, might be doing this out of some sense of… guilt, I guess. Either explanation is fucking me up considerably. My breaths are coming faster and I'm not even running. I'm standing still. And everything else is catching up with me, overtaking me…

Calm. Be calm. I retrace my steps, walking now, back up the hill desperately attempting to re-live that brief non-conversation in the void, from any angle that might explain it away. As a wrong-number, as an event without portentous meaning, without omen. Suddenly, an obvious, wonderful, realisation I hadn't yet considered overtakes me, and quietens the paranoia – Ruth couldn't possibly have my number. And this helps, it really does. I relax instantly. There's no chance.

It was nothing. My breathing is slowing; very still – regular, regular, regular.

I'm near home now and baffled as to how I could have thought it might be her at all. I've believed, and still believe, over the last two years that Ruth is, without doubt, dead. Suicide in fact. Though I've never said this explicitly to Benjamin. Beachy Head or the Dartford Bridge, the details have never concerned me, but the reason has. The reason is all. The reason once consumed me until I thought I would die. Until I realised I couldn't change anything and I had to put it away and move on. It was her decision. It was Ruth's choice.

Not to say I don't think about her often and still look for her everywhere. It doesn't matter where I am, however unlikely – Tel Aviv airport when we first arrived here or perhaps standing in line at the supermarket. It's ridiculous but I still look.

And of course I worry about my brother, about how he's coping. He loved Ruth. He needs her. The apparent new activity in his life, mentioned in his email, troubles me. But I don't care, I need him to be alright. It doesn't matter about my shame. When this all falls apart as I feel certain it will, I want the world to know that I always tried to put him first. However difficult it's been. I have wanted to protect him.

This is more than our birth-bond and more than my responsibility as the eldest. This is a protection that began the day Ben first introduced Ruth to our parents. First introduced her to me.

I'm recalling the substance of that day; details I regularly view in dreams that frequently become nightmares.

The memory always starts in the same way. I am washing up, Ruth is drying. Ben and my parents are out in the garden, looking at this year's sunflowers. There hasn't been a word between us for two minutes. Two minutes is a long time. Stationary in front of the sink, we circle each other emotionally, strategically. I'm drunk but also more sober than ever.

Ruth speaks first. "This is awful," she's saying. "Like someone's playing games with my life."

I don't respond, turning on the tap to cool down the water, then shaking suds off a pint glass – my dad's pint glass with his cricket club crest frosted on the side.

"We have to deal with this Martin," she continues. "Once and for all."

I'm listening, but anxiously checking that Ben is still outside and in no danger of returning soon.

"Well?" she says. To ongoing silence from me.

"Martin!" she hisses between gritted teeth, glancing out towards our loved ones beyond the window.

"What?" I explode. "What do you expect me to say? To do?"

"Nothing, Martin. Not to Ben anyway. Neither of us can do anything. What's done is done."

I too cannot quite believe the situation we are faced with.

"It was one night Ruth," I start.

She cuts me off immediately. "Don't – I've wiped it from my memory."

"Thanks," I reply, quickly, sarcastically. But I'm glad she's speaking so certainly. It's the way I feel too. She's not alone in wishing it had never happened.

"I just want your word," she says.

I'm not sure what word she means, exactly. But she's in no mood for hesitancy.

"Look, no argument from me. Okay. It's never going to be an issue," is what I say, when every part of me wants to be able to talk to Ben about it. To be honest.

I turn to face her, seeing the concern in her eyes – worried frown lines crinkling her forehead. "I won't. I have enough on my plate," I say. Which is true but I don't tell her that Ally's pregnant – even when this scene is re-lived in my dreams, when I could conceivably amend the details – I always imagine I'm referring only to my upcoming wedding.

We resume the washing up as Ben looks directly at us from outside – through the window. His hesitating smile. I swiftly hand Ruth my father's glass. She doesn't quite take hold and it slips through her fingers and drops to the floor. I shout "fuck" as it falls, but miraculously it doesn't shatter. We both look at where it lies on the lino. The relief is enormous. She gives a shocked laugh that it is still intact. I laugh too and in this new exchange there is release too. Release from the uncertainty brought on right from when Ben first called to tell me that somehow he and Ruth were now a definite article.

"I just don't want Ben to get hurt," she says, crouching down to recover the glass.

"He's my twin brother – it's not top of my 'to-do' list," I remind her.

"So. We're agreed then?"

"Agreed. No mention. Ever."

"Good. It won't be a problem for me." Her voice is remarkably assured – cold almost. As if she's shutting down some part of herself to say this. But almost immediately a lightness returns too; an inflection that was absent before lunch when we had stiffly acted out our pretence at a meeting, for the benefit of all concerned.

And I've kept her promise forever. And the secret has slowly destroyed me.

My mum's voice sounds into the kitchen – berating my brother for not wiping his feet after trudging round the flower-beds. Apparently "we have a mat for such things".

Dad eyes me nervously as Ruth and I rejoin them; no doubt anxious that relations have improved between me and Ben's new girlfriend. And they have. There is a new understanding. Dad relaxes and retrieves his favourite glass from its safe resting place on the stainless steel drainer.

"Time for a fresh pint," he says, trudging off to the cans of bitter stored in the garage.

Ruth and I laugh knowingly and I can see that Ben is pleased. My brother looks to mum who gives an imperceptible nod, as if it's turning out as she has told him it would; that "everything would be alright".

Whenever this memory resurfaces in my dreams, I always wake up sweating. I hate it. At the time I genuinely thought we'd handled it. I thought everything was fine. My ruptured sleep always tells me otherwise. That it was only ever temporary.

I've run back up to our apartment building desperate again for a drink – a proper drink. Like I haven't had in a long time. Even though it's the beginning of another hot day, refreshment isn't what I need. I don't think this need will ever go away.

I push open the glass doors and nod appropriately at our neighbour as she lets her cat out. I take the staircase quickly, pushing myself up three steps at a time – getting my heart-rate going (Brad would be proud) and purging my body. I fall against our door and into the flat where I head straight for the kitchen. Promises to my wife of moderation do not concern me.

What does concern me is the sight of Ally sitting there. In the kitchen once more. With the phone in her hand.

"There was another phone call," she says, pausing for a measured breath, her blue eyes unblinking.

"While you were out."

"Ben?" I say, hoping she'll nod a reply.

But her head doesn't move at all, in fact she is entirely still. Her voice is lower than normal, a deeper register I'm unused to.

"Wouldn't say. The breathing didn't sound like him, I know what he sounds like, he sounds like you. No. It wasn't Ben."

While she's speaking firmly, I notice that Alison is shaking almost imperceptibly, this strikes me as odd – trembling is my territory, though I try to hide it.

"You think it's some pervert or something? One of the kids' friends?"

"No, I don't think it's one of the kids' friends."

Oh Jesus. Please. Please don't let it be her. I start to walk over to Ally, when she unleashes another bombshell. And it is only now that I understand that she is upset in a way I've never seen. I forget about my own fears, wanting to placate my distressed wife. The woman I love. The woman I've always loved.

"It was definitely a woman," she stutters. "I'm certain. I heard her breathing."

My mouth is dry, wondering what's next – what's making her act in this way.

I manage to kneel before her, my trainers squeaking on the polished kitchen floor. The position seems appropriate, comforting but penitent if required. And only when our eyes are level do I place a tentative arm around her shoulder. It rests there unwanted, yet she doesn't pull away.

"What woman?" I offer, apprehensively. "Did she upset you? What'd she say?"

My mind is in fifth gear. Telling me I'm not here, this isn't happening. Has Ruth really come back? Is she alive? Has she said anything about...? Ally keeps her hands in her lap, not responding to my closeness. I cannot stand this any longer.

"Was it Ruth?" I blurt out. Ally's eyes widen in disbelief. She gets up furiously, exploding like never before. As if my question has confirmed everything. Everything that ever happened. Everything I have regretted for a lifetime, though I could do nothing about it.

"You bastard!"

And I think I am going to have a heart attack. Years of torment and its finally happening. Ally is sobbing now, halting on each word, not giving a shit if she wakes the kids. She knows. She finally understands.

Ally raises herself up to full height, spitting her words in my direction, not pausing, relentless in a way she never is.

"You think I'm stupid! I know about you. I know you're messing with some bitch and you have the, the, gall to try and bring fucking Ruth into it! Your brother's missing sister! That's really low Martin. Really cheap! For Chrissakes, what's happened to you? Why can't you just admit it, just fucking look me in the eye and admit it!"

And though my wife is hysterical, and upset – I relax. It isn't about Ruth. Instead, she's convinced that I'm having an affair.

Angry that I tried to bring "fucking Ruth into it" when fucking Ruth is exactly it. Exactly the problem. This is easier. She thinks I'm being unfaithful – a paranoia I can deal with. Somebody else's paranoia.

*

A couple of hours pass and we are sitting in the living room – the kids have been sent to the neighbours downstairs with the promise of yet more coke and ice cream later. I didn't have time to worry about how quickly this pacified them. My wife has calmed down considerably, she sits picking absently at the stitching on the cream sofa, looking at me across the room – the scene of our recent battle. Where I tried to make her believe that I hadn't been adulterous. The echo of earlier screams still linger in the room; and the recent memory of hesitant, accusing questions and biting retorts float above us like the smoke from my father's forty-a-day Silk Cut.

Yet progress has been made and the air is slowly clearing. Now we're talking properly. Listening in fact, albeit from opposite corners of the room.

We're working it out. Our sentences are longer and ramble in their search for lucid explanation. Self-aware psychoanalysis that the whole world picked up from *Big Brother* and the obsession of daytime tv American imports with relationship therapy.

"I want us to remember who we are Martin. Why we made a commitment. A promise." She says as if she's speaking on *Oprah*.

I remember that Ally had been fascinated when Ruth's sister Maggie had gone on one of those daytime chat show. The vocabulary of these programmes has been so rapidly absorbed into the bloodstream of modern relationships – we no longer notice it. Ben always notices it.

I go on the offensive again.

"I am committed! I work 11 hours a day for us – to prove it."

"You've been so detached lately, jumping down my throat at every opportunity – the kids think you've gone mad. I think you've gone mad."

"No they don't."

"Emily actually asked me if you were having an affair. I don't know where she gets it from, she would never have said stuff like that at home."

"Well it's you who sits them in front of the satellite tv all day, that is when you're not at the poxy spa having a back rub or whatever the fuck you do there."

"What's the spa got to do with it?"

I'd emphasised spa with all the emphasis I felt it deserved.

"If you didn't spend every afternoon – "

"It's not every afternoon – once, maybe twice a week. I'm very sorry." She's not, clearly.

"… spend every afternoon there with…"

"With?" And then she guesses "With Brad?"

I'm silent, a grin cracks across her unmade up face. She really is beautiful.

"You always go on about him," I mumble petulantly, acting like I'm outside the headmaster's office.

"I don't believe this!" she's saying.

I stand up and go for another beer.

Alison's smile fades, "No more, please Martin. For me?"

I really want one but I don't pursue it. I sit back down, placing my feet on the coffee-table. She's right. I do it for her.

"What's that smell?" Alison exclaims, covering her nose theatrically.

"Shit. I trod in some shit."

I sit up quickly, pull them off and throw the shoes out into the hallway, my aim is crap and they collide noisily with Emily's Nike trainers that cost more than mine. I'm tired of this endless conversation but Ally wants to deal with my thoughts on Mr Perfect, her expression betraying her pleasure that my 'behaviour' might be explained away painlessly as simple jealousy.

"Do you think I fancy Brad?" she asks.

I don't answer, it does seem stupid now. I'm blushing, this never happens.

"He's a nice enough guy but I couldn't fuck him."

I wince at her crudeness. This isn't Alison, or at least my vision of Alison. Maybe the fact that I have a vision of Alison is part of the problem.

'Ally.' I say, really not wanting her to continue.

'Seriously, the guy's so vain. Besides you're my husband. I fancy you. Till death us do part and all that.'

She says this resolutely, sincerely, I can tell she's not lying.

"I just don't like you spending time with him," I whine.

"You don't have to worry darling," and now it's her turn to get up and edge closer.

If this was a movie, the scene would be directed upwards; with Ally towering over me, to show who's in control. She's whispering down at her poor insecure husband.

"Look, Brad's a friend. A nice guy. I don't have many people to talk to when you're at work. This is Israel, I don't exactly belong here."

Her words are making me feel better. She's stroking my hair, moving her hand down to my chest before bringing it to rest on my shoulder. I feel like an errant employee.

"Besides, I don't stop you talking to Chrissy at the office," she says.

I decide to lighten the mood, get things back on an even keel. I stand up and grab both of her hands.

"Don't worry, I couldn't fuck Chrissy,' I say, echoing her line, not proud of myself.

"Frankly, I don't know how Brad does," she replies quickly, laughing and moving away.

"Amen," I volunteer and now we're both chuckling despite the implication that she has clearly thought about Brad fucking Chrissy and moreover the fact that we've both been rude about a woman – a friend – who is clearly not happy either – for whatever reason.

I wish I was clean. Wish none of the mess with Ruth had happened but I can do nothing to alter the past. There is no way for me to alter the reality that Ben's predicament, Ruth's disappearance and thus my fractured relationship with my wife – may all be entirely down to me. I look at Alison laughing and think of all I've put her through. She loves me, I know that and I know that I love her.

And I resolve right there. I don't want another drink. I just want to go to bed with my wife. Start the day again. Start it all again. Not to have sex or anything but just to lie down amongst the sheets, it's too hot for anything else. Just to lay there in the place where we used to feel happiest. Those years before, when we'd be happy to stay in bed all day. And so I'm grateful now that things remain hidden – it's the only way; and it almost has the chance to breathe, this dream, it's almost working, but just when I think I can deal with a life lived like this – I'm reminded that Ben, my brother, hasn't been so lucky. I don't know where he is right now. Whether he can block out his torment and move on, and ashamedly, I'm more worried about what revelations may be allowing this.

It's a direct link I'm afraid, one point to the other.

I lead Ally into the bedroom and we undress, I take off my t-shirt and get in first. She steps out of her clothes and climbs in beside me slowly. I study her freckled back as she takes off her watch and places it on the bedside cabinet. She turns to face me, the thin duvet falling sharply across one breast. I lean over and kiss it, gently.

"I'm sorry," she says "You know, for doubting you. And for getting carried away. We need to talk more Martin, remind ourselves of what's... necessary."

"I'm sorry too." I say truthfully. "I would never cheat on you."

And this is the truth too. It really is. I never have, not exactly anyway. It's more complicated than that.

"And it was probably just a wrong number," I conclude.

We're quiet then, studying each other. I look into her eyes, and sense that she's returned to the events earlier – to the kitchen, to the phone call and my reaction, and suddenly I know what she's going to say. I know what's coming. I know the question she hasn't thought to ask.

"Martin?"

"Yes?" I swallow two times, just to produce this one word. Ally notices my discomfort.

"I don't want to go on but... but why did you think it might have been Ruth? It's a bit strange don't you think?"

I just wanted to lie here, I didn't want to have to talk anymore. But I have to. Talking is demanded. Questions deserve answers. They're justified.

"I dunno. Just on my mind, I guess. It's always on my mind. You can't blame me."

But she can. If only she knew.

"You never normally mention her, that's all," Ally says.

"What's the point?"

"There's every point. We can't forget about her. As if she never existed."

"The kids have." Emily used to love Ruth – it was a mutual thing that involved secret code-names, private letters and presents even when it wasn't a birthday.

"No they haven't," Ally snaps. "That's a terrible thing to say."

I want to say it's the truth but there's no need, she knows. You can't blame our daughter – she was 11 when it happened. She asked a lot of questions at the time but a few months later these were soon replaced by other concerns. Maybe I'm wrong. Maybe I've misjudged my eldest – maybe she does wonder why? Maybe it does bother her?

I suddenly think of the joy with which Emily used to greet my every return each evening. The way she used to hold on tight as if she didn't want to let go. That eventually passed. But she went too far the other way – too distant. Too closed-off for my liking.

Ally is still thinking of her sister-in-law. Of her friend. She begins to cover herself entirely, moving fabric up until it is against her chin.

"What if it was Ruth? What if she is still out there?" she whispers, softly. Her eyes widening with just a little hope. Sudden enthusiasm. She props herself up on one elbow, the better to study me with, to monitor my reaction.

"It wasn't," I state, once and for all. On the verge of anger. Control yourself, Martin.

"She wouldn't call us Ally," I continue. "I mean if she was ok, she'd call Ben or her parents, right? It'd make no sense to call us."

"No. You're right," she concurs, before mumbling. "Why would she call us?"

And though it's not really a question to anyone but herself, I reply. "She wouldn't. And besides she wouldn't have the number," I say sensibly, relying gratefully upon the calming thought that saved me earlier. This quietens her. Ally thinks for a moment.

"Oh of course… you're right."

And this is enough. My wife brings her head back down to the pillow, level with mine, before closing her eyes slowly. I'm glad I calmed her but believe more than ever that this is only a temporary reprieve. That she'll start asking more and more questions about what, if it not infidelity, has been causing my erratic behaviour. And I realise that jealousy over Brad will not be viewed as a reasonable reason. I suspect that my allotted period of grace for worrying over my brother is coming to a close. Ally will soon, and justifiably, demand that it's time for me to move on. To start behaving normally. But how can I when it's all getting worse?

I stay awake for the rest of the afternoon, listening to the silence, willing the phone not to ring. Anxious that it might and certain that it is against me. Years ago Saturday afternoons meant only football results and lager. Not any more.

11: METASTASIS

It's Saturday afternoon and I'm still working on my feature. It's not quite working, I can't get it together. I've promised Martin I'll call him this weekend and I still have to get ready for meeting Laura tonight. I've borrowed a laptop from the office – I was informed by Rick's P.A. that it's the same model Sarah Jessica Parker used in *Sex and the City* – though I'm not sure what effect this is supposed to have on my writing.

"If someone goes missing, there's not a lot that the authorities can do. They make all the right noises but stop short of telling you that unless the person wants to be found you're screwed. If the person is an adult and has taken their possessions and passport, and appear to have exited without suggestion of violence – well it's really out of their hands. In fact, the only guaranteed involvement is that CID might ask a few questions 'just to make sure like' that no foul play has been involved. That she's not 'buried over in Epping Forest, like that bird in Eastenders'.

"I can assure you the latter scenario is a tough one to endure. Almost impossible in fact if the missing person is your wife and you promised to love each other forever. But I endured all of it. I still am…"

This isn't working – my torment isn't just about the aftermath of Ruth's departure. It's about everything we had. All of it.

Maybe I'll call Martin now. I tried this morning but his line was engaged. I got bored of trying to get through. I feel better that I'd at least sent him an email from work yesterday. I'm not that bad a brother. I do need to see what he thinks about everything I've been thinking. I am anxious to talk, I've felt lately that I've moved further from him recently than ever before. This is a strange situation for me, especially as paradoxically, I finally seem to be getting things together. It doesn't add up.

I need a better angle for my article. A better point of entry. I can be quite clinical about this. Nothing is sacred.

"I found a vibrator not long after Ruth had gone. I don't think it's pivotal or anything, even though I'd never seen it before. I don't believe that sex played a role in her departure. We were comfortably open and pretty pragmatic in the bedroom – we may have had secrets but I doubt sexuality featured too heavily in them. But nevertheless she owned a vibrator and I didn't know. I wonder if she knew about the video in my old football boot-bag. Maybe this secrecy was important. Symptomatic of some greater problem. Maybe we didn't we know each other at all…"

This isn't what I want to write. Why did I tell Rick I'd have it in for Monday? I know there's a deadline but this is pushing it.

So I push my chair away from my desk and place my hands behind my head. The wheels that propel me backwards catch on a carrier bag. A carrier bag that contains a sizeable portion of this month's wages in material form. A gift for my wife.

Did I say it is Ruth's birthday today? Happy birthday monkey – wherever you are. I have been out this morning and bought her a present, just like I used to – and, just like previous years, I hadn't known what to buy.

Make no mistake, I'm a crap shopper where Ruth – and women in general – are concerned. I go armed with all the right information. Enough to know that Marc Jacobs and Stella McCartney are her favourite designers; that she adores Clarins stuff and likes simple jewellery. Nevertheless I've rarely found the process easy. She on the other hand knew I'd love a subscription to *Vanity Fair* and tickets to West Ham.

There is some consolation however in the certain promise that this time she won't pass comment or look blank and give me the "it's fine, I love it" line (infinitely worse). The present will be added, unopened, to the small pile I have accumulated. It will sit there with the Christmas gifts and the anniversary earrings.

Don't ask me to stop. Think about it, would you? It's not denial – it's just easier to carry on. It's the thought that counts – isn't that what everyone says? The receiving is secondary.

I liked being out earlier. Bond St was deserted. I enjoyed the mission, the novelty of purpose. And I managed to buy her a beautiful dress.

It happened as it always does. On entering the shop my momentary glance around was enough to have me positioned, segmented and targeted within seconds by the relevant retail authorities. Before I had a chance, there she was. All fake eyelashes,

Ash-blonde bun and way too much lipstick on a narrow ungenerous smile. An identikit clone that had my number from the moment I paused outside the window.

"Does sir require any help?"

Of course I should have said 'No', or impressed her with my knowledge of the business but I didn't. I always find it rude to not allow them to play out their united belief that men are simply crap and in need of guidance. And to be honest while my proximity to the fashion world is fair, and I could tell you when Milan will take place – I honestly didn't have a clue what to buy.

"Yeah, thanks, that'd be great," I said.

"What did sir have in mind?"

"A dress perhaps. I don't know..."

"What size is madam?"

"I don't know – a 12 – maybe 14?" I haven't much thought about whether Ruth has gained or lost a few pounds over the past two years. Probably lost perhaps but I'll stick with what I know – it's what I usually do.

"Perfect, lucky girl," the Ice Queen simpers, preening her hair with a bony finger; a digit adorned with an ostentatious ring of rubies.

"Ruth, my wife, likes plain things. Not too much colour, not too much fussy stuff."

"What about this?"

The garment is out within a flash, waved around in front of me like some trickster peddling a game of chance to an unsuspecting passer-by. Ice Queen's spiel continuing all the while.

"It's also available in grey – not too elaborate but deceptively elegant – perfect for a range of occasions. Of course it's so important to have flexibility in one's wardrobe these days."

Enough already – I want to say. It's just a nice black dress.

"... and look at the beadwork around the... ."

Vaguely aware that I'm being stung but desperate to get away from this master as quickly as possible I say the magic words.

"I'll take it."

And that's it. £700 signed away. Ruth would kill me.

And I don't even make the standard enquiry of all men who find themselves somehow in this situation, having fallen victim to the quick sell; I don't say, in a desperate and humiliating bid to regain a bit of control over the events that have just transpired.

"If she hates it, she'll be able to bring it back won't she? If I keep the receipt?"

There's no point. Ruth won't even see the damn thing. This is money down the drain whether she ever sees it and likes it or not.

With my purchase agreed, I'm instantly directed to Deanne sulking in the corner. No further pleasantries are offered, no after-sale service is offered. I am no longer important. I feel vaguely abandoned – a sensation I'm used to. I watch the clone move off, fascinated by her stealth. Her work here is done and having exploited her lead, she's heading towards the lingerie section looking for fresh meat.

I collect myself and amble over to the till. I find myself loitering nervously, watching a bemused guy leave the counter laden with three bags and a considerably lighter wallet. I'm actually happy that I've managed to get this far with only a single item. At this moment, though I have achieved a pyrrhic victory, I have mastered the art of shopping and scored a victory over all the tactics aimed at me. I will not buy anything else – however much it matches.

"How do you wanna pay?" asks Deanne, in a soft Antipodean patter, welcome relief to my ears after the shrill equine Sloane of her mercenary colleague. Deanne is pretty. She has a lovely smile. Deanne knows what's what, I can tell that.

"Visa?" I say, receiving an affirmatory nod as I rummage in my inside suit jacket. That's right, I'm wearing suits on a Saturday. I even had a haircut first thing. Across the room the voice of the Ice Queen rings out a hideous peal of happy laughter as she spots a regular customer. Deanne busies herself with my card but I catch a mumbled phrase.

"Fucking cow."

"I'm sorry?"

"Oh! Not you… it doesn't matter. I'm having a bad day."

"Not a problem. Know how you feel."

"She's such a witch. She models herself on those bitches in that store where Julia Roberts went."

I have no idea what she's on about.

"I'm sorry?"

"… In *Pretty Woman*." Is the only clarification offered.

"I'm confused," I say.

Deanne rapidly pushes three fingers against her forehead, smiling all the while, she can't believe I'm stupid enough not to have picked up the reference. Suddenly I remember the scene she's referring to. I knew the Ice Queen reminded me of someone.

"Yeah, right – she is a bit severe. She'll get hers one day."

Deanne smiles another great wide smile it reminds me of a cross between Jennifer Lopez and Angelina Jolie. A nice mix.

"Do you have any idea what it's like to try and sell this shit?" she continues, altering her speech to an exaggerated approximation of her boss. 'Deanne – these aren't just clothes – this is high-fashion day-wear.'

"What the fuck is High-Fashion daywear for Ascot anyway?" she spits, obviously struggling to get over an earlier episode.

"It's bollocks is what it is," I say, quietly, thrilled with my bravery. I don't even look round for Ice Queen. I don't care where she is.

"Bollocks," Deanne echoes.

"Bollocks is a great word," I confirm.

By speaking to me I see that Deanne seems to have calmed down a bit. She directs me gently to a piece of paper laid out on the grey marble that divides us.

"Please sign here," she says sweetly.

So I do, aware that a queue has formed behind me. They're all men. They're all holding garments uncomfortably.

"Thanks. Here's your receipt," she says with a smile.

And that's it. It's all over. Time to leave. I wanted to give Deanne more, let her know things are okay but time was against us. She had work to do. Instead I said "Goodbye" and left her leaning there against the counter. Left swinging the present for a wife that isn't present. Striding towards the exit to meet Maggie for lunch. As I reached the door I heard Deanne whisper once again to the next customer; giving her distinctive view on the Ice Queen. Using my word now – bollocks. It obviously gets her through the day.

We had a nice time at lunch, Maggie and I, in between her repeated demands that I don't mess up dinner with Laura. She told me that Laura has been hurt too. Deliberately letting it slip about an ex-husband. I didn't know that. I'd mistakenly assigned Laura as a perpetual single. Just goes to show how preoccupied I've been. I think about Laura getting married, the hopes that must have been lost somewhere along the way.

We drank a bottle of wine before getting the bill. I didn't show Maggie what was in the carrier bag between my feet. She's not the sort of woman to be interested anyway. I don't know how would have explained that I was buying gifts for Ruth. Maybe I should have bought something for Laura tonight.

Anyway I came back home to the article, back to my words and telling my story.

*

It's 6.00pm and I'm finishing my first draft. I wrapped Ruth's present and put it away and then the words came. I'm not sure if the article says anything but I also feel like I've said a lot. That it will be published is secondary, that it is written by me is all. And regardless, I feel that I've given a lot – when I'm useless at giving and even worse at receiving.

I think Ruth would really like the dress. I think I would have surprised her.

```
To:      Rick@mentormag.co.uk
From:    Ben@mentormag.co.uk
Subject: 'MENtor torMENt feature
Rick
As promised here's my feature. Just over the word limit
and in the style we discussed.
I'm still not convinced this is such a good idea. Then
again, anything's got to be better than the incest piece
we ran for July.
It's your call.
I might want to change our names.
Cheers, Ben
```

*

I arrive early outside the restaurant, Compass – "a top eat" according to Jason, when I asked his advice about a suitable venue. He effortlessly reeled off half-a-dozen names, only two of which I'd heard of – the perennial Ivy and Sheekeys. He even gave me menu suggestions, recommended dishes and chef's specialities. I chose Compass as I liked the name. It suggests helpfulness. I wanted a place that was smart but not fussy for the sake of it. Not where the urinal could be any number of features in the bathroom and you need a degree to work out how to activate the tap. I wanted ease and direction at every turn. Compass sounded perfect. Simplicity but still, without question, one of the places to be seen, and more crucially, to be seen to be seen. I'm not sure whether Laura is impressed by these sorts of things.

I had thought about Momo's but decided against it. Momo's was our place. Momo's was where I'd proposed to Ruth – in the Kemia bar, there downstairs in amongst the crowded sound within the heavy thud of other people. She said an instant yes and I shouted our news to all around. Who cheered in a way people never cheer in Heddon St or anywhere else in London in fact, unless there's been a football match against the Germans. On a good night, like the night I proposed – Momo's felt like the centre of the universe, a metropolitan Moroccan paradise – a sensation helped that evening, July 16, by the heat of summer.

I haven't been back there since Ruth went. That betrothal night we stumbled out of Momo's into a waiting cab and went straight to Claridges, booked a room as Mr & Mrs Carter and ordered champagne accompanied by toasted cheese with Worcester sauce. Around 2am Ruth told me she loved me so much that she never wanted to be reminded of anything before we were reunited. The future, our new future, was everything. I was still drinking bourbon and said that's fine – we'll have children right away. She was pissed and didn't respond. So I said okay we'd wait a while.

Around 4 am she murmured, half-asleep "Where's my ring?" and I realised I'd forgotten to give it to her. This wasn't my intention. I'd done the bended knee thing at Momo's (thank god for Moroccan cushions); I'd gotten nervous and fluffed my well-intentioned lines just like you're supposed to; but I'd somehow held onto the white-gold

125

band with diamond inset. The seal on the deal as it were. So in our room at Claridges, with the light off, in the early hours I retrieved the ring and gently lifted her arm off the pillow before placing it on her finger. She fell back to sleep there and then with a wide smile on her face – I don't think she even checked out the stone. I stayed awake going over and over again how perfect the evening had been.

I've never been back to Momo's. And we never got round to children. I wish we had. I wish I had part of her with me.

But tonight is about Laura. About being ruthless. It's raining heavily as I enter Compass. The solitary sodden paparazzo lowering his telephoto lens as I walk past; continuing his wait for someone noteworthy to arrive. This place has got that kind of reputation. In fact, the *Evening Standard* has already published two glowing reviews and an interiors feature about the ironic use of suspended fisherman's nets and plastic lobsters inside.

While I recognise uncomfortably that I too have succumbed to the hype, and taken no small measure of pride in securing a booking on a Saturday night, I cannot help but suspect on entering that this is all a case of the Emperor's recently purchased bespoke suit. Despite the meteoric rise of Compass to the very pinnacle of the city's social firmament, and Jason's insistent praise, I remain certain that the ceramic fisherman sitting askew on the maitre d's lectern, reveals not the subtle playfulness of the playboy owner but in fact the appalling design choices of a man who really shouldn't be in the gastronomic game.

I'm directed to my seat in the back, my overcoat taken and the menu given all in one swift movement. I glance with resignation at my position near the toilet. The sarcastic smile from my departing waiter perhaps suggesting that at least I'll get a chance to view the majority of tonight's estimable clientele as they make their way back and forth from the lavatory. I'll certainly have a story or two to tell tomorrow of soap stars and weather-girls. But let's get real here, I won't be mentioning any celebrities or gossiping about who might have been here with whom. Not because I don't do that sort of thing but because I'm waiting here for Laura and I guess this is a date. The staff of *Mentor* would have a field day at the news. Maybe they already know – given Jason's revelation that everyone discusses everything. I've already garnered much comment for my acceptance of Rick's feature idea and general all-round reanimation; though I'm still some way off organising the Grand National Sweepstake or emailing everyone a comical mpeg of some granny being dragged along by her dog.

But it's not a date, not yet. At the moment I am alone and waiting for Laura to arrive and wondering whether this was such a good idea after all. Maggie warned me against bottling out. Totally changing her tune and going on about "getting out there". I told her to stop before she mentioned "plenty more fish". I smile to myself as I then remember where I am sitting – with damp hair beneath a school of plastic rainbow trout that indicates the way to the toilets.

My smile becomes external when I realise that Laura has arrived. That she is being led over towards me. It's nice to see her. She looks incredibly nervous and she also looks great. Really great, in fact.

"You look great," I say, at a loss for further words.

"Thank you," she replies "I can't believe this bloody weather. My hair's ruined."

"You're right, it's terrible. Um. The weather, I mean…"

I can't believe I just did that. Fortunately she laughs at my crapness.

"Did you see that poor guy outside?" I say, talking about the photographer, trying to win back more lost ground than the Palestinians.

We sit down and I'm suddenly trying to remember how to behave, how to relate to others socially.

"He started to take my picture – actually asked me if I was on telly." She blushes.

"Didn't give me a second look," I say. "But then I don't look like you do." I get away with that one – she doesn't wince. In fact she blushes even more, small patches of red under dark eye make-up that makes her sexy in a way I've never previously noticed.

Laura is wearing a black dress, the type that paraphrases Coco Chanel simply by being worn. And I'm actually happy and not bothered about the kind of conditioning that has left me capable of sentences like the last one. I'm glad I decided to put on a suit, one that Ruth bought me not long before she went. She always knew what looked better on me than I did.

"I like your suit," Laura compliments. "I'm still not used to you dressing properly."

"Thanks, I think," I reply, grinning. "Ruth bought it."

And that does it. All of a sudden Ruth is here as well; I've conjured her presence out of thin air. But Laura waves her away with a gentle giggle and continues the conversation unfazed.

"I think I could have worked that one out. It's pretty clear who got the good taste in your relationship," she says, good humouredly.

I can't figure out whether she's talking in the past or present tense. This is, without doubt, going to be a strange evening – for both of us, especially for Laura who is effectively having dinner with a widower, without a dead body to show for his love.

"I think I would like Ruth. I think she sounds like a good laugh."

She doesn't seem to mind talking about my wife, and crucially, I don't mind it either. There's no apology, no hesitation, no empathy – just conversation. I haven't had conversation like this for a long, long time.

I'm resolute that I want to contribute, I am compelled to join in and that I need to order some wine as the fucking waiter won't go away.

"Have you decided sir? White or normal?" he says.

Unfunny git. He's got blonde highlights that make him look like Limahl.

"What'll we have?" I ask Laura, ignoring him.

"You decide," she insists.

I order red wine. If she had said 'white' that would have been fine too.

I decide to blow the bank – one benefit of living the past two years as a hermit is the healthy state of my bank balance. I've always covered the mortgage anyway, so Ruth's departure didn't cause too many problems – she handled all the bills and the shopping. It's surprising how little resources and food one uses when caught up in a sea of grief and a constant wave of self-pity.

I've picked the second most expensive bottle on the list and the waiter looks suitably impressed. I see him study my features more intently, wondering if perhaps he should know who I am. He backs away subserviently and whispers in a colleague's ear. I like that it might be about me. But not that much. What I do like is that Laura looks happy – not with the expensive wine or the hard to come by table, but to be here with me and not to be alone.

*

I am making love to Laura. I can't quite believe it is happening, that things are happening down there, that my erection is being put to good use and I am fucking another woman. But I'm afraid that's exactly what it feels like – I'm fucking another woman. That's right, in the adulterous sense of the word. Another woman that's not my wife. There's no doubt about it, I'm technically being unfaithful to Ruth – someone that may be breathing somewhere right now and may be thinking of her husband. Of me.

There's no escape from my guilt. I'm transposing my actions, right here, to the past and believing this current betrayal to be the reason she left. But I loved her. You've got to believe me. I loved her.

Shit, where did the present tense go? When did that happen? This isn't good, this isn't helping. Put it out of your mind. But it's in my mind. Come on Ben, get back to the woman before you – and try to forget the woman before.

So, we're in my flat, we're in my bed and I'm almost in Laura. Being ruthless.

She moans as I move my right hand away from her clitoris, trailing my index finger over her body up to the soft curve of one breast. Though she's tall, I succeed in brushing the surface of a nipple with a speculative circular action I've remembered at the just the right moment from last month's *Mentor*. I wonder if Laura has read the same feature and is aware of exactly what I'm trying to achieve, what directions I'm following. Nevertheless, it works – the arch that forms as she lifts herself off the sheets clear evidence of her approval. The subsequent low moan of pleasure encourages me to move my hand yet again, this time under her, around to the small of her now raised back, better placed to support her frame. I hold her like that, freeing my elbow and slowly inching up the bed, until our faces are level, until I meet her gaze – all the while holding her, guiding my dick deep inside and grateful, so fucking grateful, that I still know how to do this.

That I haven't forgotten the steps. Grateful for chrissakes to *Mentor* and their bloody 'Fingertip foreplay' two-parter last year.

And suddenly it's there and I'm here. Mostly paying attention. Incredibly satisfied with the urgent rhythm, natural progression and serene beatific silence that follows our one mutual happiness.

*

I'm not like other guys. I never fall asleep after sex, it leaves me wide awake. Not wanting more, not unfulfilled – just awake. Eyes wide, thoughts racing but comforted by my slowing pulse. Laura however, on returning from the bathroom, has fallen asleep in my arms, her blonde hair tickling my chest with each rise and fall of her breathing.

12. FAULT

I've forgotten to wear my wedding ring. The first time ever. I had no choice really, earthquakes don't really leave you too much time to think rationally. When you hear your kids screaming for you, options are narrowed and swift decisions are made.

The roof shook first, then the plaster fell. I awoke certain that my sins were being judged. It was only as Ally screamed "earthquake!" that biblical egotism gave way to total fear for my children. Twenty seconds later, I'd got out of bed, grabbed Max and ran down cold white stairs and on to wet, sprinkler-doused grass with Ally and Emily ahead of me. Emily crying all the while – believing this to be the apocalypse, or something equally gothic. I've had better mornings. I thought yesterday's argument with Ally about my fidelity was bad, but this has got to be worse.

I stood on the grass wondering what to do. People were coming out of their buildings at varying speeds. I was deciding on the best course of action just as the crone climbed into her modified shopper-golf-cart-thing shouting the same two words over and over to us and anyone else who would listen. Max, who was relatively calm, eventually translated this as "the beach!" – clapping his hands excitedly, the boy loves the water. He's like a dolphin or something.

So that was the plan. "We'll go down to the beach," I told Ally, who was still eyeing our building nervously – I could see she wanted to go back inside. Probably for photo albums.

"No way, Ally," I anticipated. "The building doesn't look safe, didn't you notice the plaster that had fallen onto the staircase?"

She relented, defeated by my common sense. No. Go down from the mountain. Down to the beach where there aren't buildings, where everyone else seems to be going. People are getting into cars, sirens going off in the distance.

"Come on – down to the beach," I order.

Emily started to protest – screeching about after-shocks and tidal-waves. I told her to stop making a scene and she responded sarcastically "says my half-naked father".

It finally hit me. For all my usual reserve, there I was all but naked, standing in the gardens – in my underpants – exposed there for everyone to see. I couldn't believe it.

Though I'd prioritised correctly, I was mortified.

"Shit!"

I ran back inside just as Ally began to protest; however as soon as she realised that some form of clothing would be necessary (and worth the risk) – she changed her tune somewhat. Shouting after me. Insisting I grab the photo albums from beneath the coffee-table – only if I had time of course.

Into the building. Crack along the ceiling – fucking hell! Back out of the building wearing suit jacket and ripped Sunday jeans – a terrible look. I got the albums though – the pages flapping open as Ally hugged me on my return. A series of snow-scene images from a long ago New Years Eve with Ben and Ruth flickering briefly into view.

My kids huddled around – hysteria and frenzy building as people continued leaving.

We got to the beach amidst a cacophony of agitated car horns, divisive tannoy announcements and engaged cell-phone beeping, as everyone tried to call everyone else.

"Cool," Emily said, flatly, as she took in the crowds around her.

*

It's 9pm and we are in hell. Hell is other people. In this case other people called Brad and Chrissy. We are all in their apartment as our street has been cordoned off and no one can tell us exactly what the problem is. I can't remember if I locked the door.

Brad has a Playstation 2 (he would) and has set the kids up in his bedroom playing some fighting game that can't be good for their sense of fair-play. I was relieved to have them out of our hair though – it's been a long day. This relief overriding my understandable worry about the things that might have gone on in that bedroom; and the distinct prospect of sexual props being on display. I believe the things Chrissy has told me in the office.

I am nursing a cup of tea while my wife drinks Chardonnay. Chris and Brad have prepared cocktails, he called it 'fixing'. He actually made Old-Fashioneds at a time like this – demonstrating Angostura meeting sugar-cube; alcohol meeting ice.

Their apartment is spartanly dressed. Beech flooring and rattan furniture that creaks with each slight movement; fibrous strands that pierce the skin with every misguided fidget. Brad has leant me a Hilfiger t-shirt that proclaims USA in both colour and text. I'm still wearing the ripped jeans. He declared this "a great look for me" when I emerged from the bathroom.

We're all talking about the earthquake. About the phone calls we have had from loved ones back home. Ally is speaking.

"My mother wanted me to get a flight home now," she says. "What with this and that suicide bomber yesterday."

"As if London is safer," I add, and immediately wish I hadn't. I know what Ally means.

"My parents couldn't care less," Brad contributes.

"Aw, poor Brad," Ally says, leaning over to ruffle his hair, with the playful tone of someone who has a whole bottle of wine to herself.

"Actually I'm surprised that Ben hasn't called though," she states. "Martin? It's a bit strange, huh? That he hasn't called."

I emailed him earlier from an internet café down near the beach – I queued for an hour figuring he would have heard the news on the tv about the earthquake.

Mention my brother and instantly our benefactors are smiling. Chrissy and Brad love talking about Ben. He works for *Mentor* remember. That's a good thing. I straighten in my chair, the natural fibres resisting my shape, as the inevitable questions – the ones I've answered all my life begin.

"Martin – do you think he could sense it was happening? The earthquake I mean?" Chrissy's voice has been irritating the fuck out of me all afternoon.

"No," I say, though I'm not sure.

"It'd be funny if he was in London and just fell over." This from Brad.

"Why?" I say, reasonably.

"Cause of the earthquake like?" Chrissy offers helpfully, the word 'like' used Mancunianly.

"Like he'd be walking and suddenly, like, pitch up for no reason." This time 'like' is used Americanly.

The earthquake has obviously upset more than the tectonic plates – I'm turning into my brother, with this preoccupation with what – and how – everyone is speaking. no one is making any sense. Everyone is drunk except me. All I can do is notice that both Brad and Chrissy's accents use the word 'like' far too much.

Silence now.

"It is weird Martin," My wife resumes, "that he hasn't called." She just won't leave it alone.

"Thanks," I say, quietly.

"For what?"

"Everything," I am not amused. Brad cuts in.

"Who'd like another drink? Martin – another cup of tea?"

"No thanks – I'll just get some water. Then I should go to bed."

I wonder what Ben is up to this Sunday. What's prevented him from getting in touch. I believed his email when he said he'd call.

I carry out my cup into their kitchen, opening the door a crack on the kids – they're both sleeping on each other, the day has taken its toll. Ally and I are in here later as well – extra bedding and mattresses on the floor.

Chrissy has come up behind me and looks in too.

"Your kids are sweet," she says in a voice that sounds wistful. She's never professed any maternal instinct before. "I'm dead jealous."

We go back through into the lounge where Brad and my wife are still lounging around. Her bare feet pulled up onto the seat next to him.

Chrissy tells Ally that her children are sleeping like lambs. Ally couldn't care less. She's been hyper-concerned about them all day, but everyone has a limit – now nothing matters – it's only natural.

And now the subject of kids is acceptable to all. And Chrissy pours Ally more wine and says "Did Ben and his wife want kids?" all the while looking at Brad.

Not only do they like talking about Ben – they love hearing about the woman who disappeared.

"Ruth couldn't have them," Ally states, matter of factly.

I didn't know this. I react accordingly.

"I'm sorry?" I manage to stammer. Though I've just drunk a pint of water, my throat is dry. "What are you talking about Ally? You're pissed. Ignore her," I say, to our friends.

"Ssssh," Chrissy interrupts. "You'll wake the kids." As if they're hers.

Ally didn't mean to let this fact slip, I can tell. Sitting up now, placing feet back on the floor.

Brad is keeping quiet but I could tell from his face that he was willing my wife to go on – this is better than Jerry Springer.

"I'm sorry. It was a secret. Ruth told me not to tell anyone."

"I'm not just anyone. I'm your husband," I say, incredulously. "Ben is your brother-in-law." I add, before thinking about this for a second. "But it's not true," I insist.

"It is true, Martin. I was with her at the doctors. She couldn't have them."

"For fuck's sake," I shout, out of control.

Ally is sobering fast. "It's not important. She was fine about it. Just she wanted to tell Ben in her own time, so asked me to keep quiet."

"And did she? Tell Ben?"

"She was gone two months later. No. I don't think so."

"And you don't think it was important. That when the police asked us all if we knew anything – you didn't think this was important?!"

"Martin – calm down." Ally's eyes, her whole being wishing she could take back the slip.

"Why?" I insist.

"Because Ruth told me she couldn't have kids and that was that. No fuss, no upset, no big deal, Martin. She was going to tell Ben. But he didn't even want them. You know what he always said whenever he held Emily – 'glad he could give her back'."

I'm silent for a moment. Chrissy and Brad remain silent too. This is the most sensible thing they've done as a couple since I've known them.

My breathing is slowing down – there's nowhere for me to go with this.

Ally finishes her speech. "What good would it have done Martin? What good would it have done to Ben? It wouldn't bring her back. If she did go on purpose and if that's the reason – how would it help him? How?"

"I'm confused," I say. I still can't believe what I've heard.

Ally did say one thing that was true though. My brother wasn't paternal in the slightest. Maybe he saw how my life changed so early? Maybe he felt what I felt a bit too much? Maybe he viewed the way my kids impacted my life? He certainly knew who I was before they were born... and possibly, who'd I'd then become.

I can't keep up my anger with Ally because secretly I'm aware of secrets that may have played a larger role. I know all about withholding truths and cannot criticise her well-intentioned motives. I know about that too. I want to end this public debate now. There's no benefit to anyone.

So, much to Brad and Chrissy's visible annoyance, I rise noisily out of the armchair and say to my wife, "Come on. Let's go to bed."

And I remember what constitutes good manners nowadays.

"Thanks for letting us stay guys. Really appreciate it."

13: STIFF

The sun is out for what feels like the first time this year. As it streams through my bedroom window I'm reminded of the main reason why Ruth and I fell in love with this place – for the large panes of glass, the high white ceilings, the sense of space. Maximum light, minimal shadow.

Laura has stayed over and she's still here. I don't want her to leave, I don't want to let her out of my sight.

I'm conscious on this Sunday morning after the Saturday night before that the bedroom is filthy. With my head still firmly against the pillow, my eyes trace a path from the condom wrapper across the clothes strewn everywhere and I'm disgusted with myself. It's hardly a setting worthy of staging our first union – it looks like someone has broken and entered. I'm ashamed at how sordid Laura might feel if she were to wake right now. I'd already moved the photo of Ruth at university in the cream dress to the living room – it wouldn't have been fair for Laura to have faced that.

Bloody hell – it's 12.32pm – I haven't slept so deeply for months.

I jump out and begin the process of gathering up pants and shirts so that she won't be repulsed by my habits. Inevitably dropping solitary socks however tightly I hold them. Ten seconds later I'm clutching a well-intentioned and proactive pile of dirty washing when I suddenly think of Martin – and my promise to get in touch. I drop the laundry back to the floor and decide to make use of having the laptop to email him. I certainly don't want to wake Laura by speaking on the phone.

I get online and open up the email. There's a new message from my brother. He's written a lot which is unusual. A long message with one block paragraph that stretches beyond the boundaries of a single screen. Punctuation all over the place, no thought for spelling – but plenty of information. The opening paragraph tells me that "desoite the earthquake they sre all all-right. A bit shaken ip. The kids said it was lik being at Disneyworld. (sic)"

I hope other priorities are the reason for his mistakes. I'd hate to think they were beyond his control. Martin is trying to concentrate on content, not the details but in doing so is fucking up any hope of getting his message across. Further, sample sentence — "we have a crack 8' long runing parralel with the kitchen strip lght. Ran bak in hoyse to get clothes."

And though he's speaking of natural disasters, there's initially not much substance in his message. I've picked up that there was an earthquake and am relieved all is fine. It's mad how different our lives are at the moment. But then the text changes. It's as if he's trying to say more. Skirting around something, mentioning that him and Ally keep arguing and something about this "twat" he hates who is engaged to Chrissy, whom I've met once or twice, and something about wanting to just see me and go and get completely pissed like we used to.

Email is not that good for us, in fact thirty seconds face to face without uttering a word can breed more meaningful communication than a month of daily typed messages. I realise I want him to come home. To meet Laura even. Besides, it's not safe over there — the constant news about violence is ruining our mother's nerves.

I bash out a response, keen to get on with getting the house in order. Show some degree of hospitality to Laura.

To: Martin@Midaret.com
From: Ben@mentormag.co.uk
Subject: <none>
Martin
Earthquake sounds awful. Glad all is well. Really think it's a sign you should try and come back. Isn't there any work nearer to home?
It doesn't matter about Chrissy's boyfriend, I don't know why you are so hung up on him.
He sounds like a prick. Ignore him otherwise Ally will pick-up on it. Ally is the one to give your time to.
Anyway, things here are getting better. As I said going home really helped. I'm getting closer Martin. Things are becoming clearer.
Can't wait to see you all. Soon I hope. I think it's about time, don't you? Better go, I don't want to wake Laura.
love
Ben.

I send the text on its way. I mentioned Laura on purpose – I know it'd freak him out and I feel like having a bit of fun. Ben's got a new girl!

I put away the computer and head back into the bedroom to get the dirty clothes. Laura is still asleep. I've gathered them up once more when the doorbell sounds. Fucking hell, perfect timing as ever. Rather than carry the laundry with me, I undo all my good work opting to return the clothes yet again to ground, but behind the door and out of sight – just in case she wakes up.

I pace out to the hallway pulling on a pair of shorts as I go, my stomach rumbling ominously. The restaurant may have been great last night, but the portions wouldn't have satisfied a supermodel. As I tread to the door my calves are comfortably sore from my efforts; my hair scruffily fashionable – artfully unarranged in a way I would never leave the house with. I am a cliché of Sunday morning dishevelment all over the world.

I swing open the door expecting nothing in particular, prepared for anyone and anything. Anything other than a policeman which is what I get. Actually I get two – but one is in plain-clothes and looks more like an accountant. Both have half-hearted brown goatees, both are solemnly standing on my doorstep, both with serious expressions on their faces. I'm sorry to report I almost shit myself on the spot. I'm being honest. My God, it's finally arrived. The day is today. Of all days.

"Mr Carter?" one of them apparently says, though I don't notice either mouth moving. I only hear the words.

My chin moves slowly forward; down in the direction of my chest before embarking upwards once again – ie I'm silently affirming, nodding that yes, I am Mr Carter. Mr Carter is me. Satisfied of my identity, they shuffle uneasily, each waiting for the other to continue.

"I'm sorry sir – can we come in please?" Again, it's like they're both ventriloquists – I guess I'm the dummy. I could certainly say everything for them.

Badges are shown and barely glanced at. They want to come inside – they want to talk to me about Ruth.

"Sure." I say, finding my voice – though it barely sounds human, let alone like me. I open out the door and move off inside my home –

they follow me through into the lounge, I don't care that I am half-dressed, it doesn't matter. We all know where this is going, having the correct attire is utterly irrelevant.

"Are you alone? Is there a friend nearby? Someone you can call to be with you?"

An unexpected but I guess understandable question. I respond quickly – "No, I'm not alone." This time moving my head from side to side, informing them of Laura's presence elsewhere in the flat. My outstretched finger towards the bedroom attempts to clarify, but Laura's bra hanging off the armchair removes any doubt about my companion. Fuck this, I want to tell them that this is a first for two years. That I don't usually have anyone with me. That I *have* found it hard to move on.

But they don't seem to be judging me – they want to get this over with too.

"It's just we've..."

Hesitation now, this definitely emerged from constable number one. He's genuinely lost for words.

"What is it officer?" Officer! I sound like my grandmother.

"We've been contacted by Berkshire police. They've located a Jane Doe, a deceased woman who matches your wife's description..."

The other, so far silent, cop leaps in – no doubt determined to keep momentum.

"We're very sorry sir but we'll need you to come and view the body."

"When?" is all I say. It is Sunday, after all.

His palms are in the air, facing me gently, wanting me to slow down. Telling me to be calm and he's right, my breathing is fast.

"No rush. This can't be easy."

And there it is – the proud winner of understatement of the fucking decade. It can't be easy? You try it sometime.

"You really shouldn't be alone," he repeats and looks past me, in the direction of the bedroom, prompting me to get help from whoever is in there.

They're very well intentioned these guys, saying all the right things, declining a cup of tea, the uniformed officer holding his hat in his hands. I turn away quickly, leaving them there – studying my bloody shelf as I go, questioning for the first time whether it might be askew. Giving in to Ruth.

Bathed in early morning light, blonde hair complementing ivory pillow, Laura, who is still asleep, looks entirely serene, categorically beautiful. Last night she spent several minutes removing her make-up before we made love and her resting skin is as pure as anything I've ever seen.

"Laura?" I whisper.

She stirs almost imperceptibly and I realise I'm about to fuck up her day considerably. Maybe I've fucked up her life full stop. She doesn't need to be part of this. It's nothing to do with her. I need Martin, God, I need my twin brother to be here. I wouldn't have to be in charge, I could share responsibility.

"Laura," I repeat more loudly, desperately now. Which gets her attention and then immediately she's sitting up and staring at me, sensing something in my tone, her eyes clearer than I've ever seen them.

"What is it?" she says.

I brief her on events so far as quickly as possible, dropping words in my rush to avoid their meaning.

"Two policemen here – think they've found Ruth. A body." I clarify.

And only now, as I pronounce words that I've ran from for two years, am I aware of the reality of this situation and I suddenly want to get there right now. I want to get to Ruth as quickly as I can.

"Oh my God," Laura says without embellishment, just softly like that, her hand has flown to her mouth and she's upright in seconds, moving towards me but I've already moved away, uncomfortable with her proximity. It's not appropriate. Ruth is present. Ruth is waiting.

I attack the pile of clothes I'd placed behind the bedroom door minutes ago, finding a pair of tracksuit bottoms and my De Niro gym t-shirt. My denim jacket is removed from the wardrobe door handle. Laura too dresses with necessary expedience, pulling on one of my sweaters, not looking for her bra which isn't in the room. The pair of us are soon with the policemen, one discussing details and one helpfully brewing tea. Without introducing Laura or her role in my life, as frankly I'm not sure what it is, a plan of action is swiftly outlined, and I'm ready to be led, to follow instructions.

I no longer want fuss or deliberation. Within minutes I am in the car and we are pulling away. Laura remaining on the doorstop of my building, her ashen face at odds with the glorious rays sent insistently from the sky. This is a beautiful day.

I know that I must endure this alone, despite Laura's protestations otherwise. Sure, she is here for me, but Ruth is there. I repeat this notion in my mind as we leave. Ruth is there. Waiting. I'm in no doubt it's her.

I'm racked with guilt about what the policemen might have surmised about my situation, the fact that I seem to have moved on. Do they understand? The timing of all this leaves me justified in the belief that someone, somewhere, is having a laugh. Last night I was ruthless. Last night I let go of everything and experienced a sweetness absent from my life for so long. I shouldn't have bothered. Today I'm back dealing with the bitter caustic taste of reality. My ongoing reality.

As we pull ourselves through increasingly unfamiliar streets in an unmarked Mercedes; my mind alights on a new realisation. That my torment might soon be over. That there will be a funeral, that well-meaning friends will once and for all know what card to buy, what type of message to write. That I will become a widower and not simply a man abandoned. I will exist once more as a box on application forms, socially classified.

And yet, the prospect of finality unnerves me – the thought of Ruth's certain death is suddenly too much to bear. The policeman said 'found a body', didn't he? Rigor mortis is about to provide inalienable truth and the cancellation of all my hope and this naturally leads to the suggestion that Ruth possibly suffered, that she might have experienced physical pain and I wonder what I am about to see? Nausea rushes everywhere, my hands are shaking, my hands are shaking.

I lean between the two front seats. Words tripping over words like dominoes leading to total fall-down.

"Is, is, she... will she, seem, look normal?" Selfish, I must seem so selfish.

"There is no sign of outward trauma Mr Carter. Don't worry."

I fall back into the leather seat, thankful for the reassurance, no longer wanting to ask anything else at this stage. Outward trauma? Clearly he's been watching too much *ER*. A good show but a bit overrated since they decided to give each lead character a major illness, dysfunctional relative and unwanted pregnancy.

What am I thinking? Anything but Ruth. Lying there.

We slow at a pedestrian crossing – an elderly woman takes an age to shuffle the short distance. She's lived for a long time and I'm sure to her even that doesn't seem long enough. She seems alone, I wonder how long it's been like this?

I sense grief surfacing, but somehow I'm succeeding in keeping it at bay – tears held fast like flood rains against tidal defences, water ready to burst its banks and wash over me; water that may clean or drown me.

I've been waiting for this moment for a long time. I've wanted it so much, and yet I want to go back 24 hours. To sit indoors and not go out for dinner, to not meet Laura. For just the chance that Ruth might still be alive somewhere, however far, I would gladly go back. I don't want her to be dead.

You've got to believe me. I want things the way they were, even last month when I found it hard to sleep, when I found it impossible to get through the equation of the day, when I was desperate to try and get the puzzle finished.

Laura will understand, we can still be friends.

We have to stop for petrol. One of the policemen curses the other under his breath for the apparent lack of planning, for the unnecessary extension of my torment. The driver attempts to make amends by asking if I want anything from the forecourt shop. Jesus Christ. Yes please, do they sell Valium? In fact I ask for a fucking Snickers instead. I really do, don't ask me why. He seems grateful to be of use.

They pass me a king-size bar and we move off. The indicator signalling our direction. The mechanical click resounding throughout the walnut interior – regular, regular, regular.

None of the streets are familiar now. I wonder if Ruth ever knew them.

Did you notice that I'm firmly in the past tense now? There is no longer any time like the present. At least not where my wife was concerned.

*

The mortuary isn't at all like I imagined it. Vases of flower litter every available area and a receptionist sits behind a mahogany desk. If I looked up sympathetic in the dictionary it would describe this very scene.

It doesn't feel like we are in the hospital. It doesn't look like it does in films.

And then we're through a door into more clinical territory and a smell that's overpoweringly clean and dirty all at the same time. I am looking only at the floor now – the sullen gleam – the matt reflection of strip lighting somewhere above.

I am in a room, I am being held by the arm. A policeman's radio crackles and an admonishment is unleashed.

There is some material and there is a hand moving into my line of vision, about to fold back a corner perhaps. A voice is asking if I am ready. I mutter something about using dental records instead as this seems to make perfect sense.

My legs are giving way and I can't go through with it.

But I nod my head, saying I'm okay.

And I'm thinking of Ruth phoning to see if I want red or green pesto. Of Saturday mornings with the papers and us both fighting over the *News of the World*. Of our wedding night, after everyone had gone – when I had sat on the bed opening all the cards while my contented bride lay under the covers, listening to me read aloud the messages with half-asleep eyes but wide, happy smile. Of me sitting on the toilet while Ruth sat in the bath, shaving her armpits, asking me if I truly loved her.

I'm thinking of Ruth, who I did indeed love truly, lying dead before me.

Imperceptible movement. A reverential removal of cloth.

It's not Ruth. It's someone else. It's not even close.

*

Laura is still at my house when one of the policemen drops me back home. I ask her to leave. She protests but I'm quite clear on the matter.

"But it wasn't Ruth," she said.

Exactly.

BOOK II: DIFFUSION

1. CEDAR

The night is almost over but the day, Monday, hasn't yet begun. I'm still in bed. In darkness. Half asleep. Safe within these unaccountable moments. In time that is not yet defined and with breathing that is only functional. Unemotional. Before routine kicks in, before the equation starts.

In time. Shadows remove. Angles lengthen.

There.

Trace elements of anaemic light seep through the windows, hesitant and weak. Not yet enough to provoke birds that have been waking up the neighbourhood for years. Sparrows, I think, though I could be wrong. A family in the cedar tree opposite. Romantic at first, Chinese water-torture after a while. I'm hoping that, eventually, like everything else in my life, they will move on.

I'm lying in bed, in sheets that could do with a wash – wearing yesterday's clothes and aware that only one sock has survived the night. On the pillow beside me is an ashtray. This is surprising as I wasn't aware that I smoked. I certainly never smoked before.

I think about opening my eyes when I realise that given all details relating to light, birds and cigarettes just described – they must already be open. I preferred it when I thought I was still away. Not necessarily here. That I might still be asleep.

I am still married most nights. Fleeting glimpses of a life lived with another. A life regulated by commitment but liberated through purpose.

Last night I dreamed that Ruth was waiting for me outside our home. Just sitting there. Patiently.

I push the ashtray to the floor, away from Ruth's side of the bed. It lands with a certain crack. A very definite noise, testament to the floorboards that we sanded on first moving in. Original pine that unites all the rooms in the flat. A selling point. A deal-breaker when we stumbled excitedly over the threshold; shown around by an estate agent called Brendan who checked his reflection in each mirror in every room we entered. We made the offer there and then, as Ruth gabbled on excitedly about "the state of the boards" – asking Brendan if "they were original". Brendan said they were. We said there's no chain, we can move in straight away. And we did.

I'm aware of an alien object in my trousers which has been irritating me, at least on some level for an amount of time. I fumble in my back pocket, eventually removing a half-eaten Snickers bought yesterday by an understanding policeman. It smells, predictably, of chocolate. Unpredictably (given the early hour and my furry senses) I'm also aware that it smells good.

I didn't eat anything after viewing the body. The body that wasn't Ruth. Food wasn't really at the forefront of my thoughts, nothing was at the forefront of my thoughts apart from her. The poor girl. I'd opened up the fridge a couple of times but couldn't go through with it. Desperate, but unable, to get rid of the pervasive smell, taste and touch of that place.

And so I eat the chocolate fast, getting it everywhere. This scene, were it to be viewed by any casual observer, would appear extremely disgusting. I discard the wrapper in the ash-tray glad for the chance to display a degree of decorum, should anyone be looking in.

I am aware that someone is in the flat. It isn't Ruth and it's unlikely to be Laura, given the uncivil way I despatched her yesterday. More likely to be a burglar.

Or Maggie, of course. Think of the devil. My sister-in-law wanders into the room, wearing a Metallica t-shirt, smoking a fag (ashtray solved) and I remember the pair of us were up most of the night talking, mostly about her sister but increasingly about my colleague. About Laura. I notice how I've defined our relationship by our employment status alone. Colleague. I seem to have deliberately pushed the thought of Laura being anything other to me – and the pure memory of her naked out of my head. It's not difficult, the tragic woman from the mortuary, lying there cold, dead, also naked, is readily available to take her place. There's no chain, she can move in straight away.

Jesus, it's not even Ruth anymore.

As Maggie sits down on the bed, keeping a sensible distance from my odorous feet I remember more of our conversation yesterday evening. She'd kept offering me the phone, telling me to call Laura, but it had got progressively later and later and I hadn't done it.

But I sense she is more than ready to try with me again. So here she is with a cup of tea and some Monday mail that's arrived. I can't believe the postman has got up and been around already. I take the post from her, needlessly checking the names on the front. All mine. Everything is all mine. And as I rip through them, I'm reassured there is nothing exciting. This is a life-long phenomenon, I've never been one of those people to get unexpected or thrilling correspondence; to have a life-changing red-letter day. Even during Ruth, we'd only ever get water bill demands or offers for credit cards. Polling cards for election days that we were always too busy to vote in.

I remember I once made Ruth smile by complaining that "for two such interesting people, we really should be getting more interesting mail". She half-smiled and said I was stupid. That's a new memory. I haven't had a new memory for a while. I'm thoroughly pleased this surfaced. I store it for later.

And there's only five years to go until the government can officially declare her deceased.

"Drink your tea," Maggie says, offering two Anadin Extra as a chaser. She's not a student for nothing. She's also holding my phone. It's been glued to her hand since she arrived last night. It's been thrust in my direction almost non-stop. It's a nice phone, I don't mean to reject it so pointedly.

"You're going to call her," she instructs. Meaning Laura.

"Not now Maggie. Please, I just woke up. I feel like shit."

"You look like it too. I hope that's chocolate," she says, pointing to a smear on the sheet, before resuming. "Call her."

"No," I say.

"Yes," she says.

"No."

I'm really am bloody minded enough to carry on doing this all morning.

"Why not?" she says, before trying out a few insults, just for good measure. "Coward. Twat. Moron."

And that's it. I'm pissed off. Really angry, gathering up the sheets around me to better attack her.

"Look Maggie. Ruth is disappearing. When will you understand I don't want to wipe her out. There's still a chance that she's out there, needing me, needing both of us. We can't abandon her. She might be…"

I feel it's important to state that none of the above is what I believe any more. At least not what drives my every waking emotion. Of course I want to treasure my wife's memory but I know she's gone. I've been ruthless about that. And it's clear to me now that I'm acting. Using her. Exploiting Ruth simply to get someone to lay off. It's only 6.17am, you can't really blame me.

But Maggie isn't fooled.

"Moron," she repeats. There's a film across her eyes as she says this, upset perhaps at being thoughtlessly reminded of the reality of a sister lost to the void.

It was a clumsy attempt. But I had wanted to get her on side. An attempt to throw her off the scent. Speaking of scent, I really do need to wash. I scratch my abrasive armpit.

"Ben. It's truth time," she says. I see that Maggie is tired, lack of sleep creased into her face.

I owe her more than this. She must have crashed on the sofa-bed, knowing her in fact, she probably just passed out in the chair. Or on the floor.

"I'll tell you the truth," I say. "It's no longer just about Ruth. It's about not being able to deal with another person, okay? I'm not being miserable, I'm not whinging, I just don't want the responsibility of anyone. Not you, not Laura, not anyone. I refuse. I'm opting out."

"Laura won't disappear."

"I don't want to find out."

I sound so petulant.

"You'll end up alone. With nothing," she says.

"And? At least I'm used to nothing. At least that's reliable."

"It's better to have loved and lost…"

I cut her off. "Bollocks Maggie. I don't want to hear it. She's gone and I don't want to deal with anyone else. I've let her go… that's enough for me."

"You might want children. A family one day."

It can't be easy for Maggie, pushing me to move on. She's really stepping up a gear lately.

"I wanted children. With Ruth. It didn't happen. Not meant to happen."

She thinks for a minute, before sitting on the bed next to me. A warmth in her expression that betrays familial love, that goes against her natural inclination to be abrasive.

"Ruth would have made a great mother," she whispers.

"She would." I agree, much happier to wallow in the bittersweet than fight her attempts to pair me off.

"Did you talk about it?" Maggie asks, idly smoothing down a crumpled corner of the sheet which goes against everything I've ever assumed about her domesticity.

"All the time. She would have been fantastic with them, a natural."

She's got a funny look on her face. Mulling over something. Debating. Arguing the toss with herself. Then –

"Ruth wasn't perfect, Ben."

"What's that supposed to mean?"

"You're in danger of turning her into a saint. Some untouchable goddess. It's not fair on yourself, or Laura and especially not Ruth."

"I don't know what you're talking about." I pull off the solitary sock that survived the night and swing my legs out of bed, ready to turn away from my sister in law.

"I'm going to be straight with you," she says, ominously. "For your own good," talking faster now, not letting me interrupt, as if she's afraid she'll stop herself given half the chance.

"… Ruth couldn't have kids. There was never going to be a family, at least not one that you both conceived." She looks terrified, saying this, but before I fully comprehend, she's moving on to the reason behind her words. "What I really mean to say is that you need to follow things up with Laura. It could be good, it could be bad – but that's just the point, you don't know."

"Couldn't have kids?" I say, understandably stuck on this revelation.

"Laura's who you need to focus on."

"Fuck Laura, Maggie."

There's finally a silence between us. The birds outside have started, the morning has broken. Along with my heart which I thought was already in shards. I'm supposed to be getting ready for work and I've heard this.

"Yes Ben. She couldn't have kids." Maggie's back to full-strength, pushing her black hair off her forehead, out of wilful eyes that keep my gaze.

"How do you know?" I demand.

"She told me."

"She never told you anything." Maggie looks momentarily hurt. But I don't say sorry, and she continues.

"Well, she told me that. She'd kept saying she was going to tell you. But you were always so keen."

"I can't believe this."

I'm stunned, turning over this truth in so many ways, wondering what it means to Ruth's departure.

"Who else knows?"

"I don't think she ever told anyone. It didn't upset her Ben. It's not important."

"Who the fuck are you to tell me that? Why didn't you tell me before. It might have helped."

"I told the police."

Silence from me.

"They took it on board."

"Took it on board!"

I suddenly remember, the police's obsession with Ruth's likely mental state, endless questions about our childlessness, about her hopes, ambitions. About whether she was depressed. In those days of fraught questioning and terrifying nausea – our long-term hopes for a baby were entirely not relevant. Not to me, and not, on the whole, to a woman who might have been abducted. I was on tablets by then – dothiepin – nothing got through.

"Might have helped me?" I say. This is the heart of my annoyance.

"I don't know. I really don't. I didn't see how it would help. It would only have added to your guilt," she says.

What does she know about feeling guilt?

"I can't believe this. What I'm hearing."

And yet it makes sense, it would have driven me mad to think of Ruth feeling pressure. I had been talking of kids throughout our marriage, fuck it even on the night we got engaged.

"She didn't leave because of that Ben." Maggie is holding my hand. "I wish I hadn't told you."

"Well now you're going to tell me everything you know about it."

"No," she says, "I promised."

This makes me laugh bitterly.

"Ruth promised to stay forever," I say. "She lied. I'm past believing in promises."

I'm extremely angry. So angry.

"Alright, she had an abortion at university. Before you came along. Never thought anything of it…"

She pauses, considering, until –

"… but there were complications and…. well, Ruth was unlucky. It was like a million to one chance."

Abortion?

Maggie continues. "She always said she'd done it for the right reason. She wasn't guilt-ridden about the baby, so don't do that to yourself."

"Oh great, I feel much better," I say sarcastically, unable to go further.

"She was at university, she was 20, she wasn't meant to have a child then."

"I used to talk about children all the time Maggie. What must that have done to her?"

"She was fine Ben. She was happy."

"So happy she left me."

"If she left you."

And there it is again, the terrifying prospect that she didn't leave on purpose and it's too awful to face so we retreat back a few paces. I certainly begin to retreat into my memory – to the things I know for sure – with this new information.

"I remember that she wasn't around at the start of the third year. I used to look for her everywhere."

"She didn't tell anyone. She just got on with it."

"Who was the father?"

"That rugby tosser she went out with on and off. He never knew."

The one she was looking at in the photo. I always hated him.

My poor Ruth. I had no idea. How could I? We weren't together then but I had noticed. I remember visiting Martin and him telling me to get over her, that she'd probably dropped out. But she came back, mid-way through the first term – as the months, our final student months, were slipping away. And I was finally thinking about myself – making plans for life after. Aware that Martin would be living with Ally so getting on with getting the grades and a career sorted.

Neither of us speak for a while. Until –

"I want you to leave," I announce, coldly. To Maggie.

"Oh okay. Like that's the answer."

"Unless you have any more revelations." I can't even look at her.

"You're such a bastard sometimes Ben," she says. "Fine. I'm going."

And she's gone. Slamming the door. Causing the room to shake.

What am I doing? What the fuck am I doing?

*

By the time I get to the office, I've feel as I've been up for hours. Partly because I have. I'm almost amused to find that I am one of the first to arrive. Now this is unusual. I'm bothered to notice that Laura is not at her desk and hope she'll arrive before anyone else. I'd like to make things good as soon as possible. Maybe then I'll get round to Maggie. How I feel about what she stored all these years.

"Ben." A voice sounds, startling me.

It's Rick. Coming over with a big smile on his face.

"Good weekend? Get up to much?" he enquires, with genuine interest, like the good man manager he is.

What I want to say is –

"Not bad thanks Rick. I shagged one of your valued staff-members, then some policemen arrived who took me to view a dead body, which fortunately turned out to be some other poor bastard's girl. I came back and decided to dump the aforementioned colleague without any explanation – all before finding out that my wife was sterile and may or may not have ever gotten over it."

Instead I answer "Not bad." And leave it at that. Not quite the lie that it feels like.

"How was the restaurant? Compass wasn't it? With Laura?"

Fuck, Jason's got a big mouth. I'm close to reverting to my previously held opinions on him. Especially with the way the day's

153

going. Rein it in Ben. Calm down – he was proud at helping me secure a booking so late in the day, probably just showing off about that more than anything else. Which reminds me, I said I'd buy him a pint today. He wasn't looking forward to the weekend. While I was making plans, he was having an emergency summit with his wife.

What's Rick waiting for? Oh yeah, my verdict on the restaurant. Think back – it was only Saturday night.

"Yeah. Good." I say. "We had a nice time." This part isn't a lie either, and oddly the thought of the evening warms me, acts to calm the maelstrom in my stomach.

"Great bottle of wine." I add, remembering that too. And the way Laura smiled as she appeared out of the rain. But I don't share this. I keep it for myself.

"Is Laura in yet?" I ask, trying to sound as casual as possible.

"Got the day off – phoned in sick. Women's stuff again." As Rick says this we're both looking at her empty desk. Only one of us wistfully, only one of us seeing the forlorn postcard that I'd sent her from Finland by now hanging desperately to the bottom of the monitor by one corner.

"What did you do to her?" Rick jokes, almost laddishly but this isn't really his style. He raises his palms in the air. "Don't tell me. I don't want to know."

He really doesn't.

"Nothing," I say, feebly, feeling terrible at pushing her away.

"I'm pleased about you and her Ben. She was so alive on Friday. Happier than I've seen her for ages."

Oh God. What have I done? I'm a total git.

I move off, heading for my phone and an apology I need to make sharpish.

"Ben, wait a sec. I wanted to have a word."

"Sorry." I say, pausing, wondering why my boss is smiling so effusively at 9.46 on a Monday morning.

"I read your feature. On the weekend. We both did, Tabatha and I." Tabatha is Rick's glamorous, annoyingly intelligent, extremely well-connected, art-dealing, wife. It's widely held that Tabatha, rather than the deputy-ed is the real number two on the magazine.

I'd forgotten all about the piece I'd written.

"She loved it. I loved it." He's really smiling here. "It's a great feature."

"It's not a feature." I want to respond. "It's my life."

But I don't. "Thank you," is what I say, and this time I guess, is also what I feel.

It is a feature that I've written and I am pleased he likes it. I can allow that. It doesn't feel wrong.

"We're changing the flatplan right now." He says. "Male anorexia is going down from three pages to one." He doesn't see the funny side so I don't point it out.

"I mean it. Such honest fucking writing. Such a new approach."

He doesn't swear much usually. The expletives jar; at odds with his soft, measured diction. It's kind of embarrassing to hear.

"Good work Ben. Really good work." He finishes.

And I walk over to my desk and allow a degree of satisfaction to flourish, unchecked by anything at all.

*

Laura's house is in a nice quiet part of Dulwich. Close to the college and its immaculate grounds. Close to a coffee-shop which I want to believe might just be the only one of its kind. Jumping out of the cab, I instantly regret not having been here before. A bittersweet sense of loss, mourning all of the potential clear mornings and lazy afternoons, now passed, that could have been spent here while instead I self-obsessed and did... other things.

Wasting time mostly.

She has a front gate that requires oiling. I make a mental note to bring some WD-40 with me. Inside the gate however are signs of due care and attention. Signs of Laura.

A guy answers the door. He's eating a sandwich and holding a human skull. He looks like one of The Monkees but not the English one.

"Yeah?" he grunts.

"Is Laura there please?" I feel like I should be asking for my ball back. I'm not sure what I feel about the skull.

"Laura!" he bellows into the house, before trudging off into the interior.

After a moment, I see her at the top of the stairs. My heart beats irregularly.

"Oh," she says, scraping strands of blonde hair that haven't fallen behind an ear.

"Laura," I say "I'm so sorry."

"Shut up Ben. Come in," she instructs. "And make sure you slam the door hard, bloody thing gets stuck on the mat."

I go up.

We've been talking now for a few minutes but the time has been mostly spent lying together in silence. I'm studying her ceiling, she's studying me. I'm stroking her hair absently. This is all very nice.

"Gavin's as polite as ever," I say, referring to the guy who'd answered the door.

" You can't judge him on that one night."

"I can."

Gavin had come to a *Mentor* do last year. He'd got into a fight with a bouncer.

"He pays his rent on time. He's alright. Gav's just stressed. His final exam is coming up."

"He's a med student?" I say, thinking of the skull and that I really should know decisively, given the proximity of mine and Laura's working relationship and realising yet again how self-interested I've been.

Laura's laughing at my query. "Gavin? Don't be stupid – he faints at the sight of blood."

"What's with the skull then?"

"Hamlet."

"You're kidding?"

"Wish I was."

As she says this my eyes catch the basket in the corner. Samuel's basket. Laura's recently deceased dog. She follows my gaze and turns away.

"I know it's stupid to keep it."

"I don't think so."

"It is. It's stupid to keep a dog basket when you don't have a dog."

"Not having the dog is why you keep the basket," I say.

"I'll throw it out this weekend," she says.

And then I kiss her. Several short kisses that build and build. Rapid breaths and stumbling hands.

Reverential removal of cloth.

It's not Ruth. It's not even close.

And that's a good thing.

In the afterglow, I tell Laura about Rick's reaction to my article.

"It's going in the next issue. It'll be on the stands in 10 days. In fact…" I say, looking at my Bvlgari watch "… It's being printed now."

"There's no going back," she says.

I pull the blankets over us both.

2. BROKEN

Emily has just ended her longest ever period of silence. Five days, three hours and twenty-two seconds of silence to be precise. I'm not getting my hopes up – she's only letting me know there's a phone call. I'm not stupid. I can detect her complete and utter dejection at having to communicate with me; marginally more than the disappointment that it's not her friend Margi calling to discuss the new Eminem video.

I still don't think its right for her to have a tv in her room. Let alone the internet.

To be further precise about our 'conversation', I didn't actually get any words out of my daughter. Just a grunt, followed by a rolled pair of eyes when I said "thanks darling". I know I sound lame trying to be so enthusiastic all the time but Ally has told me to act normally. That she'll come round. That's fine for my wife to say, she gets hugs, cuddles and offers of cups of tea. I don't even know what normal is anymore.

I hope it's Chrissy on the phone, I hope that she's heard when we can finally get back to work. That they've given the office the structural all-clear. I pad over. Fed up with being in the house, fed up with not being able to get to my email or my voicemail messages.

"Hello?" I say, as my retreating daughter slams her bedroom door and my eyes dart immediately to the crack in the ceiling as if her actions might make it rip further across our home. Our landlord doesn't think it will be a problem but I can't stop studying it – fearful of how much it might grow.

"Martin? It's me."

"Jesus. Ben?" It is. It's Ben.

"How are you?" I say, words rushing fast. My question finally getting through.

"I'm good. Very good," he says. "You?"

"I'm okay," I say, suddenly wanting to offload every worry, every diseased thought in my brain – to use this opportunity with my twin for all the reassurance I know he's always been able to bring. And all my desires to ask if he's okay, to discuss how he's doing, and who Laura is, vanish out the window.

"What's wrong?" he says, picking up on my tone. "More to the point – what's wrong with Emily? She barely said two words to me."

"She's 13," I deadpan. "Apparently it's going to last some time."

There's an excitable pause between us – I'm so calm talking to him, I'm so protected – nothing's the matter. But it really is. It really is Ben. Why don't you know? I want to cry. I feel so fucking sorry for myself – it's humiliating. Especially when he sounds happier than I have heard him in two years. Why do I want to drag him down?

"Everything calmed down after the quake?" he's asking. "We watched a report on the news."

"Yeah, no real damage done. I'm off work though."

"Lucky bastard."

"Oh yeah right, its great fun sitting at home with one kid who hates me and another who's taken to climbing in the toilet bowl at every fucking opportunity. The sooner they get the office made safe the better – it's killing me."

I don't dwell on how I don't like to go out too much at the moment – the new attacks down in the south, scaring me. Making me feel like I need to get my family out of here.

"I'm sorry I haven't been in contact much," he says.

"It's okay. I understand." Do I?

" So much has been happening Martin. So much. Can't wait to tell you."

"It's cool," I say. Cool? Why am I trying so hard to sound diffident; asserting myself as the elder, untroubled brother. What's wrong with giving back a bit of unease?

"Anyway, every time I try to call you at home you're always bloody engaged," Ben says, laughing down the phone.

"Emily has discovered the telephone," I explain. "But her mobile has been confiscated."

"Oh," he says. "And you wonder why you're getting the silent treatment?"

"You sound like Ally."

He's right. But I hate the fuckers. I decide not to tell him that when Ally first suggested we buy Emily a mobile – I initially thought she meant something to hang over the bed. With Disney characters or similar. Luckily, Ally thought I was only joking. Evidently no one could be that stupid. I got away with it.

"How's Ally?" Ben enquires. I can tell he's eating something. Multi-tasking. This phone call isn't everything to him at this moment, when it's everything to me.

"Okay. She's okay." I say. "She's at the spa. As usual."

"Not with All-American hunk Brad?"

"Dunno," I say, when I do. At least I think I do.

"Why don't you go down there?"

"Me at a spa? Don't be stupid," I say, trying to sound casual, wanting to get off this subject immediately. Despite my desire for Ben to look after me, to make things right – broaching my marital discord has been a step too far. It's unfair for him to have to hear me talk about my relationship. Not when I've still got a wife to experience discord with.

But this is Ben. My brother. My other half. We're supposed to be honest. I swallow a couple of times, preparing to convince him I'm fine.

"Martin?" he says, sensing. And I'm off, taking a deep breath and letting it out.

"We just seem so far apart Ben."

"You talking about you and Ally – or you and me?" Ben says.

"Ally. Me and Ally," I cut in, a little too quickly, "of course." But I'm not of course.

"Do you think she's having…?" he leads, his voice trailing off – not wanting to say it.

Just then I look up, noticing that Emily's door is now open, a thin strand of cerise light from her lava-lamp breaking through.

"No I don't," I reply, firmly – steadying my tremulous voice; speaking loudly, for my calm control to be heard.

"Have you spoken to her?" he asks. "You're not drinking are you?"

I'm not sure which question he wants me to answer. Which question I want to answer even – for the admission of both will convey much of my current character – much of my current fears – much of my current inability to breathe.

"Just talk to her," Ben says – through the void. To me.

This is appalling. I'm actually making my poor, abandoned brother counsel me.

"Talk to her while you can, Martin," he says.

How can I put him through this. But he sounds so strong. So assured. So in charge. I realise I haven't had him around for a long time. I haven't had his support – as he clearly needed all of mine for so long.

I look at a shadow move near Emily's door, I have to stop. She's listening. Fuck it, it feels like everyone's listening.

Control.

"I'm sorry," I say, lightening my voice unnaturally. Trying to convince someone who can see all of me. Wondering if it is like this for all twins.

"Anyway, what's going on with you Ben? How's London?"

"I'm great," he says reluctantly, accepting that I'm changing the subject. And confirming what I've known for some time, what's been clear from the measured, even tone of his voice.

"You're kidding?" I say. "What happened to Ben – hate-all-the-bastards-Ben?" I know he's about to tell me about this new girl. Laura.

From within my daughter's room, I hear Max exclaim "Daddy swore" and the muffled shhhing of Emily. So that's where's he's been hiding.

"Nope, I'm being serious. Things here are going well. I mean it. Things are great. No choice in the matter. I've been fucked over but this is where it ends."

Fucked over? I stop myself repeating this out loud, but the phrase resonates in my head for eternity.

"In fact," he continues…"I've…"

"Ben," I say, stopping him in his tracks as door keys make their familiar sound in the lock and Ally returns – sunglasses on forehead, all-over healthy glow – swinging her sports bag like a tampon advert. In a micro-second, the kids are everywhere and loudly happy – nothing like the zombies they've been for the past couple of hours. Ally's brought back sundaes – this has gone down well.

"Ally's back." I don't say this because I want him to stop talking but because I want him to understand how uninvolved I feel in the scene unfolding before me – like I'm on set in a soap opera but no one's given me my lines or my motivation.

But Ben is fine to end the call.

"I can hear," he says. "No worries. I've got things to do anyway."

"Okay."

"Go and talk to her Mart," he says. "I'll email you soon. Bye."

"Bye."

I let him go. Deeply unsatisfied. A certain type of character.

"Who was that?" Ally asks, offering me only a harried cheek when I move to kiss her hello.

I don't answer – momentarily stunned by the sudden activity taking place in the room, of my son climbing onto worktops to look in the carrier bags and Emily dancing around her mother.

"Uncle Ben." My daughter answers. She actually throws me a dirty look when she says this, forcing me to avert my gaze.

Ally claps her hands together in laughter "Hah! Uncle Ben. Just like the rice. Never thought of that before. Have you?"

"No," I say.

Her eyes fall on our youngest and she sing-songs "Uncle Ben" to him a few times. My son, who is too young to understand nevertheless thinks it's hysterical too and starts a braying laugh that I'm sure he's picked up from his sister. A noise that bothers me immensely. That's not right, is it? Believing your own kid's laughter to be affected.

Ally continues to smother him in love, showering kisses on his forehead. She's such a good parent. She'd win awards.

I withdraw from the scene. Exit stage left or something.

"Martin?" Ally shouts after me. "How was he?"

I don't answer.

Someone's left the bathroom window open and the netting down – there's a bug on the toilet seat. I kill the fucker and sit down. I mull over the conversation with Ben. Wondering what I would have answered to Ally, had I been able. The question about how Ben is.

*

I think about how long I have been with Ally. A long time. I can't remember life before her. Not really. Not the stuff of days – not the long-term sensation of being unattached. Instead I can recall certain isolated evenings, events that I have kept secure. As days unfettered by anything. As days when I was just Martin. Single, on my own, in charge of my own destiny.

Most of these moments are of visiting Ben at university. Although visiting Ben isn't really an appropriate description. I'd travel down. We'd go back to his digs or room and watch some tv, then I'd go out with his housemates while he sat in and read or worked on assignments or whatever. He rarely came out. Rarely went to the pub, when the pub was everything I had ever wanted – my drinking at furious rates even at that age.

I used to leave Ally and come down – we were already in a shared house by then. Just the two of us. Student home-makers. I did love the life. I loved her, don't get me wrong – but it was occasionally nice to wallow in the hedonistic fun that my brother so effortlessly enjoyed. I wanted the chance to be seen by others as just Martin Carter, nothing else. Not even Ben's twin brother.

Mart Carter – what a stupid name.

Sometimes people just don't think things through.

3: HOPE

It's been raining again all day and everyone, except me, seems to have a plan on how best to deal with the conditions. Raincoats, umbrellas and only occasionally a taxi, and all long since hailed.

The sky is black. Covering a world thick with bodies rushing to escape. To get home for quiz shows, microwaves and other people. It's elemental and everyone's prepared.

Unlike me who's drenched but having fun and past the stage where it's a problem, in fact revelling in how far this will all go, letting the rain cover me like I used to when I was 14. At least I can still do that. Even if I can no longer run indoors to have relations exclaim and fuss. Or rub my hair dry with a towel saying "get out of those wet things, your dinner's in five minutes" while I shiver in the bathroom, teeth chattering out Morse code, waiting to hear the usual line – that I'll catch my death. The last admonishment always worrying me slightly, knowing it was just a phrase but even as a kid believing there's no smoke without fire. Remembering now the nervousness with which I'd study my mother as she intoned those words automatically, while mixing Bisto. Furiously getting dry to appease her and fearful of the imminent grim reaper.

Just then a beaten-up Bedford van – with a scar carved into its side – screams past, sending up a tidal wave of water over me. A pensioner rolls his eyes.

That's enough. It's no longer fun.

*

I'm in a Starbucks having just ordered an Americano. Unfolding my *Evening Standard*, I find a stool in the window from where I can watch the world stream by with the calm acceptance it affords a man who appears to have a reason to be somewhere. Which is all any of us really want isn't it? A reason to be.

Jason comes in a few moments later, armed against precipitation in standard issue long Burberry trench coat and a black Dunhill umbrella. He's carrying two holdalls and a carrier bag from Paul Smith. He further wears an expression of desolation that I entirely recognise.

"You sure it's alright to stay mate?"

"I'm sure."

He orders a latte and sits down.

"So. A trial separation then?"

"Yep." He says, his tone suggesting that this arrangement is in no way his idea or preference. I muse that trial is an appropriate word for all involved. I have a sofa-bed and I owe Jason a fair hearing; it's the least I can do.

*

So he has moved into my living room – Annabel having finally decided to come home but still insisting on some time apart. So he was forced to leave. Choosing not to tell any of his friends as "things might blow over". I'm not insulted at all about where this information places me in his social circle. It makes perfect sense. When Ruth went, I didn't want to tell those we collectively knew. I didn't want them to form any opinions or viewpoints which would forever more be irretrievable. We would always have been known as having that episode where Ruth left for a bit – however strong or perfect our marriage then became.

After a while, and there's no set time, you suddenly realise that it doesn't matter what anyone thinks, you say fuck it, and go to the other extreme, deciding for no good reason that its best to broadcast the news that things might not be okay at home to anyone who'll listen and even some who won't – the postman, the supermarket checkout girl or even the cab-driver who only really wants to know if "you saw the game".

Neither extreme is ideal. I understand not wanting to give something power – to refuse to name it. I also understand it's not helpful or constructive to hide things away. It's fucking ironic that when you're fucked over, you feel trapped from telling the people who can put you straight quickest. The fact that they care too much for you, puts them (initially anyway) off limits. This with hindsight you understand. I realise I've learnt much. I'd do many things differently if I had the time over, but that goes without saying.

Ruth used to hate discussing problems with other people. She sometimes saw words as weakness. This never interested me. Yes, words sometimes didn't work – via misguided intention or misread inflection and, true, sometimes you couldn't even find the right one – but I've always believed, I still do, that an attempt to explain speaks as much as the skill with which you pull it off. It's the thought that counts. Ruth thought entirely otherwise. She believed many words were said without thinking. It was better to keep quiet until you were sure – which explains a lot.

Anyway, Jason is standing in my hallway, still gingerly checking out the surroundings and admiring various details I've never thought much of. I show him the bathroom and where we used to keep the towels. Doing the tour that Ruth used to do if anyone was staying over. He comments favourably on the 'surgically reclaimed' washbasin.

As I finally trudge off to bed, I check in on him in the living room. In the half-light I notice his outstretched arm poking out from under the spare duvet, fingers tracing the metallic casing of his mobile – willing it to ring.

"Goodnight," I say.

"Night mate," he says, immediately – his voice intrinsically alert "really appreciate this."

What happened to us? To men? This didn't happen in the 1950s.

The next morning is strange only in its immediate normalcy. We wake, we eat some toast, and each knock back one of those effervescent vitamin things (Jason's) before making the journey to work together. Like clockwork. It may take me a while to get used to the grunting sounds emanating from the bathroom – relief descended when I worked out that he was just working through his morning stretch and sit-up routine.

So the revised equation worked just fine. In fact, I felt like I was in a sitcom.

When we get to *Mentor*, only then do things become awkward and stilted. Real life sets in. Sure we fight against it but it lands like so much dust. Jason instantly takes control of the office, of his freelancers and staff writers and anyone else in his domain – marshalling, running straight off for a features meeting. I'm left alone, to make my way over to Laura.

"Morning," I say.

"Hi," she says softly. "How did it go?"

"With Jason?"

"No – with the Archbishop of Canterbury. Yes with Jason."

I'd texted Laura to say what had happened from my bed last night. I'm finally succumbing to the practice – it's so much easier when you've got someone who responds.

"It was fine," I say. "He was a bit down."

"What's happened?"

"Annabel had an affair."

Laura exhales in shock, slowly digesting the information as if she were the Sarlacc Pit in *Return of the Jedi*. I wonder if Laura knows what the Sarlacc Pit in the *Return of the Jedi* is. I bet I could ask every guy in this office and he'd know. Weird Tim in the corner would even take off his baseball cap to proper respect the mention of Boba Fett's demise.

"She didn't!"

"She did. Jason's been trying to make it work for ages but it's all come to a head."

I decline to tell her that it all came to a head because Jason caught Annabel giving her new bloke head (while in their bed) – the rhyming not indicative of the seriousness with which I regard the details.

"Don't take sides," is what I say instead, knowing that Laura who although she has never much cared for her colleague, is fiercely loyal and will have already damned Annabel to the gates of hell forever more.

I'll never ask what she thinks of Ruth's actions. If she believes them to be actions that is.

With this thought I don't want to think about that – or Jason – and I just want to go to the gym. Jason ate his breakfast in his boxer shorts this morning – I hate that he still retains control over his love-handles. I'm acquiring the dimensions and form of the FA Cup, with the winner's ribbons attached. I have lean-ness envy. More to the point, I want Laura to be proud of me. And if we're going to be having sex on a regular basis these things matter.

"I'm going to the gym," I announce. "If anyone needs me."

"Its 10.00am Ben. And who ever needs you?" She says playfully, hoping I'll playfully hit her.

"I know."

So, 10.30 and I'm in the gym once again. As ever there's no air and the usual array of usual suspects. My kit has not improved. I lie flat on a mat and spend the majority of the time counting the polystyrene tiles in the ceiling. But I'm doing the odd sit-up in between.

I think its time I texted Maggie and apologised.

This is enough to make me head for the showers. Not that I needed an excuse or anything.

*

At the end of the day Jason keeps me waiting for ages while he's in with Rick. I can see our editor asking concerned questions, probably offering to do what he can. Saying take some time off. There's an arm around the shoulder and Rick's Hennessy is opened. Glasses are poured.

I busy myself with the 50 most stylish men in Britain. Take comfort in the fact that I am still younger than at least half of them. I'm sure we did something like this only three issues ago, or was that the 50 coolest men? No one seems to notice, or if they do, no one seems to mind. Especially David Bowie who's come out top yet again.

Eventually I see that Rick's door is open and Jason has come out looking ready for a fight. I think its best we go straight home. I ask him no questions. He tells me no lies.

*

Despite an earlier offer of dinner with her in Dulwich, I blow Laura out that evening as it's only fair to Jason that I stay at home. He protests that he's fine but fuck it, I can't abandon him. Not after all his efforts in my direction over the past two years.

He's in my bedroom on the phone to his wife. Apparently the trial separation has immediately led to a trial union between Annabel and her suitor, some banker-wanker, in their marital home. She has made up her mind. She's unmade her bed – let her lie in it, I think.

Jason is shell-shocked when he returns, but at least he's calm.

"I just needed to know. That's all," he says. And he means it. "The worst is over," he concludes and I pass him a can of beer.

And I see again that it's the 'not knowing' that is the hardest thing. The death-throes of tortured final days as couples try to keep it going, when the actioner has already moved on but selfishly refuses to give the other their total decisiveness; just in case they haven't made the right decision. That's the nightmare to endure. When it's finally irreversible, when the perpetrator grows up and lets the other one go – that's release.

That's all it takes sometimes. And sometimes the perpetrator won't do it simply because in doing so, they see that they are making you stronger than them.

Three hours later and the pair of us are pissed, sprawled on floor in front of the tv where some shite is on and we're routinely slating anyone who dares venture onscreen. A weathergirl has just received some particularly harsh treatment about her tits, but it's all forgotten as our diatribe segues into an analysis of who would be better in bed – Cagney or Lacey? It's not as cut and dried as you'd think, especially when diverting special-guest stars keep appearing. And then there's a panic after an agreement is reached, over which one was actually Cagney and which one was Lacey; a detail you'd have to get right before you could reasonably make your choice.

This is fun.

All night Jason has kept saying evangelically that we're like Lemmon and Matthau. I thought for ages that he meant that German footballer from a few years ago and that he was making some analogy about us being defensively expert, clinical and ruthless. When I worked it out, I realised that not everything is about me.

He's really happy to be doing this, drinking and having a laugh. I thought he'd be moping, and I thought I'd be counselling but sometimes you just want to be rid of all the crap.

There's room for discussion. But not much. Not enough to interfere with beer. I think this current stage of the conversation represents something of an epiphany.

"So Annabel wants to fuck about a bit. I don't. Maybe that makes me a nutter. Maybe I should sow my wild oats and all that too. Maybe I should enjoy being free," he says.

"Annabel sounds like a spoilt bitch who wanted her cake and eat it," I declare.

"No she isn't."

"Don't you mean no she aint?" I say, a sly dig at his mockney which has been slipping of late.

"No she aint," Jason tries again. I piss myself laughing.

"Why did she sleep with that guy then?"

"It's a good question Ben." Jason raises himself up on an elbow to make a serious comment. "Look at me mate. I've got a good job. I go to the gym. But sometimes everything in the world isn't enough. Can't do nothing else about what she wants. So I'll do what I want. That's why I want you to be the first to know I'm leaving…"

"I know." I slur. "You're here mate remember. Not there. He's there. You've left already."

Shouldn't have reminded him of this I think, he looks momentarily waylaid but regains his footing. Though drunk, he's giving a passable attempt at walking in a straight line, conversationally speaking. But I haven't understood.

"No. I mean really leaving. All of it. *Mentor*. Leaving London."

"You what?"

"I'm going to New York, got offered a job a while back and I think now, yeah, fuck it. I'll take it. Fuck her."

"You're just pissed. Don't make any rash decisions." He's evidently thought this through though. From every angle.

"And I wanted to tell you that I think you should go for the job." He's saying, pointing at me furiously with his beer bottle. "I've already mentioned to it to Rick this afternoon. When I told him I'm going. I said Ben's the one for the job."

"Me?" I say. "As features editor? It's hardly likely Jason. I'm chief sub…" I'm slurring badly. Why am I so drunk? Why I am I going red? When I should be taking all this in properly.

"Trust me. Everyone likes you Ben. You've got integrity."

I spray beer everywhere, choking. Jason laughs too, continuing, sounding oddly sober now just as my inebriation fully kicks in. "I mean it mate. You'd give something new to the place. You'd have to interview, mind. And dress a whole lot better."

I look down at my attire. "And cheer up too, you miserable git."

*

Jason wasn't lying. I'm sitting on the sofa in Rick's office, waiting for him to finish on the phone to the boss – Lewis. He's got him on 'hands-free' and they're arguing the toss over a CD covermount of Bacharach classics covered by post nu-metal guitar bands.

"Come on," he says to me, when the conversation is over. "It's a nice day, let's do this outside."

"Okay," I say.

We find a park bench, I sit down first then stand up, wondering what the etiquette might be in this current arrangement. We've bought some sushi in M&S (which I thought was very features editor) and a couple of bottles of water. I've got a hangover the size of Pamela Anderson's implants. "First of all, I want you to know that we are looking at other people. We want to fill the vacancy ASAP but legally we have to advertise. That being said, I think this could be something that's right for you."

"Thanks," is all I say.

"You'll be interviewed like everyone else. Lewis and I also want you to prepare the following – five typical *Mentor* feature ideas, your three best and three worst aspects of the current issue and a general presentation on the direction of the title over the next 12 months."

I suddenly realise I should be writing this down. "Shit," I say, rummaging in my bag.

"What?"

"I didn't bring a pen."

He raises his eyebrows as if to say "lesson learned" and I contemplate crawling away but I actually want the job (I think) so I don't.

"It won't happen again," I say humbly.

Christ I want this so bad, I let him know I'm contrite and have taken this on board. In fact I'll be like fucking Noah if I have to. Everyone and everything can come on board if that's what it takes.

"Right, let's eat," he says and we discuss other stuff unrelated to men's lifestyle. We discuss what school his eldest should go to. I respond like it's my favourite subject in the world.

*

I spend the next three nights going over my presentation materials with Jason. The first evening Maggie comes over and, whether she's trying to get me back for my recent behaviour or not, acts like she has a crush on my colleague. She senses an instant ally and the pair of them proceed to wind me up so I end up telling them to fuck off. Then Laura arrives and there's no chance of getting anything done. The four of us, an odd quartet, wind up ordering pizza and playing drinking games. Maggie playfully arguing with Jason over which is Led Zeppelin's best album. I put on Ruth's Carpenters album to drive them mad like she used to and my wife is suddenly here as well – but in a good way.

On the third night Jason agrees to go and see a band with Maggie at the University of London, there's nothing in it other than the total abandonment of doing something you haven't done for ages. I was tempted to join them but I want this job so badly. So badly. I feel as if I've been glued to my desk. Typing away at home, under the City Lights bookstore poster from San Francisco that a friend – Will – had framed for me years ago. I think about calling him too – making contact again.

I keep typing. Working.

Integrity. That's what it needs. A fucking conscience. I feel like Tom Cruise at the start of *Jerry Maguire* and then remember Jason saying that if *Mentor* were a movie that's what it would be and I suddenly think no it wouldn't – it would be *Escape To Victory* – the crap wartime football movie with Sylvester Stallone, Pele and half of Ipswich Town FC. I've always believed it to be a classic. It was the best and worst of films.

I know I may experience some difficulty in the interview. Some resistance to the bullshit. And I can't pretend to be something I'm not, even if I have now realised that not everyone there is, necessarily, a wanker.

*

The day of the interview starts like all the rest. Except three hours earlier. I get out of bed at 5am, the birds in the cedar-tree opposite are still sleeping and Jason's sit-ups are in no danger of happening any

171

time soon. In fact he's snoring heavily as I tip-toe past.

I get the first tube into work, which means I get a seat. I should do this more often. I buy a newspaper and a coffee, and generally get prepared. I've worn one of the new suits I've bought – nothing too flash, nothing bespoke but credible and comfortable all the same.

And I'm so nervous. I haven't been nervous in this sort of butterflies in stomach way since that night when Ruth came to the nightclub. The night I ended up losing my part-time job. The night my life changed forever. The night of my, of our, second chance. In fact I even get butterflies in my stomach even thinking about the way I was when I saw her again. Not believing my eyes.

I'd been working in Albatross, on a temporary basis for almost six months. At least in my mind it was temporary. It helped to pay the rent. I'd figured I'd be going out in the evening anyway (I was 22 remember), I might as well be paid for the privilege of being amongst drink, music and women. Eagerly making up for lost time, for University years spent mildly. And over-compensating for Martin who was settling down fast.

I was a crap barman though. On the night that Ruth came in with her fellow PR pack I was on an official warning for various misdemeanours. Let's just say I was far from being Tom Cruise on that occasion. My heart was never really in it.

I remember the moment it happened. The club was crowded, a thousand people moving across three floors of chrome and frosted glass. All united in the belief that right then, at that exact moment in time, Buffalo Stance by Neneh Cherry was the best record ever made. Strobing blue, white and green lights shuddering in time to the swagger of pure 1980s retro that pulsed out of speakers all around. In the time it took the bassline to unravel, a multitude of relationships began, were consolidated or ended.

In the midst of so much chaos there were pockets of calm; the newly-formed couples tucked into dark corner booths trying to make their opinions heard; toilet cubicle confessionals with friends soothing abandoned friends; I can remember the colleagues hiding in the back offices attempting fleeting stolen cigarettes. For the most part however, the noise was conquering all – I couldn't hear myself think. It filled every inch of available space – making conversation a challenge. Even outside, where the insistent beat was muted, it always managed to bleed through. The walls only part-muffling the music from the line of eager customers queuing anxiously down the street. I used to go home every night with a headache. I had a headache that night.

That particular evening I'd been trapped up at the top corner of the bar, forced to constantly service, in the drink sense, a group of girls from a hen party – the glitter make-up, three buckets of cheap champagne and bridal veil all giving the game away. I distinctly remember wondering if the bride-to-be was aware of the L plate stuck to her back. The condoms tied to her dress, another predictable touch. And though they were having fun and Albatross decidedly wasn't the sort of club where one bothered too much about being sophisticated – I just wasn't in the mood.

I'd been endlessly checking my watch and for some reason my eyes drifted from the female hen-party as they inflated a life-size blow-up man, to the dance floor below and initially the sight of at least 75 percent of the clubbers moving their arms structuredly, like a battalion of airport ground staff getting a plane to taxi – all vogueing now like it was still 1990. When it wasn't.

And there, in amongst it all, she was. Ruth. Not looking at me. But there, all the same. Right there, looking the same.

I left my post immediately, ignoring a request for six Malibu and Cokes and engineered a meeting next to a pillar. Fuck it. This was the opportunity of a lifetime, an opportunity – dare I say it – meant to be.

As I edged nearer, fate was on my side, the music became slower and quieter and the crowds parted magically as if Moses was somewhere on high orchestrating things.

She turned and saw me, her face immediately flushing scarlet. I didn't care about this, it didn't faze me. To be honest I'd expected her to have no idea who I was. But I had the confidence of an employee in a place that he's seen in the daylight. The setting was far from intimidating. This was my turf. Ruth's mates, sensing an 'approach' might be on the cards, closed ranks more effectively than the German world-cup winning side. I plunged in as Ruth checked her escape routes.

"Hi. It's Ben," I opened. Directly. She registered this information for an age.

"I remember," she'd said, finally, not bothering to raise her voice to be heard above Prince, making me struggle to hear.

"You do?"

"University." She paused to take a swig from a bottle of water she was holding, I noticed her hands were trembling.

"Yeah. University," I repeat for no good reason other than to give myself time to work out what to say next, I love you and think I might always have done, not really appropriate. Not yet. "Can I get you a drink?" I offered hopefully.

"No. Thanks," she said.

"It's no problem, I don't even have to pay. I work here." It seemed like the whole club winced with me. A terrible attempt at cool nonchalance.

"We're just leaving," she said, unconvincingly.

"You've just arrived. Come on, let me get you a drink. For old times' sake."

"What old times?" she said, coolly. It was a good point. "Just leave me alone. Please?"

Her friends had started laughing but I could see they had softened in the light of my politeness, they weren't hovering quite so closely. They could see I wasn't a total lunatic.

"Come on. I've always wanted to buy you a drink."

"No."

"Come on." I insisted,

"Go on," one of her mates said, "We'll be over here."

"I don't want to."

"Please," I said, as sincerely as I could. Pleading.

Her friends moved off, abandoning her. She followed reluctantly to a booth.

We sat facing each other, Ruth looking everywhere except at me. Playing with an ashtray set into the centre of the table.

"I've only got 10 minutes," I said, aware that I didn't really have anytime at all. In fact according to my manager when I'd arrived earlier for my shift, all the time I had was already borrowed.

"You work here?" she'd said, disinterestedly.

"Yeah, the money's useful. I'm a struggling journalist."

"I don't know why I'm here," she said. "I only came out under duress. It's like a nightmare."

"Well I'm feeling the exact opposite," (I actually said that) "The whole time at university I would have killed to do this. Be here – with you."

She looked at me then, intently, like I've never been looked at before or since. And smiled. Only a little. A sad smile. But a smile.

"How's your brother?" she said, after another difficult pause.

"Martin?"

I wasn't even aware that she knew I had a brother. But twins on campus are hard to ignore.

"Martin? Looks like you."

"He's good. Married with a kid and no time to do anything but work."

"Right."

I remember thinking I didn't want to be talking to Ruth Carmichael about my twin. How I wanted to bring it back to me.

"Maybe we could go out for a drink sometime. Dinner even?" I'd said hopefully, also by now fiddling with the ashtray. Hurt when she quickly withdrew her hands, placing them on her lap, out of sight.

"Ben," Ruth had said then. "I do like you. I mean I did. Back then."

Eh? … did the world just stop turning?

"I'm sorry?" is all I manage. "When did this happen?" I managed to splutter.

"You were so fucking shy," she's continued. "Anytime I went near you, you'd disappear or move off acting weird."

"I um… I um… .this is very strange. I was strange. No, I mean I was interested. In you."

There was no way to articulate that as my brother seemed to be so married, so young – I had probably, deliberately run away from anything that could end up being permanent too. Knowing I had a similar capacity to just meet the one and have that be it forever.

That back then I still didn't know who I would end up being. That I had things to do before I became one half of another pair. And that only now with my own life forming, did I feel individually strong enough. And satisfied with who I was becoming and could be. Confidence in myself and my own life.

"It doesn't matter now. We've grown up," she says resignedly.

"No."

"It's too late. We're different people." Her eyes were so piercing and utterly desolate as if she'd been leaving on a ship the next morning for Australia or something. "I've had a bad day at work. Sorry. And I hate my flatmates."

"No. It's not too late," I stammer, still stuck on the revelation. Still unable to comprehend how far this short exchange had got me after years of patient futile inactivity. And certain that the tragedy of me not following up 'Ruth Carmichael asking me the time', at the time, with more courage and more action would bother me forever.

It was certainly too late for my bar-job. Just then my manager had appeared with Mickey the bouncer in tow. Mickey who I'd have a laugh with. Not anymore evidently.

"Out! You're fired," he'd wheezed, like the fat fucker he was. "Come on, out, what do you take me for? Out now – the pair of ya."

Ruth had begun to protest but it was no use. She'd looked round anxiously for her mates but they had vanished into the dry ice. There was nothing to do but leave together, escorted to the door there and then to the sound of another ballad not meant for us.

We'd stumbled onto the street, freezing cold and united now in our venom towards the club and its staff. As the door slammed shut behind us, there was nothing to do but laugh at the unfairness of the situation. Well, unfair to Ruth anyway – they had a reasonable case for dismissal where I was concerned.

I gave Ruth my coat and we walked slowly off in the direction of an all-night café.

"What time is it?" Ruth asked, as we'd trudged onwards.

I checked my watch. And on this occasion, on that night, Ruth Carmichael listened to the whole of my answer.

Minutes as well.

Evidently it wasn't too late.

*

We are doing the interview in Lewis's office on the floor above ours. It's a huge corner deal with two sofas, one dining table and an area that looks suspiciously like the reading-corner of my old infant-school classroom. I look around for the A-Z alphabet banner but instead see only several blown-up covers of issues of *Mentor*, *Tank* and *Friction* on the walls.

"Shall we start," Rick says, in a gentle tone that worries me as I think oh shit, him and Lewis are going to play good cop, bad cop here. Lewis will probably shine a light on my forehead and wrench my arm behind my back.

"Yes," I say, only the words don't come out, instead, helpfully, a dry rasp that sounds like one of Marge Simpson's elder sisters emerges. Lewis raises a patronising eyebrow.

"Have some water Ben. Relax," he says as he leans back into his executive reclining chair – hands crossed behind his head – I notice he's still having trouble with his sweat problem. He's wearing this huge bracelet full of gold and silver links. It falls from his wrist excessively.

"Yes, yes," Rick repeats, like he always does. I wait for the interview to begin. My laptop expectant, at the ready.

Lewis clears his throat dramatically. What the fuck is he going to say? I'm ready with my printed handouts too but he's having none of it. He's deviating from the script like the contrary arse he's known to be. Free-styling as he calls it.

"Ben. Tell me," he opens. "Which of the following words would you use, in copy, to describe a *Mentor* reader – lad, bloke or fella?"

Eh?

I look to Rick for help. Rick studies his boss uncertainly. Lewis doesn't care, he leans in, rubbing his palms together like Wile E Coyote trying to get an ACME dynamite stick lit, after the matches, and the fuse, have both failed.

"Who are they Ben?" Lewis elaborates, without elaborating at all, now patting his stomach as if he's just eaten.

"Who?" I say, genuinely puzzled, wondering if he's channelling some distant spirit, having maybe decided to leave the trifle that is this interview, behind.

"Our readers."

"Oh."

"Lads, blokes or fellas?"

"They're um… they're um…"

Rick is willing me to succeed, crinkling up his eyes, slowly nodding his face up and down with each "um" that I expel. I can see him trying to mouth something – he reminds me of an anxious mother standing in front of her child during the school Christmas Carol concert. But I can't make out what he's trying to say.

"Yes?" Lewis coaxes.

"Well they're um… they're… men." I say, unimpressively.

The word sounds like the death-knell it so clearly is.

"Men," Rick repeats solemnly, reverentially.

Men.

In the time it takes me to speculate that if my computer didn't make it through the building's glass, I probably won't either; a smile at least equal to the size of one underarm sweat-patch, breaks across Lewis face.

"Men," he reiterates to himself. "Men."

Before I know it we're standing, shaking hands furiously and I'm being ushered out to cries of "very impressive presentation." The last 25 mins were a blur as I jabbered on about everything I hated with the magazine and everything I thought it could be. Basically everything I think I should be. In reality. In the real world.

It bothers me to think that I did well perhaps just because I've made Lewis think I've come up with a new fashionable approach. It bothers me to think that my accidental "men" might have carried more weight than my entire presentation.

But fuck it. And it doesn't bother me that I will be able to write and, most importantly, decide what we write. At least to some extent. And I know that given all the details relating to sweat, patronising smiles and chunky male jewellery just described – that at least my eyes are open.

4. PERFECT

It turns out that Chrissy and Brad haven't had sex for six months. I know! It was like finding out your mates don't earn more or that other blokes freeze at the urinal too. All unspeakably satisfying and immensely reassuring. Anyway, she's sitting in our kitchen right now telling my wife all about it. Ally – sympathetic and comforting, Chrissy – distraught and hammered, working her way through a bottle of Gordons. In the last few minutes it further transpired that the crisis is less about Brad not being interested in Chrissy but in women full stop. By the time she'd got round to listing the magazines she found and the internet sites he's been visiting, I decided to leave the room. Okay, Ally made me go – kicking me under the table just as I was settling in to hear the scandalous details. And though there was some fascination in hearing of Brad's marital imperfections, it was distressing listening to my colleague sob that "there were videos too" and that "she'd watched one, just to make sure" (apparently the cover shot of three half-naked guys in naval gear not enough indication of the subject matter – *Able Seamen: Vol. 6*, she said it was called, I may have the spelling wrong). As I made for the door I resisted the urge to ask if she'd found it difficult to get into the story, what with not having seen the previous episodes. I don't blame Ally for asking me to leave.

I'm sitting on my bed wondering why I'm so elated that Brad isn't actually Mr Perfect after all? Or at least not Mr Perfect for a ruddy lass from Lancashire with women's needs. I am sad for Chrissy but I've always believed she can do a whole lot better. Turns out a straight guy would have been a good start. I notice my reflection in the long mirror that hangs behind the door. More significantly I notice that I'm smiling and in fact that it's Ben smiling back too.

And then Ben disappears and I feel only sadness that Brad has endured a life of secrecy. A life, no doubt, of denied emotion and want. A life of hidden torment. This moves me. He doesn't deserve that, nobody does. Except perhaps for me, I feel that my own particular brand of torment is all my own doing – not the random selection of some biological hand of cards but the result of one insignificant occasion that eventually turned out to be so much more.

I turn away from the mirror and tune back into the soothing words coming from my wife when the phone rings. There's a cautious answer from Ally and subsequently a loud shriek from Chrissy. Try as I might, I can't make out the hushed words. Eventually there's silence of a sort.

Ally appears in the doorway.

"It's Brad," she confirms. "On the phone."

"I guessed."

"He's all over the place Martin. He sounds really weird. Funny breathing. Not saying much."

"He always sounds weird."

"Not helping."

"And?"

"Will you go and talk to him? He's at the flat."

She's got to be kidding.

"You've got to be kidding," I say, thinking I might as well be honest. "No way Ally," I continue.

"You go. He's your best mate. Maybe you two could go to the spa and talk all about it."

I sound like a five-year-old. Evidently my wife agrees.

"Don't be so childish – I can't leave Chrissy. Please Martin – he sounded awful. I'm worried he might do something stupid."

"Jesus Christ."

And she knows I'll go because I'm stupid like that too. I pass Chrissy on the way out, she's scared. So scared about being left alone.

*

I swore I'd never come back to this apartment, not after our enforced stay following the earthquake. But here I am lowering myself into rattan armchair, regretting that I am wearing shorts but regretting more however many hours this will take.

Brad hasn't said much since I arrived. He looks like he hasn't slept. Rather disconcertingly he still looks better than me.

"Brad," I say monosyllabically, preferring to stick to safe ground – not really knowing what I'm supposed to contribute here – recognising that his name, therefore, is a good place to start.

"Marty," he replies, only this time it doesn't annoy.

"You okay?" I query, feeling more confident now in my ability to offer syllables.

He doesn't answer. The smashed laptop in the corner does. I remember Chrissy dragging me to the shop to buy it for him last year. It was going to be the sacred vessel for his masterpiece. Now it's in pieces. I think about what Ben told me about throwing a PC at his office.

"How is she?" Brad says meekly, after an age.

"She's..." I search for the right word. "She's upset. Is what she is." This is like having root canal work.

"I tried to tell her it was research. For a book."

"Oh."

"But it wasn't. And I couldn't carry on with the lies," he says.

I'm surprised he's not crying. I had him down for crying.

"Right," I say slowly, not really wanting Brad to have time to hear his own words; but unable to find suitable replacements. He assumes I'm giving him space to elaborate.

"I do love her Marty," he leads.

"I know you do," I say, jumping in, taking the bait but wondering if I do. All the while studying the anguish in his face and the nervous scratching of his neck. Wondering if real love needs to be 100% all the time.

Yeah, he does.

I believe him.

"It's just... you know how it is?"

"How what is?" Uh-oh, I know where this is going and wish I'd paid more attention in recent years to various significant episodes of US sitcoms.

"Stuff," he says, hesitantly.

Stuff? Stuff?

"Stuff?" my mouth repeats; echoing the unhelpful voice in my head.

"It's just sex," he says.

I'm confused. Stuff is sex?

"What do you want to say?" I say, wishing that I had a phrasebook where each of us could just point to our own translation. Brad to Martin and Martin to Brad. It would make it all a lot easier.

"It's not an emotional thing," he insists. "It's not my heart."

This is an interesting thought, sexuality existing separately, or at least acting independently, to the emotional ties of a relationship. I dismiss it though, firstly as the desperate idealism of a man repressed and secondly because I don't really feel comfortable thinking in such terms. It's not me.

"Brad – can I get you a drink? Let me get you a drink."

He shakes his head.

Well I really need a drink. I need to get out of this rattan chair too but I'm nervous that any movement in his direction might be misconstrued as a call to arms. A hug to be precise. Not nervous about him you understand, I don't think he's going to jump on me and declare his undying love – no, I'm nervous about being tactile in general. I'm certain that even when closeted, Brad was big on hugs. And I wouldn't have wanted one then either.

I decide to be direct in a different way. It's not hard to try and get to the truth when it's somebody unconnected. Or somebody so keen to unload their burden.

He's saying, "Chrissy needs to understand it's not who I am. I hate it." He's whining.

And just like that, I cut in.

"Brad... stop pretending." He stops dead. "Its denial" I conclude, with all the decisiveness of Poirot in the 85th minute of a 90-minute BBC drama. Why am I distracted?

I know about denial and Brad hears me, but doesn't respond, collecting his thoughts, his face distorting oddly, as another wave of self-pity threatens to engulf the room. I have an inappropriate urge to fart. Why do people never fart in BBC dramas.

"I hate myself," he eventually murmurs.

I know about that too.

"Chrissy will be fine. She's upset because she feels she didn't know you. That all this time she thought you were somebody you're not. You just need to work out who you are. What drives you. What you want…" I trail off, unnerved by the fact I'm busily constructing sentences and moreover, that he seems to be listening to me intently. Christ, he's really paying attention and I don't know what the fuck I'm talking about. Shit. I shouldn't have said all that. Should have offered general support using words like "mate". Should have steered clear. And now I realise that you can't just offer something like this to an upset Floridian without having the psychological insight to back it up. He's already brightened with the prospect of imminent counselling that my monologue has suggested.

He's waiting for me to continue. He's not expecting me, therefore, to cut back to the chase.

"You're gay Brad. Right? She's found out you're gay."

Shit. He expected more babble, more blustery dialogue mentioning feelings and touching on esteem-issues and parental influence. Not straight (if you pardon the pun) definition. He draws his feet up off the floor, stung into action. Levelling his back and facing me across the room. Arms folded. The best form of defence and all that.

"I'm not. And its not denial, despite what you think," he says, prissily. Ironically it's the only time I've ever seen him behave in such a camp manner. He stomps over to the window and stares out at Haifa beyond. I check my watch and realise that my weekend is almost over. How did I get here? I didn't need to be here. I need Ben. He'd help. He'd know what to say.

I can't let this drag on any longer. Finish what you start for once Martin, I hear my Dad say. And I resolve not to let him down. I continue, for all those Airfix model Spitfires I abandoned half-completed on the bottom shelf in our shed in the back garden.

"Brad. Reality-check. You're gay. Come on, Chris said you haven't had sex for six months."

Shit. Another bad choice. The man needs some dignity. He rocks from one foot to the other, still with his back to me. Shit, it's hot in here.

"Look, no one minds anymore. It's okay to be gay," I say.

But I'm lying. It's not. Not everywhere. Brad knows this too. I know he's calling on a familiar image of quarterbacks, cheerleaders and prom-night pressure. Its cliché but I'm guessing it's not so far off the mark.

"Let me guess – some of your best friends are fags?" he sneers.

"Nope. You're the first one I know," I say, bluntly. I think about saying Ben knows hundreds but it's not appropriate or even particularly helpful.

"Marty, I'm not gay. I'm just..."

"Brad. The videos."

Another humiliation. Bringing up his videos again. Resorting to the hard-facts; the insurmountable evidence. A humiliation not in content-terms (he can watch what he likes) but because it must be awful to be so understood by everyone except yourself. By contrast I'm lucky, at least no one knows my torment. At least I have that. At least I can avoid ever wearing my heart on my sleeve; or rather I hope I can.

Brad's face has crumpled and he falls to the floor in a heap. Something about this reminds me of the Wicked Witch of the West on Dorothy's ingenuity with a bucket. This can't be good. Up to now nothing in this scene has been textbook.

I'm doing all of this really badly. Ally only sent me round to stop her friend killing himself. Here I am sending him hurtling along the fast-track to a breakdown. His face is no longer twitching nervously, but his eyes have a look in them. I have no idea where he currently stands in relation to suicide as a reasonable lifestyle choice.

"I love her," he whines, between strangulated sobs – like the air being slowly teased out of a balloon.

"I know you do," I say.

"I'm guess I'm bi-sexual," he grasps, with manic fervour. "No, wait – bi-curious." I can see him processing these descriptions, trying to work out which is the least damning – when it really doesn't matter anymore. I contemplate helping him out, agreeing with him, saying that definitions aren't important. But I don't. What I do say is -

"Chrissy just needs a bit of time. Then you'll talk. Things will be fine."

"I want to talk to her now."

"Not a good idea."

And then we're both quiet. Thinking.

"I want to be truthful Martin. I want to face things."

And right there I see that he's a braver man than me. He's further along. He's going to try to be honest. I stand up and rethink hugging him. But I don't, partly because he hasn't finished speaking but also as he's not Ben. It's Ben who I'm foetal with. Only Ben.

And then it's like he's reading my mind. Eyes lighting up, changing the direction of our conversation, invoking my brother, who's at the forefront of my thoughts.

"I'm going to be like your twin," he declares unexpectedly. "I'm going to face whatever it is I have to face."

"Sorry?" I say, my throat tightening unexpectedly.

"Ben. His article."

"What article?"

"In the magazine."

"My brother doesn't write articles."

"He does now."

"About what?"

"About Ruth. All about everything."

And before I can panic, he's retrieving a copy of Mentor from the floor, from over there near a shard of his now-smashed keyboard – the debris from his night-time dramatics. A tiny remnant in which I can see only the following letters:

R T Y U

    H

Clear as anything.

Brad's handing me the magazine. It's been well-read.

Turning the pages, he continues, energised by the welcome distraction from his sexuality.

"I read it over and over last night."

Read what?

By way of answer, pages are found. Brad isn't making it up. It's an article written by my brother. Brad relinquishes his grasp and leaves me to read – sitting back down on the floor. I remember to avoid both the rattan armchair and Brad's wide-eyed, you-too-can-see-the-light, gaze.

And I'm scared.

I'm about to read what my twin has got to say for himself. For himself is the key. There's his name. The feature runs across three pages. Photos as well. One from their wedding day, where they climbed up on a brick wall outside the reception. And another shot – older – of Ruth, from university, with some people I vaguely recognise. She's standing slightly to the side.

Above all else, I'm taken aback by the title. By its directness. At odds with my current perception of my brother.

Getting... and losing the girl.
By Ben Carter
I have no idea why my wife left me. I wasn't unfaithful, I've never been violent and I'm optimistic fairly sure that I wasn't that bad in bed. That sex wasn't always in bed reassures me of this; it suggests spontaneity and passion. Ruth and I definitely had passion. We fucked on a train once.

*

… I lost the girl.
Two years of praying. Nothing makes sense. Only that she isn't here. Nothing else adds up.

*

I put down the magazine to see Brad still staring at me. He's nodding vehemently. The light has disappeared – only darkness seeps through the window. I re-read the final lines.

"Sometimes you just have to accept things the way they are, I guess," Brad says, from across the room, shrugging, like a man accepting his fate and ready to face it head on. "Sometimes there isn't a solution."

And then I'm hugging Brad. And I'm not sure if this is for me, or for him. There's nothing in it. It's an unconditional hug when I haven't had an unconditional thought for two years.

There's a noise at the front door. I pull away, ashamed that I am embarrassed about holding a man. But I realise that Brad seems equally uneasy.

And then Chrissy's flown into the room with Ally trailing behind. It's a torrent of red curls and arms outstretched. Tears and competing voices all up an octave, all charged with emotion. Chrissy gathers up her new best friend and tells him not to worry. It's palpably clear that things will be changing. Brad doesn't protest and they don't kiss. At least not the way that Chris always told me they did.

Ally loiters in the background, watching nervously – her good nature and kindness fully invested in navigating this partial reunion. It's clear that they'll look after each other – which I guess is the main thing.

Satisfied that Chrissy and Brad are okay she inclines her head towards the exit.

"Ready to go?" she mouths. I nod imperceptibly. I'm still holding the issue of *Mentor*.

I take Ben's words with me, I don't ask Brad's permission, as I presume he's finished with it. I follow Ally out of the apartment, signalling that yes, I am definitely ready to go.

Home.

5. LAURA

Martin is coming home! That's what the email says. I think about replying but Rick calls me into his office. I close the door behind me, thinking we are going to discuss Jason's leaving present and goodbye party.

"Ben. I won't beat about the bush…" he opens.

I laugh involuntarily, reminded of a joke.

"What's funny?" he says, knocked out of his stride.

"Nothing. Sorry." I say contritely, wondering what he wants to discuss so seriously. Why I had to close the door.

"I just wanted to let you know you've got the job."

There's a pause. I hadn't expected this.

"You're kidding?" I respond, eventually. I think it's safe to say I'm in shock.

"Nope. You're the best man for the role. We all think so."

"Even Lewis?"

"Especially Lewis."

"But I hate him. I mean I think he's… um…" and I'm laughing again.

"Ben. A word of advice…" Rick's face is deadly serious. "Respect," he says.

He wasn't lying. It is just a single word he gives me. Not even repeated.

Respect.

"I understand," I promise.

I have the job! I literally run out of his office, call my mum – she's distracted with her wisteria but seems happy for me. I spin Laura's chair around and receive a round of applause from everyone else.

Even Alan – the deputy features ed who must have gone for the job – but is only 24 so fuck him – seems happy. We order champagne and everyone stops what they're doing for a while. Jason comes over and claps me on the back.

"Well done," is all he says.

"Thanks."

"I'd better crack on. Loads to sort out."

"I understand."

He's leaving today, so we've already done our goodbyes. He's staying with family for his final weeks in England – making the most of his time. Something I've been universally, spectacularly crap at for so long.

As things settle back down in the office, I sit back in my chair and think about everything I'm going to do. All of it.

It's a good day. Everything adds up. The formula makes sense.

*

I have given Laura a set of my keys and she is in the kitchen. I knew I'd be late – a long drawn out meeting with the ad team for *Mentor* where both sides seemed to spend the entire session being as defensive as possible. I think I handle the editorial case well – suggesting we hold a launch to entice a new breed of advertisers. And my suggestions were heard and appreciated – something it will take me a while to get used to.

Judging by the aroma, Laura's been cooking. I kick open the door and am met by a Sydney Opera House of supermarket carrier-bags along one worktop and, lower in my line of vision, a rogue watermelon that has circulated to the floor.

"Get out!" Laura shrieks as she clocks my appearance.

"Charming," I say, sounding like Darren in *Bewitched*, with my boss coming to dinner and any second Laura will be forced to exercise Plan B. Crinkling her nose and conjuring a culinary masterpiece out of nowhere. She didn't mean to be rude in demanding my exit. I can see from the earnest hope in her eyes that she is doing this for me.

"Sorry," Laura says. "I just want it to be a surprise, Ben. Please? Go wait in the other room."

"Fine," I say. "I'll open some wine."

I trudge out, pull off my tie and instead become intent on appropriate musical accompaniment. I think about what would be best. I browse REM's 'Green', I dismiss Marvin Gaye out of hand and decide on Joni Mitchell, 'A Case Of You' in particular. My favourite lyric of all time untangles itself from the speaker on the shelf that Laura never passes comment on.

With this out of the way I demand further amusement. Intriguing sounds and smells are wafting in waves from the kitchen and it's all too much for me to bear. I head back determined to secure more information about dinner. Besides, I'm starving. "What are you making?" I shout, with enough force to penetrate both Joni and the glass of the kitchen door.

"A mess," she shouts in response, with typical good humour and only a hint of exasperation.

"The takeaway menu is in the second drawer," I offer. I don't add that I know it off heart or that Mrs Mann in the Golden Dragon always gives me extra prawn crackers. Out of sympathy.

"Fuck off," Laura says back deadpan, through the door, and I'm shocked. I've never heard her utter profanity of any kind.

"You swore!" I say, sounding like exactly like I did when confronted by Martin after I'd persuaded him to eat a beetle. We were twelve and Martin had said cunt.

I'm genuinely shocked. Perhaps also by what this suggests about the development in our relationship and perhaps even more owing to the fact that I'm definitely, without qualification, considering this a relationship.

I wait for her to (completely in character) apologise for her outburst. But it doesn't arrive and I like her even more. I hear the cold-water tap turned on and there's the hiss of steam or hot oil or something and I decide it would be perhaps more useful to keep to my earlier promise; and leave her alone.

I head over to the wine-rack, next to the stereo with the speaker that sits on the askew shelf. I'm reaching for a bottle of red with right hand when I notice the globe that sits on top of the wine-rack. I haven't noticed it for months. It's not small. It hasn't ever moved and yet I feel like I'm seeing it for the first time in ages.

I spin Australia into view. The globe is stiff and only Perth makes it. I place my fingers against the painted plaster and manually feed the rest of the continent round – even allowing the edge of Fiji to appear. Long ago Ruth and I used this globe often – to talk of visiting St Petersburg or to settle dinner party disputes about where, exactly, Dubai was in relation to Baghdad and Beirut. On the latter occasion I'd embarrassed myself by responding to a question about whether "the United Arab Emirates were dry states" with "No. I'm pretty sure they all have a coastline."

Ruth's friend Anita had honked like one of those boys turned into donkeys in Disney's *Pinocchio*. I didn't know they meant alcohol. How was I to know?

"Laura," I suddenly shout, reminded of my purpose. "What do you fancy?" But she doesn't answer. Anyway, Joni is preventing my query getting through so I grasp a bottle of Rioja that Maggie brought round last month along with a four-pack of Guinness.

I still have the fingers of my left hand on the Globe and am therefore connected to the past. Nearer in my memory, I recall showing my niece Emily where Israel, her new home, was. Proud of the education I was imparting, I almost choked as she, in turn, jabbed a finger at Palestine and spoke deeply, knowingly, about the Gaza strip and its tempestuous history.

It was their goodbye dinner and I was in no mood to entertain. Martin and his family were about to go to Israel. Emily spent the night transfixed by Ruth's globe, trying to get me on my own to discuss it and I'd remember what it was like to be 13 and in the company of annoying adults. Every time Martin, her Dad, had come over she'd got frustrated.

"You gonna open that or what?" Laura barks, having arrived with laden plates and cutlery.

Dinner is evidently ready.

There at the table, leaning against the bowl with the floating candles is a congratulations card. From Laura of course. It's very nice to receive and I say so. Laura beams back at my words.

We eat quickly. Lasagne with aubergine and some other stuff. There was ciabatta too but it had been done with olives and wasn't the best really. Laura wasn't hungry but she watched as I ate, getting through two and a half glasses of Rioja before I'd finished – and I eat fast. Ruth always said I had all the table-manners of a peasant.

Laura and I stumble from the table to the bed and into each other's arms. We're missionary again and there's a zeal and devout purpose to my actions. I'm both the saver and the saved. Condom is on and we're fucking. Just fucking. I hold her shoulders gently as things draw to close. And then I'm grasping fiercely as my soul shudders into hers. Absolute absolution. She's smiling and I'm so happy. I climb off and take her in my arms – stroking soft breasts through the fabric of half-removed bra still lifting and separating in all the right ways, even at the moment, as she lies tousled against me.

"I don't want you to say anything back," she says, prefacing solemn words that fall effortlessly from her beautiful mouth "… but I love you."

I don't respond. And that's fine. But I would like to give her something in return so I mouth the words "Thank you", lingering as I do so, allowing the vowels to breathe. And that's more than fine too. She's happy with that.

6. DEPARTURE

I get to the airport early, determined to make sure I get on the plane and make it home. Ally was still crying when I left but it doesn't matter. Saying that the kids are still disturbed by the earthquake and the crack along the kitchen ceiling is growing and that they need me around. It was the last comment that made me laugh the most.

In time she'll understand. I have neglected this for too long. She has no idea of the level of neglect. I feel sad that she's no doubt registered that she's secondary right now, that I've decided my marriage is secondary. That they will have to follow behind.

I have to let it go. I only hope it will survive.

The airport is cool when all else is insufferably tropic, over 100 degrees in the shade. My appearance is scanned and my legs frisked and I'm through. Homeward bound. Five guys with beards are detained while my passport is barely looked at. They're being asked to remove their shoes.

There is a problem with the in-flight entertainment which is a bugger as I've left the latest Dan Brown in my bag overhead and I can't be arsed to move the teenager snoring next to me. His yarmulke has slipped and is slightly askew as my brother would say. I ponder whether this is a fashion statement – whether one is allowed to experiment with positioning and colour? Whether what I'm thinking is sacrilegious or just plain inappropriate? So I have time to think about what I am doing and the situation I have left behind. Time to think about what I am going to say to Ben. More specifically, how far I am going to go.

All the way.

I'm not proud of my life. I'm not happy with the way things have gone. Maybe I married too young. Maybe Ally and I weren't meant to do what we did. But I rushed us into marriage. I fucked her without a condom, wanting a child to be born, wanting to start anew. And I was only 22 when I became a Dad. 22? I knew nothing of the world. Nothing about commitment. And yet I'd allowed myself to get tied down at university. I wasn't ready. And made worse in that it had been Ally who had said, "Let's wait. There's time." And I'd insisted. "There's no time to waste."

We taxi down the runway and lift effortlessly into the air.

I close my eyes and think back. To a time when we were living together – even as students, even so young, domesticated in the extreme. What was I doing?

I did love her. But I was just a kid. A kid making up for mistakes. Mostly making up for being unfaithful to my girlfriend.

*

The pub is so crowded – heaving Wednesday night masses, all the returning sports teams back from matches against rival universities, all congregating in town. The student mob spilling out into the high street in a kinetic mass. I need a drink. Desperately. I've travelled all this way for chrissakes and my own brother wants to stay in and watch a re-run of Abigail's fucking Party. Picking Mike Leigh over me.

I enter the Black Griffin on my own. I order two pints on account of the long queue at the bar and turn to face the crowd, leaning against a quiz machine. It's a wild night. Everyone's up for a laugh and I wish Ben was here with me. I don't miss Ally. That's not a bad thing. Its just she wouldn't approve of this. Ally is more at home having a nice meal with friends, not hawking around on tables shouting along in time to Dexy's Midnight Runners, however much she appreciates the talent of Kevin Rowland.

I don't recognise any of Ben's friends in the room which is a shame as I'd like to be part of this group. A girl on one of the tables is vaguely familiar, like someone I've seen in the movies or something, so I make my way over, accidentally knocking over a snakebite and black and only throwing an apology. The girl falls off the table into my arms and there's uproarious laughter. She says thanks and I say "No problem." – next thing I know we're kissing. No other conversation. And I'm glad that Ally doesn't like coming to pubs and I'm relieved she's hundreds of miles away.

*

The District line lurches into Embankment and I leave my seat, pleased to get away from the tosser who's been leaning over me all the way from Hammersmith, swinging his Nike rucksack in my face at every opportunity. His ipod headphones unsuccessfully containing the insistent pound of some dance track I have no chance of recognising; that sounds (in its current form) like the whine of a dentist's needle. Jesus, I'm sweating – this is the 21st century and I'm struggling for air. Pinpricks of electricity almost fizzle on my forehead as nausea sets in. Is this what they call a panic attack. Is this how it feels. So self-aware? Yet, I long to give in, let it wash over – consume me – take hold.

I am about to see Ben. My brother – my better half is heading to the same destination. We're meeting at Embankment tube and going out straight away. I expressly asked for this arrangement. Avoiding his home, his office or our other places too – like a cinema where we saw Woody Allen or a bar in which we'd stayed all night. Me, drinking, back when I was allowed to drink.

I think most of all this needs to be tackled away from any space that has Ruth imbedded within it. She is going to be invoked enough as it is.

I'm clutching the issue of *Mentor*. I could recite it by heart by now. There was even a guy reading it on the train. Avidly.

We are now properly aligned in the station. Doors about to open, expectant crush of faces on the platform, all eager to stand where I am right now. In these few seconds of calm before the storm I browse through the expectant crowd on the other side of the glass, instantly aware which ones will try push on before I've had time to disembark. I find a candidate, the desperation etched on her Shirley MacClaine face. The doors open. Sure enough the woman with the short hair streaks past, not waiting for me to get off, not listening to the instruction of the platform guard – somehow finding a space under my right arm. I turn round and watch her fail to get the one vacant seat. It's already in the process of being occupied by a large Chinese lady. I openly laugh at her humiliation, at her failure. It was only fair. The Chinese woman had been standing with me since West Kensington. It was only fair.

*

Chrissy had questioned whether I was doing the right thing. I'd joined her yesterday for a fag-break after I told management that I was going home due to family needs. They weren't too happy – we're behind after all the lost time when the office was shut. Chris exhaled a nuclear mushroom of smoke, saying, "Explain to me again why you're doing this?"

"I can't."

"Oh that's right. You mean you don't know."

"I just need to."

There's no way I could have gone into the details. That I've been going slowly mad for twenty-four months. That I thought her Brad had been screwing Ally. And then the guilt I felt for not trusting my wife. I can't tell her that somehow I believe my kids see through me. See my shame and don't respect my choices. That Ruth is haunting me.

I don't explain that I can provide information, can give Ben something that might make her leave me alone. And of course it might, in the long run, help him too and perhaps even me. Something's got to give.

I mostly can't tell her because she doesn't really want to know any of it. She's in the middle of trying to work out what to do herself. Brad is still sleeping in her bed, they're hugging like brother and sister and its killing her. She hasn't told me this directly, I've just pieced it together over the past few days. Chris has lost all of her energy. It's all drained away. She's throwing herself into work – spending all hours at her desk.

She'd stubbed out her cigarette and lit another immediately.

"Hey – go easy on the fags," I'd offered.

And she'd laughed uproariously, for the first time in ages. "Is that supposed to be funny?"

I saw what she meant and laughed too as the Scandinavians walked past, mumbling something in perfect English about time-wasters. Chrissy gave them the finger.

"How is Brad?" I asked.

"I'm not sure," she reckoned. "He's writing though. Properly now. Sat at the poxy PC all night. Said Ben had inspired him."

"He's not the only one," I'd said, before asking "What are you going to do Chris?"

"I don't know Martin. I really don't."

"Promise me you'll go easy on yourself. Things will get better."

She didn't look convinced.

"It'll work out. New stuff always comes up."

"What's stuff?"

"You know what I mean."

We left it there. Me feeling like I wasn't helping. There wasn't much to say. What do you tell someone who loses the one they thought might finally make an honest woman of them. Someone who realises their love was never honest. Not ever.

The plane hits a bit of turbulence, the seatbelt sign comes on and I recite the Lord's Prayer. Don't ask me why.

7: ARRIVAL

I give my money to the guy and take the magazine. I say keep the change which is only eighty pence from a two-pound coin so I don't feel particularly benevolent. The seller is about my age, fitter, healthier even perhaps. Clean-shaven, wide-smile – polished teeth as if he were some American tv-movie actor struggling to make his big break; keenness and enthusiasm personified, seems like he should be called Zack or Ryan but his badge says 'Henry'. It's a normal name at odds with his LA persona and in fact his eyes betray another truth, a truth entirely washed out, tired with the relentless reality of a homeless place in the world. His clothes are a little too worn, however cool 'destitute-chic' is in again at the moment, according to those ridiculous fashion stories in *Mentor* – which I'll be doing something about, believe me. I've just commissioned a piece on three men locked up in Burma for broadcasting their own internet radio station. Times are changing.

"Be good," Henry says in parting as I make the climb down the steps from Hungerford Bridge, clutching a Big Issue, dodging the tourists staring at the Millennium Eye across the river. I've been on the South Bank for the past hour, at the National Theatre, browsing the book shop, killing time, waiting. I'm good at waiting.

I roll the magazine and stick it in my back pocket, Henry's parting words lingering as I enter the station. Ruth always said "Be good" whenever we had a goodbye and I always said "I would" in response. Out of habit more than anything; a rhyming couplet that emerged each time I left for work early – or went to the pub without her.

If I had known that "be good" would be the last thing I'd ever hear my wife say, I would have begged for more, for some extra syllables. Extra pieces to pad out the phrase. That last "be good" and my automatic "I would" which, frankly, never made any sense, have added to my ongoing sense of duty. To my need to be faithful to my wife and our marriage. I've interpreted it as an instruction. Ruth asking me to be good. And I've tried. And I've since wondered, what's good? Am I being good by getting on with things? By developing things with Laura? By remembering to send her mother-in-law, Stella, a birthday card despite our estrangement? Was "be good" intended to keep me faithful; to stay true to her and her alone?

Sometimes I imagine that maybe Ruth knew these would be the last words she'd say. Not even that she was giving me a deliberate instruction – simply that she knew it would be a permanent goodbye. And I ponder her hidden expression. Was she smiling or crying? Perhaps she was simply trying to get the conditioner out, unaware of the fate that may have befallen her later that day.

It had been a final conversation caught on the run. Ruth said "be good" from behind the shower curtain as I ducked my head back into the bathroom and said to her "You'll be late tonight, right?" I'd been halfway out the front door before remembering she was going out that evening with workmates. I'd wanted to remind that I remembered. I'd rushed back in, simply to confirm that I'd wait up.

"I won't go to bed till you get back Ruth."

She'd simply responded then with, "Be good."

And I'd said, "I would."

Aside from the minimal content of our last conversation there was nothing noteworthy about Ruth's final delivery, nothing memorable in her tone. "Be good" – the two words segueing sing-song style into each other amidst the rush of water. My "I would" was equally uninspired, a monotone affirmation caused partly, if I remember rightly (and believe me I've preserved the entire scene) because I had deliberated first about telling her off. Criticising her inability to place the mat close enough to bath. I can still see the water that had been rushing – as usual whenever she showered – down the side of the tub onto the floor and through the minute cracks between the floorboards. This carelessness used to piss me off (it wouldn't anymore). So you see, I almost said to her "don't you remember what I said about the fucking mat? If the place floods we'll know who to blame".

In this light, her "Be good" and my response "I would" is an acceptable and preferred dialogue. It doesn't seem insufficient. It's positively Shakespearean in comparison. And I'm so grateful that I held my tongue. Grateful for the brevity we chose. I remember I decided against a tirade because somehow I knew she was expecting me to say it – there had been a definite pause before she'd spoken, an intake of breath as she perhaps tried to imagine what domestic-neurotic statement I would make this time.

Maybe she believed I'd run back simply to pick her up on the error.

Isn't that terrible? I see her now, hearing me charge back in – perhaps trying to work out what she'd forgotten to do. Replace the toothpaste cap? Open the window to let steam out? Or the fact that she'd been taking longer and longer in the shower every day – "how clean can you make yourself?" I'd said only the day before. But somehow for the first, and unfortunately the last, time in my whole marriage I'd realised I could be a bit of an idiot and caught myself in time. Over-bearing. Irritating even.

Not to escalate my trait. I was house-proud, actually scratch that – house-fascist – I was a bit too hard on her. But any extreme behaviour on my part was mirrored by her total inactivity. Ruth never saw mess, did little to help round our home. She only noticed if shelves were lop-sided. She didn't mind dirt or dust at all. And she didn't really mind me complaining. It didn't faze her. She'd just look at the floor say "sorry", or say "that's why you love me", flush a sheepish pink and promptly forget all of my 'instructions'. I'm a bit embarrassed admitting here that I gave her instructions. In my defence, and to even out the dynamic of our relationship, I had my own from her – about how much milk in her coffee, what volume the tv could be after she'd gone to bed and how much money I was allowed to take out with me. We were balanced, I need to make that clear.

Ultimately, the dialogue that immediately preceded our separation was from her to me. "Be good," she'd instructed. "I would," I compliantly replied. And I'm left wondering if I have kept my side of the agreement.

"I would."

The *Big Issue* seller seems surprised by my response. Shouting something else which I don't hear as I am already inside Embankment tube. I stop at the cash-point in the entrance and draw out 70 quid, this is going to be a long night. I am going to see my brother for the first time in six months. I'm going to tell him about Laura, about how great she is. And about my job. He will be pleased that things are progressing – that I am being good to myself. I know Martin will be late so I think about going to grab another coffee, think about how much milk to put in as Ruth is still on my mind but at least I'm letting a woman similar to her height and build walk past – resisting the urge to go and check for any sign of her staring back at me.

It's seven o'clock and Martin's plane landed at Heathrow over 90 minutes ago. He's getting the Piccadilly northbound to Hammersmith, crossing the platform and coming across town on the District Line. We'll walk up Villiers St, to a pub right at the top near the Strand. I offered to meet him at the airport but he insisted we connect here – saying he wanted to be able to talk as soon as he saw me, to not have to travel together amongst others inhibiting us. And not wanting me to be driving and unable to look him in the eye. This all makes sense, I guess. So we're re-joining here – in a not-so-quiet pub that we used to meet in before I got the train home after work to Ruth, back when we used to live south of the river. In Blackheath – when we first got together.

I'm leaning against a shuttered station kiosk. I've bought a coffee from next door and have begun reading the *Big Issue*'s regular page of missing cases. Absent souls that have departed without leave, word or any forwarding address. It is a relentless tide, every week more faces appear, somehow selected from extensive files. How do they choose who to feature? Maybe the most vulnerable and maybe there are some that are always passed over? Maybe there are some who haven't got anyone looking? Sometimes people leave because they don't want to be found. Part of me wants Ruth to fit into this category.

But fuck that, I want her to be found, want her to need me and want to be the one to make things better.

There are four faces on the page. They all look pretty regular, nothing unusual or extraordinary. I have looked at so many of them over the past months and it has left me numb. The random snapshots carefully selected as the best likeness – initially spontaneously taken snaps, now precious images – handed over from relatives anxious that they will get the photo back; if not the relative, but of course willing to offer anything that may trigger a discovery.

I appreciate the way that the blurb accompanying each photo is resolutely present in its tense, even when someone has been away for six years. A simple but genuine sign of respect for those departed and for those left behind. It's a comforting approach, one that resolutely refuses to acknowledge finality. Alex *is* now 30 years old, he *is* an engineer for British Telecom. His family *are* desperately worried.

Alex where are you? He's been missing for six years. Ruth still has some way to go. I still have some way to go.

The final sentence in the ad doesn't work for me. Family are desperately worried is not up to the job of conveying the inner turmoil, as far as I'm concerned – but what phrasing or combination of words could? How do you convey the sheer terror and constant turmoil that surrounds every part of endless days that pass without news. And the subsequent succession of sleepless nights that turn into years; units of time in motion that do little to prevent the nagging onslaught of insidious thoughts and fear eating away at your very soul.

At times like this, it's not hard for me to see that it will still be tough to reconcile my professional and personal existence. But the interest I place in the reviews page opposite suggests I can increasingly accept that more trivial matters, including those relating to my magazine, have their place. I am allowed to be swayed by inconsequential things. It is okay. As long as respect is involved. Everything is relative.

And it follows that on my journey today people were allowed to be pissed off if they missed their train or if they couldn't get a seat. They aren't pathetic – they have a right to be bothered. I do not have a monopoly on anguish. Justified or otherwise.

The National Missing Person's Helpline number is 0500 700 700. Registered charity 1020419. They urgently require funds. If you would like to help, please send donations to The Missing Persons Helpline, 284-286 Upper Richmond Road West, London, SW14 7JE.

I finish reading. Quite a bit of time has passed. Daylight has disappeared, commuters have begun to swarm over the station, forcing me to retreat from my position. Martin is late. I check that my mobile phone is still switched on before heading back outside for no other reason than a change of scenery. I want to see Martin before he sees me anyway – want to be in a position to watch him appear from behind the ticket gates. I keep thinking of how the moment will go, tears appearing in the corner of my eyes which I fight away.

I'm staring back into the station now, but my body is outside. I'm next to a flower-seller – the red glow of a thousand brake-lights racked up along the river road beside me – the interminable crawl home. Across the traffic is the river which is mostly empty. I look back up at Henry – still selling his magazine. He's done quite well. Fewer copies in his hand than before.

I check back inside, no Martin, before pacing back over to Henry with my copy in hand.

"Here. You can have this back. I've read it."

"Eh?"

"Sell it again. Make another..." Check the cover. "£1.40."

"I don't make £1.40," he sounds rude, but he's still smiling.

"You will from this one. I've read it through. Waiting for my twin brother."

Why am I telling him this? Why am I continuing? I must sound like an arsehole. "I just thought it'd be a good idea. It's not charity or anything," I justify, feeling the unease Jason might have, in recent months towards me.

"Yes it is," Henry says. "It is charity. But thanks. I'll take it."

"Cool," I say, honestly – not crappily, like that word always seems when written down without inflection. Or when used by people who should know better.

And then some pretty young girl stops to buy a magazine. Henry takes her money, flashes her a winning smile and tilts his head for me to hand over my copy.

She says "thanks" to me, and is gone.

Henry says "Cheers mate."

And I turn back, having passed something on while passing something back. In both directions.

And just maybe the girl will know Alex, missing for six years.

I step back into the station and there he is. My brother – wearing his glasses – heading for the exit barriers, looking nervous. I'm wearing contacts.

Martin. Looking around for me.

He looks just like our Dad at this moment and I realise I must too, though the glasses are adding to the impression.

I suddenly wonder why he's here. Alone. It doesn't make sense. I hadn't thought before.

Straight away I worry for Ally.

And then I spy the copy of *Mentor* in his hand, the way he's gripping it so tightly. I think ridiculously of Patricia. My mother's friend from Grays.

I look at Martin closely. Seeing right into him and afraid of what I find there.

And so I walk away.

8: POINT

He's walking away from me. I see him leave the station just as I manage to work out how the ticket machine operates.

"Ben!" I shout, above the throng of people. He stops dead in his tracks but doesn't turn around which is odd. I catch up with him, knocking some people out of the way in the process but fuck them. I grab his shoulders from behind and he almost recoils. "Ben!"

Then we're staring at each other and I see that he has lost weight and I think of everything I have done, everything he has been through. And debate whether I can put him through anything more.

"Hey!" he says, managing a smile. But that's all.

We move off silently, our steps together, slow even paces heading out into the rush of London. Up Villiers Street and towards the Strand.

"Let's find a drink," I say.

"Typical," he says, as if he's being funny, though there's no humour in his voice.

We make it to a pub and nab a spot in the window. I ask Ben what he wants and head off to the bar, leaving him peering out of the window. I see him put his mobile phone carefully down on the table – as if he's expecting a call from someone. I couldn't tell you who.

The pub is empty, a young couple at a table near ours and a barman idly waiting for something to do. I'm served instantly and return to my brother, marvelling at how expensive London is nowadays.

"Why didn't Ally come back with you?" Ben asks accusingly, not even letting me sit down.

"Why would she?"

"Let's see. She's your wife. Mother of your children. She hates it over there. Do you need any more reasons?"

"What's with the aggression?" I say.

"I don't know. I'm just pissed off."

When we were growing up Ben would never get pissed off. It was always the other way around. At least it was before. I see so much anger in him right now.

He seems to have learnt a lot of aggression since Ruth went. Most of it, unfortunately, from me. Indirectly – but from me all the same. And I know this is my doing. And that I will deserve his fury.

9: COUNTERPOINT

"Why didn't Ally come back with you?" I ask Martin accusingly, not even letting him sit down. In fact, the fact that Martin is here in my life right now – which has been moving along nicely – while his wife is waiting in Israel, is entirely pissing me off. It's like something's has gone off in my brain.

A warning sign.

"Why would she?" he's saying, as if it's a ridiculous question.

"Let's see," I sneer. "She's your wife. Mother of your children. She hates it over there. Do you need any more reasons?"

"What's with the aggression?" he pleads, and I feel like maybe I should give him a break but also want to break his neck. Venom coursing through me like never before. Warning signs going off everywhere now. I feel like there's both an angel and a devil beside me – and neither of them seem to know what to suggest.

"I don't know. I'm just pissed off," I say and it comes out a little too harshly. All I really want to do is hug him for ages but we don't need to. But maybe we need to do something normal. Something 'twin-like' because none of this seems normal yet.

Maybe it's because I've realised there's an agenda in his visit. Maybe it's the way he's holding *Mentor*, which he never reads. Maybe because I can read, if not his mind, then his body language and maybe I don't like what I see.

I've never felt like this with Martin, especially after not having seen him for so long. Aggression is usually his territory, but I can't control myself. Can't keep this at bay. I am pissed off to see him throwing things with Ally around so lightly, doesn't he realise you have to hang on for dear life? Hasn't he learnt anything from my mistakes?

"I wanted, I needed, to come back on my own. To see you Ben."

"Why? I'm alright. Things are alright. Is Ally alright though? With you coming back, I mean?"

He ignores me, "I read your article. In *Mentor*."

"Oh." I say, not wanting his opinion.

"It's very good," he says.

"Thanks."

"Why didn't you tell me you were writing it?"

"It wasn't a conscious decision not to. I tried. Anyway, I just did it and then moved on. That's all I'm trying to do Martin. Move on. So what does Ally think?"

"About the article, I don't think she…"

"About you fucking being over here – while she's there!"

"What's your problem Ben?"

"I don't know." I really don't. I'm stalling – some sort of diversionary tactic to throw him off what he wants to do. It's like I want a fight.

"I came here to speak to you. To talk," Martin continues.

"Maybe that's the problem." It's true. I feel sick about what he wants to talk about. Worried about what he wants to discuss. I certainly don't want to talk about *her.*

"Do you want to tell me why the fuck you're drinking?" I say, settling for an easy target.

"It's one beer Ben. Calm down, eh? Stop trying to change the subject."

"One beer? Does Ally know you're drinking again?"

"Fuck Ally will you!" he says.

"Like that American guy, eh?" I can't believe I'm speaking like this. Then he looks like he wants to kill me. But he doesn't. I just don't want to confront what he wants me to face.

"Ben. Brad's gay – he's not the problem." Martin sighs then, and I see how tired he is. "Look, I'm tired of running away. Of looking to other things."

"Welcome to my world brother," I tell him. "Want to know how exhausting life can be, fuck it up with Ally. Let her go. Make her disappear."

"My kids hate me," he murmurs. "My life is falling apart."

"Enough with the self-pity."

Finally provoked, he squares up to me.

"You don't have the monopoly on wallowing Ben," he sneers. "Poor Benjamin – his wife disappeared."

At this there's finally silence. I notice that the nice young couple on the table next to us have moved to the other side of the room. The barman is whispering to his colleague. I realise Martin's ripped the label on his bottle of beer to shreds. Pieces of damp paper litter his side of the table.

"Your kids don't hate you," I say. "Emily's a teenager and Max is just impressionable."

He's grateful for this. But he's not really listening. I can see he's getting up the courage. I stall him again. "What's really going on with Ally?"

And finally he answers directly.

"I can't explain it. We just don't connect. We both try so hard but we just end up snapping. And I don't know whether a marriage works on good intentions alone anymore. Somehow it just goes wrong. It's like there's these little gremlins, determined to make everything go not quite right. I'll accidentally sit on her new sunglasses and break them or someone will call when we're just about to sit down for a quiet meal together, having spent three hours getting the kids to go to bed. It's just going wrong."

"You can't blame anyone else."

"I'm not!" he roars, so loudly that it looks like the barman might call the police. "That's why I'm here. Other people just get in the fucking way. I wish they'd all just leave us alone. I do trust Ally, I really do."

"You sure?" I say, thinking of Jason's experience but also thinking of Ally and knowing that whatever else, the security of her children's family-life will always be her number one priority.

Martin has his head in hands. "I'm not sure of anything. Everything is slipping."

"You shouldn't be here. Why are you here with me? You know I'm fine."

"I'm not here for you." He raises his head, looking at me. "I'm here for me."

And I feel sick again, total fear. I can sense it. Sense something I don't understand.

"I need another beer," I say, rising and heading to the bar on unsteady legs. Martin pushes back in his chair, the noise screeching violently, watching resignedly.

I know I'm prolonging the pain. I should let him do whatever he wants to do. Hear whatever he has say.

"You okay?" The barman says to me, as I arrive at the counter.

"Not sure."

"You twins?"

Surprisingly this is the first time I've had this one in years. Used to happen all the time. People asking the most obvious question in the world.

"No," I say, "I've never met the fucker before in my life", I finish rudely, unnecessarily, and head back to the table with two beers. I hear the barman mutter "prick" and I hate myself.

"Now you're feeding my habit?" Martin says when I return with his pint.

"Something like that."

I take a long swig of lager and avoid his gaze.

"Ben," Martin says, his new beer untouched.

"What?"

"We need to talk. Or rather I need to talk. To you. I need to tell you something."

"No Martin. You don't." I'm sweating profusely, worse than Lewis at work.

"I do." He really means this. His voice flatter than I've ever heard.

"It's about Ruth."

"No. I don't want to hear it. I don't want to know. I don't. Okay?"

"I can't go on."

"You'll have to."

"No," I say.

It's like I'm suddenly in a fog, like everything is obscured – hazy and unclear and I've lost all my bearings. I need to get out of this situation.

"Ben. I'm here..." Martin's saying. "I'm here because there's things you don't know."

I try to regain control. "I don't need this melodrama Martin. Just leave me alone."

"I'm your older brother," he says.

"Fuck that – you're not. You're 30 minutes older. That doesn't make you my older brother."

I can see this wounds him. Since we were little I'd given him that, acceded to his age and told anyone who'd listen, partly because it was cute, partly because I felt he liked it, partly because I liked it – that he was my older brother.

"We're the same age Martin," I continue, as if this is the most important thing in the world to say.

"Fine. Whatever." He shrugs, he doesn't care anymore.

"I need to go. I'm meeting Laura," I say. Her name is a way out, a path through the fog. The thought of her calms me. I could go and see Laura. Leave this and go to her.

But I can't. Martin is adamant. And in distress and my mind's racing and I need to face this. Bizarrely the image of Patricia, the neighbour from Grays comes into my head and I don't know why. And then I do.

"I slept with Ruth," he says.

If you've always believed in fidelity and wondered how you'd feel if the love of your life is suddenly presented as otherwise, I can tell you it's not how you think it'd be. At least it wasn't for me. I didn't shout, or rail against the injustice, my heart didn't implode into a thousand fragments, the earth didn't stop spinning. None of the above. Maybe I was in shock. Maybe infidelity just isn't the worst.

But then the seconds pass. The truth sinks in.

My twin brother. That's something else. That's almost impossible to process.

Martin is looking at me. "I'm sorry," he's saying, over and over again. Repeating it and making me think of my editor.

"When?" I ask, as if this matters. Actually it does.

"When?" I say again.

10: EVERYTHING'S RELATIVE

"I'm sorry" are the only words that will do at this moment. I'm just repeating it over and over.

"When?" Ben asks, as if it matters and actually it does. When is crucial. It both absolves and damns me.

"When?" he asks again.

"It was a long time ago. Before you were married." Knowing that should, by rights, help the situation, but it doesn't. And that's it. I'm past the point of no return.

"When Martin? I want to hear you say it," he persists.

And suddenly I see that somehow he comprehends. About a night I spent alone in the pub at his university. About meeting a girl he'd admired for months and months. A girl he desperately hoped would one day notice him.

A girl who had noticed him. Ruth.

"She thought it was you." I'm saying. "I knew all the time she thought it was you. She called me Ben. And I went along with it. I wanted to be you so much. It was never about her. It was about you."

He's breathing deeply. Suddenly I want to take it all away, say I was just kidding. I want to erase it all and go back to how it was. But actually I don't. There's a weird kind of relief in confession but a horror at what this revelation will do to our subsequent lives. How could I do this? When he's been through so much and come out the other side.

"You knew I liked her. I loved her Martin," he's saying.

"I was drunk. I didn't mean for it to happen. But the point is she didn't cheat on you. Ever. She thought I was you. She didn't know the truth."

His eyes close. Unable to look at me.

"But you Martin…" he says, slowly. "You knew. And it's not just me you betrayed. Or Ruth. You cheated on all three of us. Ally too."

"You're right," I admit. And there it is, everything encapsulated in one sentence. I cheated on everything I held precious.

"We were young." I say eventually, searching for excuses. "You weren't together yet, it's not like you were in a relationship yet; you and Ruth," I say. Trying to further mitigate his pain and yes, my guilt.

"We were together. You and me. Brothers. Twins. That's supposed to mean something."

"I wanted to kill myself," I tell him. "The next morning. I still do some days, when I think of how much its messed Ruth up. When I wonder if that was the reason."

"It all makes sense." He's murmuring to himself, not acting at all how I thought he would. Mention of my depression not registering on his sympathy scale.

He sits upright in his chair, folding his arms.

"When I met Ruth again. At the nightclub. She'd said she'd always liked me, even back then, and I didn't ever really believe her… But it was me that night Martin. Me she'd liked. Not you…"

His voice trails off, waiting for me to speak further.

"I wanted to tell you," I say.

"When? On my deathbed? Just to make me feel really bad? You went up to the girl I'd liked and decided to stab in me the back."

It wasn't like that, I want to say. But maybe it was. Maybe I knew it was the girl from his photograph, God knows Ben had made me look at it enough times. And maybe, possibly I did resent her. The hold she had on him. The perceived hold Ally already had on me.

"Don't do this Ben. Please," is all I can say; wanting to stop what I've started – but he's still waiting for more.

So I carry on. "The next morning I told her that I wasn't you, I was Martin. And she wouldn't stop crying. Just wouldn't stop. It was awful. She said she'd liked you from the moment she saw you. That she'd got her mates to find out lots about you, even watched you ask questions in your lectures when she should have been in her own. And she always knew you liked her. Said it had made her feel special. And now it was ruined… I tried to tell her it wasn't."

I look up. Ben's not crying. He's not moving at all. Just listening to me.

"And when I… met her… she'd been so happy that you'd finally made a move. She was a virgin… ." I can't believe I'm telling him all this. It's a fucking nightmare.

"… she wasn't," he cuts in, immediately. "She always told me she'd slept with eleven guys at uni."

"Ben, she was a virgin." I insist. And his shoulders slump, defeated. I see that he believes me, see the defeat in his soul.

And I fully realise just how much damage I might have done to

Ruth – as if her eventual disappearance alone isn't evidence enough.

"I didn't know what to do Ben. Everything snowballed from there, I started drinking. It was like I was being punished."

"Shall I get the violins?"

"I don't blame you for hating me."

"Did you tell Ally?"

"No. I went back home and have never done anything like that again. I proposed the week after to try and make a clear break. It was the only way I could tell you – without telling you – that Ally was the only one for me. That honestly no one else, including Ruth, could ever be significant."

"You used Ally."

"I didn't. I loved her. I still love her. I just accelerated things…"

This isn't the time for clarifying my thoughts about Ally. Ben abruptly stands and heads off to the loo. He's gone for ages. But eventually he comes back and sits down. I carry on talking straight away.

"… And I thought it was all over. Except two years later you go and bring Ruth home to mum and dad. We had to make a pact to never discuss it. And I thought we could handle everything. But obviously she couldn't."

He listens motionless to this. No more histrionics. Nothing.

"It was only one night after all; it was only one mistake," I continue. "You weren't even together." I repeat.

Ben sits still – I notice his knuckles – white, gripping the edge of the table.

"Except it wasn't just one mistake," he says. "Abortion." His eyes fixed on me, coldly. "She had an abortion Martin. You'd got her pregnant."

And I think I'm going to be sick.

"Oh God" is all I can say.

"It was yours."

I don't say anything. I don't need to.

"You got her pregnant."

"Ben. I had no idea."

And I see him putting everything together. Making it all make sense, whatever he's been trying to solve for the past two years.

"… And then she's unlucky. Then she can't have kids. Ever."

His voice is strange. Like a robot. Like he's talking only to himself.

And, all of a sudden I'm throwing up everywhere. Like I was on that New Years Eve all those years ago, when Ruth and I had to continue the pretence of getting to know each other – which in a way we were – while our happy partners sang 'Auld Lang Syne' and saw in a new year of promise as I drank and drank to forget all the time before and all the time in the future. And her knowing that she had to live in close proximity to everything I would forever represent and remind her of.

Abortion.

*

I didn't know about the baby. Ruth never told me. I hope that one day Ben believes me. I don't need forgiveness. I don't deserve that.

And other things make sense now.

A week before Ruth disappeared I'd gone round to their flat to drop off a video that Ally and I had borrowed. I had a key to their house and let myself in.

I didn't think anyone was home. There was a noise upstairs. I went up slowly, pushing open the door to their bedroom. I don't know why I didn't call out, let anyone know I was there.

Ruth was standing in front of the mirror, naked, looking at herself. She was crying violently – a look on her face of disgust. When she noticed me, I saw final, utter defeat in her eyes. In a second she had attempted to cover herself. I moved in and held her for an age. Wanting to take the hurt away. I didn't even know what was wrong.

I just held her as my sister-in-law, that's all. That's all I ever wanted her to be.

And she must have wondered how all this had happened. And what kind of purgatory had me – the person who had brought about all this pain – find her.

And then my daughter. My daughter had come in from the car, where I'd told her to wait for a moment. My 11 year old daughter saw us both. Saw me holding her aunt.

Ruth saw my daughter too. She screamed. A noise I'll never forget. A death-wail.

Emily was Ruth's favourite. Ruth was hers. Emily was purity and innocence. But no more. Even that must have seemed spoiled.

11. THESEUS

I think about the kind of God that put Ruth and me – Benjamin – back together again in that year after we graduated. That puts a woman so damaged back into the fire. I have to hope it's because we were meant to be one. That our love was destined to be stronger. Intended to overcome.

Except it wasn't. Clearly.

What must she have thought when I approached her in the nightclub?

Later she'd told me on our honeymoon, after the big Dean Martin wedding, that she believed we were always meant to be. That our reunion meant everything was preordained. I just thought she meant the fact that the pair of us had been too stupid to see Eros and his arrows at university. That we'd been given a second chance to put right what both of us were too crap to get going first time round.

I never imagined my twin brother was the one getting in the way; the one that she had no chance of ever getting past – not when he's here forever in my face, my voice and body.

But I had pressured her. My persistence had won her over. She was resistant. We'd walked from the club to that café and I'd decided to tell her how much love I could give her there and then. And I can see with hindsight just how she might have thought we could make it all right. Martin and I are different in so many ways. As much as she knew that Ally could never choose – or want – to be with me.

And I can reconfigure that time at my parents when I first introduced her to my brother. How she didn't want to go. How she fought against it. How I'd left them alone in the kitchen and how they must have come to an agreement. How painful that must have been for her.

And to never tell anyone. Not a soul.

Jesus, I think of the drive home after she met them all. How she'd cried – and the extra hurt once I'd encouraged Martin to announce Ally's pregnancy at the table. Especially then.

I think about what that must have done to Ruth.

And I think also about when I proposed that passionate night after Momo's. How I'd talked of kids.

*

Walking away. Along the river. Up onto Waterloo Bridge, London all around – too many things all around. Not sure what to think. Where it all begins or ends. I guess it never does. Our lives never stop bleeding into each other – even after death.

I left Martin in the pub, the barman cleaning him up. I couldn't look at him. Couldn't touch him. He was crying for me. Saying he didn't know about the abortion and I guess – like me – understanding so much for the first time. Apologising over and over, as he retched.

*

Ruth and I used to listen to this old Dino song all the time. 'Two Sleepy People' I think it's called – one of those instances where you never actually check the CD cover to learn the title. Anyway, it's a story of a pair of lovers who enjoy their bed. Not in that way. More innocent than that. Just a place for lying together. For us, Ruth and I, it captured the simplicity we aimed for. It was the most hedonistic thing we could think of. To get into bed and just be. Me looking after Ruth and her looking after me. I realise now it was the purity we wanted. The lack of interference, of the outside tainting our world.

I'd say that was our favourite place in the whole world. When we first moved into together, in a flat in Blackheath, South London – we'd stagger in from work, tired and cold – and I'd repeat-play the CD over and over and I'd take any excuse to drag her under the sheets and stay there.

It's always winter when I remember the song. Winter in Blackheath. White, unbroken snow. Those were some of the happiest months of my life, even when her Dad used to say we were throwing money down the drain renting or when it was a bugger to get home to from the centre of town.

They're all nice memories. All the ones of Blackheath. It's still one of my favourite places in the world – the long plain of grass with its views over Docklands or the village with all of its shops and restaurants. Ruth and I would spend Saturday mornings just wandering around, enjoying being together. Everyone who came to visit, the friends who'd stay over, would all end up wanting to move there.

When I go in a cab now to Laura's in Dulwich, sometimes I ask the driver to cut across the heath. The lowering skies above and the beautiful isolated church on the south side. A church in which a couple we knew later got married. I wonder how they are. Two perfect kids and a happy life.

Today, the heath is littered with circling crows that remind me of Madonna's video for 'Frozen'. I recall how they swooped on Ruth one night as we staggered pissed back home, after yet another Friday tikka masala like so many couples across the land. We'd passed the officials preparing the heath for the London Marathon which starts here and I'd made Ruth laugh by pretending I was crossing the finish line. The crows had other ideas. And she'd been really freaked out. In her drunkenness, worried that they were a portentous omen – saying that she was 'bad' and that their cawing and black feathers could see into her soul.

These memories have all made me stronger. They aren't wrong, they aren't false. They aren't anyone else's. There not even Ruth's. They're mine. And therefore it's fine that I sometimes share them with Laura but I'm always careful not to dwell. Not because I think she minds hearing them but because I don't want to dilute them by drawing on them too often. It's just nice to know they're all there. Some happier than others. I like it best when things surface that have remained hidden for years. I like to surprise myself.

And I'm learning that there can and will be new memories. I laugh now when I think of her flatmate answering the door with that skull. Fucking weirdo. He passed his exams – we went out for a celebratory drink and he ended up getting into a fight with a bus driver. We weren't even on a bus.

*

What do I want to do? It's what everyone asked me after Ruth first went. People were prepared to accept any choice – I had the right to behave however I needed to. If I wanted to let off steam that was fine. Crying was acceptable. Wandering, looking, doing something – also good choices.

"What do you want to do?" Suzie asks me again. Her office just like I remember it. Chaise longue instead of a couch. She's grown her hair long and acquired a pregnant bump in the time since we last met. The room has been repainted, it looks fresh, but its still magnolia. It's still neutral. Mental health books line the shelves.

I want to make things right with my brother. But not yet.

Laura is important. We've grown closer and closer together. I'll be honest and say that I don't know if it will work out long term. I'm not sure if I can last the distance – but that's probably obvious. Only the days passing will show me if I can trust again. And I'm wise enough now to accept that it will be a lot for Laura too – for her to decide whether to commit to a man like me. A man who wants to remove the picture of his wife from the bedroom but can't bring himself to spend the night alone. Despite the woman next to him.

And even if I did. If I put Ruth away in a drawer. She'll still be in my mind.

This is partly Martin's fault. He's set me back. All the reasons I'd come up with, all the reasons I'd discussed, debated in a bid to understand why she went, were wide of the mark. Just when I became ruthless, just when I didn't care.

But even then; if I persecute Martin, if I berate him for what he's done and assign blame. Even then, I can't be totally sure that that's why she left me. *If* she left me.

What after, all this, if she was just taken away? No choice in the matter. What if that night had nothing to do with it and I end up hating Martin forever?

So mostly I know he's set me free.

12. OVER

My mother is there at the station when I arrive. She is wearing regulation countryside green wellingtons and a quilted bodywarmer that makes her look like she's about to join the royal shooting party.

"Martin," she sings at me as the train pulls in, unembarrassed about raising her voice at such a sleepy station.

I'm in no mood to sing back but raise a hand to let her know I've seen her. I pull my suitcase off the train and step down onto the platform. She rushes over, still sprightly despite the horror stories of arthritis that have frequented all of our conversations in the past six months. It's a beautiful evening, the smell of Norfolk lavender everywhere, including on her.

"You smell nice," I say.

"It's local," she says, by way of eccentric explanation. "Come on, the taxi's waiting."

She bundles me into a Ford Mondeo driven by a kid who looks like he's Emily's age. He has the broadest Norfolk accent and says "are we now going?" in a way that makes me laugh for the first time in twenty-four hours. As the car pulls away my mother smiles across at me exclaiming "Oh. Almost forgot. Would you like a Murray Mint? How about a tissue?" I've been crying, again, she can always tell. Before I can respond, she's produced a packet of both and is thrusting them in my direction.

"Mum. Calm down, eh?" I say. It comes out all wrong and I sound like a rude, ungrateful son. I see the driver's eyes in the rear-view mirror clocking my surliness. He's not impressed.

My mother is unfazed. "You love Murray Mints."

"I do. You're right," I say, and take one – only to struggle with the cellophane wrapper; revealing my nervousness.

"Fantastic scenery Martin. Don't you think? Didn't get this in Grays." My mother twitters on for the whole 10 minute drive to her home and I see that she too is nervous. Nervous about the circumstances that might have brought me here alone. Both without Ben and without my own family. Ally and I have almost been together for over 15 years and it's hard to remember life without her. Or me without her, I should say.

Yet, it saddens me that I can't remember spending anytime alone with my mother, just us two. There was a moment at my Father's funeral – as Ally put Emily to bed upstairs in the room I grew up in, and Ben went out for a walk with Ruth – that my mother and I stood chatting in the garden studying his last crop of sunflowers.

"I'm going to miss him Martin," was all she'd said.

"I'll look after you," I'd responded.

And I wonder if I have?

We arrive at my mum's house and I'm instantly struck by how quiet it all is. Our house in Essex was never quiet. There was never a moment's peace from our friends or neighbours who'd call in for lingering cups of tea or Patricia doing one of her updates on all the local gossip – conveniently forgetting her own scandalous indiscretions which were well-beyond the scope of anyone else in the area. Pat chose instead to relate twee episodes of vicars receiving speeding fines. I never liked her. I got the sense she never liked me. She always had my number – even before I slept with my brother's unrequited love.

"Take your bag up to your room," my mother says, as if I have a room. I don't say anything different as right now it is nice to think of this cottage as my home – though I've never slept here. I walk up the stairs, reassured by the old-fashioned cream carpet-runner that must have been here since the war. My mother's made the bed and thoughtfully left the latest Dick Francis by the bedside. I also see a stack of my brother's magazine in the corner and smile to think of her as the sole reader of *Mentor* in this small village, avidly showing around the racy articles and glamorous pictures to all of her friends who'd no doubt be polite but entirely baffled. Good on her though. She's supportive to the end, even if she doesn't understand all the details.

Her support and unconditional love never wavers. I guess it's why I'm here. Running to my mum when things have gone bad. In reality it's also a practical decision. Ben left me alone in London and eventually I got it together to call Ally.

Only for my wife to say three words down the phone that cemented the madness of that day.

"I'm leaving you," is what I heard.

The police picked me up off the streets a few hours later, dragged me to a cell from where I eventually managed to call my mother. A cab then for the train station – I went immediately, dragging my case with me, still wearing its baggage stickers from the airport.

*

My mother has appeared in the doorway behind me.

"I've made you a cup of tea. There's some lemon cake too."

"Great," I say and trudge down the stairs after her, passing a photo of my Dad hanging in the hallway. There's one of me and Ben next to it, we were dressed as Arab sheiks for Halloween.

"Now. I want you to start from the beginning," my mother says. "And I don't want you thinking that you'll spare me the details. I have lived a bit you know. You boys think you're the only ones to be young."

"I'm not young."

"Stop stalling Martin."

"Where do you want me to start?" I really have no dignity left. Now that Ben knows everything, and with everything I've learnt over the past twenty-four hours, I understand that sometimes there's nothing to be gained from ever withholding the truth. Not from those who can guess its hiding there, deep down, just by looking at you.

And so I tell her. All of it. From Ben to Ruth via Brad and Chrissy and drinking and all of the lies that have been built on that one mistake. About an act of betrayal that spiralled out of control. That had a wilful mind of its own.

My mother only exclaims once. When I recount that Emily, her grand-daughter, saw me consoling Ruth. Then she almost drops her tea-cup, the spoon clattering where she'd rested it on the saucer. Aware what Emily must have surmised and how unchecked, bad things have a way of continuing to spread.

I bring her up to date with the news that Ally has left me.

"She wants to try counselling though," I say, trying to give her hope. She addresses the suggestion briskly.

"It's not a bad idea. Harriet in Grays did it with her Daniel. Best thing they ever did."

The grandfather clock chimes the hour. The ring reverberating from the hallway. Regular, regular, regular.

"How can I go back mum?"

"Don't be so stupid. Of course you can go back. Honesty is all you've needed."

"It wasn't all a lie," I say, anxious now that my mother doesn't think that all of my adult life, with Ally and Ben, has been unhappy. Ben too. I want her to realise that we've still been close, we've still got a lot of time that was untainted, despite the disease eating away at all of our lives – threatening now to consume my daughter with its pervasive guilt.

"I know that," she says, softly.

The light has faded from the room, her profile now in silhouette. She lets out a gentle yawn and I can see her age. It's been a lot to take in. She needs time to adjust and I accept that.

I hope that Ben and I will regain what we have. In fact here at my mother's house I can begin to sense him again, that perhaps he is out there. It's weak, but the signal is coming through – stronger up here in rural Norfolk than in London. You can't get a mobile phone reception though. And predictably, for this I'm glad.

"You'll stay here for a few days, but then you should go back," she continues. "Your family need you." She doesn't say if she means my Ally or my Ben. But I know she means my wife.

It's twilight outside; the foliage of her garden losing its definition. She levers herself out of her chair and crosses the room, drawing the curtains and switching on a large ivory lamp that made the journey up from Essex with her.

"You know" she's saying, matter of factly "all this has been caused by guilt. That's all. You made a mistake Martin. A long time ago. But you're not solely to blame for what happened after – to Ben, or Ruth or anything else. Sometimes life has a habit of getting in the way all on its own."

"Thanks," I say, it's nice to hear, even if I don't believe it.

"I haven't finished," she says, her voice taking on a stern tone I haven't heard for years. "Most of all though – Ally's not to blame. She never has been."

*

Funerals are supposed to be conducted in the rain; memorial services likewise – not like this, not in bright Mediterranean sunshine. Yet here we are – a small band of ex-pats gathering in 37 degree heat to say a collective goodbye. The church is white, recent construction, beautifully landscaped grounds. It reminds me, bizarrely, of the end of *The Graduate*. A sensation helped by the whispered presence of hushed Americans – including parents – amongst us. A congregation paying their respects here, before the body, for that is all it is, returns to home soil.

How did we, I mean how did I, get here?

The physical details first. I was sitting up, past midnight, with my mother playing gin rummy, the old card game from our childhood. I had a winning hand when the call came.

From Ben.

"I've just spoken to Ally," he'd said. And then the world stopped turning.

"Suicide." I completed his sentence for him.

I'd repeated the term, unable to believe what I was hearing, causing my mother to come and stand by me. Holding her heart – her relief palpable when I said it wasn't the kids or Ally or Ben.

I got him off the line and dialled my wife immediately. Ally was crying. Saying she was incredibly sad. Of course she was I said. It's understandable. It's a horrible nightmare.

I was surprisingly calm. Life gets in the way sometimes I said, before telling her I was coming home. The first time I'd ever called Israel that.

Within 25 minutes I'd booked a flight for the morning and my brother was on his way up to Norfolk.

"It's the quickest way Martin," Ben said. "There's no trains. I'll get you and we'll drive straight back down to Gatwick." He was remaining in control. I didn't protest.

Just over two hours later he'd arrived. My mother meeting him out on the moonlit gravel as if this was a normal Sunday afternoon visit. They embraced for ages. I could tell my mother noticed the difference in him and didn't want to let go. Like a weight had been lifted from her shoulders.

He came into the warm amber glow of the hallway and we stood there awkwardly, facing each other. My mother disappearing to make us a flask of coffee and clucking loudly, to fill the silence, about Ben resting for half an hour.

"You alright?" he says, his finger tracing the side panel of the grandfather clock.

"Yeah," I say. "You."

"Yeah."

And then we're driving to the airport at top speed in his Clio. Both concentrating on our goal. I just wanted to get to there. Thinking of what pushes someone to suicide and, oddly, both of us knowing. Understanding and feeling immensely sad that sometimes, in this instance, people give up.

"I can come with you," Ben kept saying. "I know how it feels."

And I said it was fine. I didn't need him. Not for this.

The lights of the motorway strobed through the sun-roof; sending intermittent flashes throughout the darkened interior of the car. Regular regular, regular.

I kept mulling over the information that Ally had given me, about how the body was discovered. It all seemed so unreal. Like it couldn't possibly have happened. Going for a morning jog and never coming back.

After 90 minutes of the journey had passed so slowly – Ben said. "I believe you Martin."

"About what?"

"That you're sorry."

"Oh," I said.

"You should have told me though. Back then. Back then when it happened."

"Ruth begged me not to. Each time, every time I wanted to – even that afternoon, at mum and dads – always – she always told me not to. That it was better this way."

"I mean when it first happened. The very next morning after you… and her… All of this would have been different."

"I know," is all I can give him.

"We're twins," he says, in response. "We don't do that."

And he's right. I broke the rules.

"I know."

"It's such a nightmare. It's like something out of some poxy soap-opera. How we can get so unlucky. You couldn't make it up. You'd have to be twisted."

He's almost, but not quite, irreverent here.

And I agree.

I think about turning on the radio, but decide against it.

"I can't imagine, can't guess what it all did to her," he says.

"I know."

"But that's just it – I can't guess. All I know is she's gone. And that's the same thing I've known from the beginning."

"I did tell the police Ben. About that night. I tried to do the right thing."

"It doesn't matter anymore."

Suddenly it all seems such was a long time ago, but I finish anyway.

"But they didn't understand. I didn't even understand." And then my words are rushing out. "I didn't know about the… baby, Ben… you have to believe me."

He pulls into the services for some petrol. I offer to pay but he declines. I watch him walk over to the cashier window. He turns back and asks if I want anything. He doesn't actually say anything, but I know that's what he's asking. I shake my head but am glad we're still reading each other.

London edges nearer, the distance finally falling away.

I decide to tell Ben the last thing. About that day just before Ruth went.

Me finding my sister-in-law crying, looking at herself in disgust. Perhaps for a one-night stand that had ruined everything that was pure.

"It's not necessary," he says but he doesn't stop me, staring resolutely at the road before us.

Then I tell him about Emily seeing. This alone registers.

"Poor Emily." He turns to look at me in the passenger seat, shaking his head sadly.

"Give her my love when you see her."

"I will," I promise.

As we pull into the airport, Ben looks over once last time.

"I'd wait with you mate. For the flight," he says. "But I've got a big meeting. I can't miss it."

"Oh god – your new job. Well done. Mum's been telling me. I can't believe it."

"Thanks," he says. "You understand, right? That I have to go?"

"Of course. It's not long now," I say, checking my watch. The flight's in six hours.

I jump out of his car, with a final wave back.

"Be good," I say, to my younger brother, meaning the meeting.

"I would," is all he says, before driving off. I don't know what this means. But I've accepted now that that's fine. That's how it's should be sometimes.

I boarded the empty flight, closed my eyes and didn't open them until we landed. I didn't sleep. I just couldn't face seeing.

At arrivals, the relentless humidity hit me as though I'd never been away. The soldiers with guns at each door. The palm trees outside the glass of the terminal windows. The clear unbroken sky above. I think of Ben in his meeting, in London – being listened to and enjoying it – and I feel so proud.

I think of Ruth. Momentarily. My stomach remains calm. It has to, Ally is waiting. I find a trolley for my bags and wheel through customs. And there she is, my wife.

She meets me with the determination with which she's facing everything at the moment. Squarely in the face. We embrace, holding each other for dear life – her breaths coming fast into my shoulder, her body fragile, at odds with her defiance, as if it might collapse.

"The kids?" I said, holding her out in front of me.

"With Mrs Gelt downstairs. But Emily's being great. Playing with Max. They're staying overnight. I didn't know what you wanted to do, where you wanted to go."

I don't respond. I'm not sure either.

We begin to walk through the terminal to the car, Ally striding two paces in front.

"Who found the body?" I asked, as we strapped ourselves in.

"A neighbour. There was a note too."

"What did it say?"

"Not much. Saying that the truth too much to bear. Oh Martin, it's so awful. All of it."

I want to say it'll be okay but I know it won't. I know the next few days and weeks are going to be painful. I think about one friend dead and another friend devastated. I think about how this could have happened. Whether I could have done anything more? I think about how much more devastation will be unleashed – and how I can try and stop it.

"Let's go home first," I say. Everything else can follow.

We get to the apartment. It's dark and cool. The air-conditioning throbbing unseen giving total relief. Ally switches on lights and moves into the kitchen, pouring me some water. I'm comforted to see the maintenance people have repaired the ceiling – up where the crack had been. There's only the faintest trace of its existence above us.

"I'll sleep on the sofa," is what I say.

Ally starts crying.

"You don't have to. I don't want you to. I want you to be with me."

"We'll both sleep on the sofa then," I decide, attempting to get a smile from my exhausted wife.

And we did. With no sheet to cover us. And in the morning I tell her everything. All of it.

Less than a week later we are here, at the church for the memorial. Our role is important. We have to look after the bereaved. It's not about just us. I know that now.

I'm standing to the side while Ally has her arm around Brad. And I don't mind – the guy is a wreck. He's not coping. He's sedated on something.

And Chrissy, my friend, my lifeline from all those years ago in Aberdeen onwards, is lying over there in a coffin. Dead. Unable to go on. The line stops here.

I'm standing to the side because I'm about to speak. I'm trembling but this is something I really want to do.

"I knew Chrissy would be good fun from the moment I saw her. I'd started my first job and remember how nervous I felt, walking into the office looking for a mate. I'll be honest in saying I never expected my mate to be a loud redhead from Manchester. I'll be honest and say I never expected her to be a girl. But Chris, from day one, was my mate. My friend. She was kind, honest and true – the most loyal person in the world. She was also extremely loud and sometimes annoying. She also never knew when to shut up. But she was Chrissy and I wouldn't have changed her for anything.

"Perhaps the best thing I could say about Chrissy is that we'll miss her so much. And if that's the case well then I guess she made her mark on the world. She'll never be forgotten. And that's what Chris would have wanted."

The rest of the service was a blur. Brad didn't speak and I don't blame him. Unfortunately I could see he had decided blame should be evident in every element of his being. I knew that no matter what I said, I couldn't take it away from him. Not yet.

But Chrissy didn't kill herself because her husband was gay, or because their marriage was a lie. I understand now, as I hope Brad will in time, that she killed herself for her own reasons. Just as I know that Ruth was ultimately her own person. Like we all are. Looking back I can see that Chrissy was unhappy. I even that think perhaps that she always knew about Brad – they were all just further layers to hide behind. Maybe she 'used' him too. I think of her now, on yet another cigarette-break, anxiously biting her fingernails, juggling her keys, whatever. I think of times when she'd come and visit Ally and I and the kids. It upsets me to think that I could have looked beyond myself and perhaps seen her a bit more clearly. But sometimes we can't. It's just the way it is.

I think of her probably calling me early in the morning – perhaps while Brad got their gear ready for a 6am run, that she didn't want to do. Picking up the phone and dialling a friend – and then not speaking – only breathing silence into space. And I had no way of hearing her either.

After saying a goodbye to Brad and his family, we leave and make our way home. I'm sure I'll never see him again. He's finished his book though. I ask him to send me a copy and he promises, saying he'll sign it for all of us. And that it's dedicated to Chrissy – his biggest fan.

Emily is withdrawn, taking my hand as we leave and squeezing it tightly. I notice that she's got her ears pierced while I've been away.

Ally takes my other arm.

*

I sit with my daughter in her room. This is long overdue. I see the posters all around, I see a girl slowly turning into a woman. I toy absently with the switch on her lava-lamp, nervous about quite how to begin.

"I just wanted to check you were alright," I say.

"I'm fine, Dad. Honest," she says. Not only are her ears pierced, she's dressed all in black. This wasn't for the memorial service, Ally told me that she's been doing this for a while now. Somehow it hadn't registered before. She's also wearing heavy make-up, dark mascara on her eyes.

"It's okay to be upset." I whisper.

"I know," she replies. "And I liked Chrissy, she was nice. I understand what's happened."

How did my daughter get so old? I'm worried about where her innocence has gone. I'm torn between blaming MTV and myself – wondering how much of my life has seeped into hers and how much she has been affected by my inability to cope. To be a man.

I hold her and I sense that though she's acting like she's letting me do this – for my benefit – she needs it as well. She's just a child.

"Emily," I say, "I want to talk to you about something."

"Dad. It's not a problem. I get it."

"Not about that. About Ruth."

"Oh," she says.

"About that time you saw me holding her. Do you remember?" Maybe she's forgotten, maybe she thought it was no big deal. Maybe all of her resentment is just because I have been a crap father?

"I don't want to talk about this Dad. Please," she's sighing.

"It's not what you think it is."

She gets up and shuts the door. I should have let Ally do this with me. She'd said it would be better if Emily heard us both say it. But I couldn't face that.

"Ruth was upset," I continue. "I don't know why. I don't know if we'll ever know why she went. But that day, the day you saw us – I wasn't doing anything wrong. She wasn't either. You have to believe me."

I've never spoken about Ruth's departure to my daughter. Certainly never discussed her seeing us that day. And I should have – it would have stopped my shame – stopped me pushing my kids away and resenting their unannounced presence.

Any talk of Ruth was Ally's role. In the months after her disappearance, Ben was my priority.

I can see Emily thinking about something. I move to wipe away an eyelash that has fallen and she allows me. Her skin is so young, so soft.

"Look, Ruth is okay," my daughter says, after an age.

"We just have to accept that she'll probably never come home," I continue, not listening to her. A recurring theme.

"I know what you're trying to do," she says, inflecting her voice at the end of the sentence like all of her friends, reminding me how impressionable she is.

"You understand then?" I persevere, "you understand that Ruth might be… .like Chrissy?"

"She's not dead," Emily announces gravely, but still looking like the child she is. Her tone is forceful yet light – as if she were only insisting that Father Christmas really lives in Lapland.

"No Emily. We don't know what happened to her," I say slowly. Wanting her to comprehend.

"Don't speak to me like a child Dad. That's always your problem. I am not a kid."

"I know you're not darling."

"She wrote to me."

"Who? Chrissy?" Fuck – I don't want my daughter dealing with her own personalised suicide note from my friend.

"No," she says, quietly. "Ruth."

I don't hear anything else. I'm not even sure if I'm still breathing.

"When?" emerges finally. Solitarily. The urge to vomit once more paramount and I wonder how much more of all this I can take. But there's also, somewhere in this revelation, the euphoria of hope – of a chance to make things good. Not even necessarily good, but maybe just the release that a knowledge of life… continuing might bring. For my brother and, yes, for me.

On this day of mourning. Hope emerges.

"What do you mean ? Wrote to you? When?" I'm asking all this hushed; anxious not to scare away the optimism before its had to time to take hold.

"A while ago." Emily's not refuting or backtracking or saying she was kidding. My heart is pounding. I flirt briefly with the idea that she's making it up – seeking attention.

"Just before we left England. When I didn't want to come here.

When you were making me leave my friends. I knew I'd hate it… but you weren't listening. Always worried about Ben. Never listening to what I say. And then Ruth wrote to me. Just to me."

"Emily. Are you being honest?" I can't believe what I'm hearing.

"Yeah, are you?" she fires back offended – like the 13-year-old she is, but also sounding just like Ally.

"You're not making it up I mean. For attention?"

"Dad!" She retorts, angrily.

And then she's rummaging under her bed, amongst her secrets. Retrieving a simple box, wrapped in silver ribbon – the words PRIVATE tippexed all over it.

And from within she's handing me a letter.

She's giving me hope. It's dated some seven months ago.

Dearest Emily,

This is a very hard thing to do. I first of all want to ask that you don't tell anyone that I've written. It wouldn't be fair. Too much time has passed. You have to understand that I had no choice.

I just feel so bad that you saw me that day in my bedroom. I only want to apologise and make you promise me that you won't think you had anything to do with my leaving. You are in no way to blame.

I won't write again but I'll think of you always.

Love
Ruth

*

It takes me a while to work out what would be the right thing to do. I find it strange that my number one concern is for my daughter. To reassure her that she has done the right thing in giving me the letter.

That she has done the right thing.

13: LAURA

It's the opening night of the London Film Festival, the gala black-tie screening – I've got two tickets through my new found status as features editor. They were biked over to the office earlier today, along with invites to a party at Somerset House afterwards. Work's been hectic for the past few days – I haven't had time to think about anything else. Pressures of a new job.

My mother's called a few times. She hasn't pushed it or anything. Hasn't demanded anything at all. She has, however, been sharing a few details, unasked, about my twin. And I haven't necessarily told her not to bother.

I could get quite used to this. It's the full works – the red carpet , the A-List stars, the minor royalty and the phalanx of photographers. Laura looks stunning – she's wearing this Versace dress in bright red. She's worn her hair up like Grace Kelly and, I know I'm biased here, but she outshines all the women in the room. As we enter the Odeon on Leicester Square, the screams of the crowd behind swell as the film's leading man arrives.

It's all a bit of a disappointment inside the cinema, the magic outside makes you momentarily believe you've stepped back into some golden age of Hollywood glamour; yet when you step in you see just another cinema, popcorn stand, cardboard promotional cut-outs and a well-worn carpet – albeit crammed with tuxedoed celebrities, it's a faintly surreal experience.

Laura kisses me lightly on the cheek as we make our way to our seats, squeezing my hand gently when a very recognisable film-star asks us if we know where the bathroom is. We're in the middle of a row and it takes forever to sit down, with everyone so dressed up, people take an eternity to move and let you through.

As the lights go down and the film begins, I think of Martin. Wondering how things are going in Israel. Wondering how the service went yesterday. I sent flowers – I knew Chrissy – she was Martin's friend and, well, I'm Martin's twin brother. When nothing else adds up, that's what counts.

*

The drive to Cheltenham is fairly uneventful. Maggie plays Bruce Springsteen's Nebraska, maybe her taste is mellowing, and we loudly berate the drivers of other vehicles for no good reason. I've been covering a lot of miles lately – making the most of my time.

Maggie's, sorry Ruth's, parents, are waiting in their conservatory for us. Both dressed up as if we might be turning up with cameras or something. Cecil and Stella. Panama hat and blazer; twinset and pearls. Maggie looking like mutant offspring in this polite company.

Cecil offers me a drink which only ever means Spirit and mixer. Stella tut-tuts over Maggie's hair, her dress-sense, skin, nails and diction – especially when Maggie mentions that she's off to use the "lav".

Maggie responded, "Could have been worse ma, normally I say bog."

Stella looks as though she might have swooned.

On walking through into the conservatory I passed a shrine to my wife. Several photos tastefully arranged – wedding, graduation, school and baby. None of them were Ruth's favourite shots. I remember her mother saying "that's not the point", when the photos were criticised by Ruth. Back when they lived separately, in albums, alone. Long ago, before they were congregated together – now positively catholic in their collective dramatic import.

Cecil hands me a drink and I inhale deeply, steadying myself for what I am about to share. What Maggie already knows. What Martin told me over the phone breathlessly. Cecil however has something he wants to say first – I can't believe that the thought of news, any news, which surely our joint presence must indicate can take second-place next to whatever he has to offer. He takes off his hat and clears his throat. Stella eyes him nervously.

"We um… saw the magazine," Cecil opens.

Eh?

"The magazine. Your magazine. What's it called?" he barks.

"*Mentor*," Maggie and Stella chime in unison.

"That's the one. Must say…" He's gone bright red. "Didn't much appreciate your tone. About Ruth."

Shit. It didn't even occur to me to think about what they must have thought. The line "we fucked on a train once" leaps into view. Shit, shit, shit. In all my ruthlessness about my wife, I discarded the truth that she was their daughter. Everything affects everyone.

"I'm sorry. Genuinely sorry," I say.

"Yes. Well. It's done now," Stella says, remarkably. "I just wish you'd used a better photo, I have much nicer shots."

"Sorry," I say. "To you as well Maggie."

"It's alright," she says, and I'm appalled to pick up that she too might not have appreciated my piece.

I suddenly realise I have been cut a lot of slack and feel more humble and respectful towards Ruth's family than her years of pleading that I just try and get on with them could ever have achieved.

"Now," Cecil says "This news?", motioning for us all to finally sit down. He remains standing.

That there is news to impart isn't such a new thing – we've had a couple of occasions where sightings have been too detailed to ignore but now they have understood that I have something worthwhile to share. That they're not screaming at me to tell them just indicates how inured they've had to become. How desensitised Ruth's departure has made them.

"Ruth wrote a letter," I say. "Seven months ago. To our niece."

It's like a bomb has gone off the room. Stella is up and then down again. Maggie is shouting at them to be quiet. Cecil is holding his heart and his hat.

"What do you mean? Cecil, what does he mean?" Stella pleads.

"I mean that Ruth is alive and out there. At least she was seven months ago." I can't believe the calmness with which I'm relaying all this.

"How do you know? What did it say? I don't understand?" Stella gabbles.

"Emily has only just shown Martin. Ruth made her promise not to. It's definitely from Ruth, she's signed it, Martin described the signature, and it just is – I know it."

Maggie cuts in, "It said that she was sorry for leaving, that's all and that Emily wasn't to blame herself."

Maggie and I had agreed that this was all we'd share of the letter's content. The rest was unnecessary.

Cecil faints.

*

When I was a child I knew my place in the world. At Martin's side. I found it hard to grow up, to make my way on my own. The fact that we went to the same university says much.

There comes a time when you have to stop.

I'm glad he's returned. That all of them, his family, are back here where they belong.

Everything in its right place.

Jason has emailed from New York – keeps saying I should think about taking a job over there. Telling me that I'd love it and I am seriously considering it. He's got an amazing place on Sixth Avenue.

And the fact that I'm seriously thinking about it, makes it easy to understand that I'm fine when Laura tells me she might want to take it easy. To slow things down.

It's nothing to do with anything else, just two people treading carefully. Trying to do the right thing.

I'm only thinking about it. But that's what I'm best at.

My calendar, a present from my brother, tells me that today will be three years. An anniversary. A reminder that doesn't sharpen the pain and doesn't scream to be heard.

EPILOGUE

Leaves litter the path to my home. It's October which means its autumn – season of mists and mellow fruitfulness. The season in which Ruth and I were married.

I love October, it's my favourite month of the year, it reminds me of football; of darkening skies in late afternoon. Of the dying of the light.

I struggle for my keys, not remembering where I've concealed them, conducting an exhaustive search of every possible hiding place, patting my pockets one by one. If I lost them I'd be screwed, it's never happened though – they're always somewhere. I always find them eventually.

Only then do I notice that she's sitting on the step. Waiting for me out here rather than letting herself in like usual. She smiles weakly and for a moment I wonder what's wrong. What's happened?

When it hits me, a rush of noiseless energy assaulting my senses; louder than the car back firing in the distance and brighter than the three o'clock sun shining aggressively against the glass of the front door.

It hits me just before I hear her say.

"Hello Ben."

And I want to respond only the words don't come out. They aren't even half-formed – my heart has stopped in my chest, my lungs have given out. I can't even breathe.

I don't touch her, I don't even look at her eyes. Instead I find my keys immediately and open the door, letting her go in first, watching my wife remember to take off shoes that are entirely clean. I follow behind, trailing wet leaves and everything else I've walked through.

ACKNOWLEDGEMENTS

Lyrics to Coldplay's 'The Scientist' reprinted with kind permission by BMG Music publishing. With thanks to Estelle Wilkinson. Various lyrics from Radiohead's 'Kid A' reprinted with kind permission by EMI Music Publishing. With thanks to Julie Calland & Bryce Edge.

Thanks to my parents: Demetrios 'Yianni' Demetriou, who I know is somewhere smiling proudly and forever more. Thanks Pops. Geraldine Demetriou who taught to me read, encouraged me to write and as a result has had to put up with all of my words over the years.

Thanks to Emma and Paul Tait; Greg, Tara and Jonathan Demetriou.

Thanks to the following people who read, listened and offered direct advice: Cemal Arman, Seema Barker, Bill Borrows, James Bradbury, Mel Brodie, Sam Copeland, Richard Collins, George Conyne, Jo Cosbert, Mark Dunn, Jane Edyvean, David Gould, Ali Gunn, Paul Fletcher, Liz Hoggard, Helen & Keith Ivens, Stephen Jenkins, Ruth Katz, Jason Lamont, Trish McGregor, Mike McNally, Claire Steele & Will Misata, Christian Moody, Julie Pease, Ian Simons and Alex Weston. Thanks also to Mike McMahon, Tony Wadsworth and all my friends. I owe you so much.

Liza Butler who was there from the beginning. Lucy Nichols who was there at the end.

Rachel Stones – thanks for Brightness Falls and the beer. Couldn't have done it without them – or you!

Paul Lenz and Andrew Chapman at **reverb**. Thank you for taking me on when I was worried this story might disappear completely.

And finally, and most importantly, thanks to Sarah Ivens. Who is in every word and on every page. Nobody said it was easy, but she made it all seem effortless. And made it all worthwhile. She believes in this book, and me, more than anyone else.

www.stefandemetriou.com

Kishkindha,
by Robert Turner

ISBN 1 905315 05 8 • £9.99

There's a bizarre atmosphere, growing beguilingly familiar, amongst these rocks which bathe still hot in the moonlight. There's such a weighty sense of gravity that even the sky seems to rest lower. The ghost world keeps its silence, and the law of the jungle shadows the superstitious children working in the fields. The carved gods have been deserted by history, but the mischievous monkey spirit lives on.

In June 1991 Robert Turner arrived at the ruined South Indian city of Vijayanagar, which lies in a bend of the Pampa river known as Kishkindha, the mythical Kingdom of the Monkeys and Bears from the epic love story of the Ramayana. His visa had expired, he had very little money and good reason not to return to the UK. He ended up staying for four years.

Robert has superbly documented the landscape, history, myths and people he encountered there, from the local Raja and a mad sadhu to a vengeful hunchback and a capable country harlot. Interspersed with the tales of Kishkindha is the astonishing story of how Bob came to be in India in the first place after a colonial childhood that lead to a youth detention centre; a three-year sentence in a Lebanese jail; and many other adventures besides, across Britain, Pakistan and China among others.

Intriguing, compelling and surprising – you will not read another travel biography like it. In Robert's own words, "To err is human – and to get away with it is fun."

C M TAYLOR

cloven

reverb

Cloven,
by C M Taylor

ISBN 1 905315 04 X • £7.99

It was cow country, and beyond the garden stretched the fields, each stocked with a herd of creamy bovines, mooing and lowing and ruminating away between twice-daily milkings. Udders swayed from the cows' bellies, pendulous and unwieldy as over-stuffed shopping bags. And who can say, perhaps it was this early exposure to cows which was to prompt the years of cattle madness that the unusual Buxton brothers were to experience?

Paul Buxton had always hated the countryside, believing that cash machines and night clubs were innately superior to nature, and that a cow was just a failed horse with tits. So it was disturbing, to say the least, when his sinisterly vague boss made Paul a weird and lucrative offer to research human reactions to BSE.

To the merciless amusement of his veggie brother Chris, Paul begins to research the millennia-long human relationship with cattle. And aided by his beautiful anthropologist sidekick Jane, Paul reluctantly enters a world of rodeos, cave art, holy cows, hunting, domestication and, finally, foot and mouth...

Why are cows in fields and people in offices? Why isn't it the other way round? How come humans fed cows sheep brains? Why did we kill millions of cattle during the foot and mouth outbreak? Why do we buy Friesian-patterned knick-knacks? If you've wondered about any of these questions, Cloven is the book for you.

It's gripping. It's unusual. It's moojestic.

Light, by C M Taylor

ISBN 1 905315 00 7 • £6.99

"Before you know it you've read 100 pages in a sitting. Extremely compelling and delightfully unusual, it would make a wonderful bitter sweet film in the vein of Withnail and I."
Time Out

Light is a poignant story of love, loss and English summer. After the death of his father and the loss of his job, Ben's reacquaintance with a childhood friend pitches him into a glamorous life among a wealthy, rural set.

In a milieu of infidelity, corruption, cash and unrequited love, the narrator inadvertently achieves artistic fame. Through revelations of long-buried love, mix-ups and malice, an accident occurs and an innocent party takes the blame.

Inspired by the art and media world of the late 1990s, when an idealistic and transient glamour created millions for the elite of the new economy, Light has a strong claim to being the English *Great Gatsby*.

The Group, by Ravinder Chahal

ISBN 1 905315 01 5 • £7.99

The Group is a book that talks to people who are successful in an economy that they do not believe in. Aimed at those for whom it is fashionable to be knowing, it tells the story of Khaled, an arch-cynic for whom everyone is a fake or a loser. The only problem is Khaled has done very little himself that he can be proud of and is beginning to bore himself.

Faced with the prospect of drifting through life in obscurity he dreams up a satirical scam to reveal how easily people can be manipulated, and how thin their dreams and aspirations are. But rather than escape The Group, his scam only serves to show how hollow he has become, and how he needs to completely recalibrate his own life.

The Group is a dark and wickedly funny book about people who tell lies and people who believe them.

www.readreverb.com

Grief,
by Ed Lark

ISBN 1 905315 02 3 • £7.99

Juan has left his past behind for the seductions of the city and the Crystal Realm – a world of ever-changing fashion, daily plastic surgery, mind-altering drugs and bizarre sex.

He effortlessly climbs the social hierarchy, gaining money and power until the city thrills to his every move – but something is missing from his life, which perhaps only the picaresque troupe of troubadours who are trekking across the desert in search of him can explain.

Grief is both a unique dystopia, or perhaps an interpretation of the present, and a remarkable psychological fantasy, disturbing, witty and moving by turns.

Who Needs Cleopatra?
by Steve Redwood

ISBN 1 905315 03 1 • £7.99

"Where does a circle begin? When I met Bertie and we made our first journey through time? Or was the real beginning when I stumbled across that astonishing 16th-century notebook in an Italian farmhouse? But then long before that, in a way, I had provided a wife for Cain, and so allowed myself to exist in the first place..."

What made the Mona Lisa smile? How did Rasputin die? And what *really* happened at Roswell?

Despite the best attempts of the sardonic narrator 'N' and his hapless sidekick Bertie to solve historical mysteries, all they find is constant danger – and the sneaking suspicion that they have inadvertently created the very events they are supposed to be investigating.

This richly comic novel does for history what Jasper fforde did forliterature – join Leonardo da Vinci, Boadicea, Cain (and Mabel) on arollercoaster quest through time where the future (and the present) of humanity itself is at stake.

aboutreverb

reverb isn't a traditional publisher. We think of it as a cross between an online community of readers and an independent record label. Why a record label? Because we publish books that have broadly the same 'sound' – contemporary literary fiction with an edge. This edge can be humorous, it can be thought-provoking, but it is something that makes the book stand out from the crowd. We hope that if a reader has enjoyed one **reverb** book then they will enjoy the others.

reverbforwriters

Unless they are already successful, writers tend to get treated pretty badly. At **reverb** we are trying to do things a little differently:

- **Give new writers a chance** – we are committed to publishing 50 new writers over the next five years.
- **Fast but meaningful feedback** – most traditional publishers will leave unsolicited manuscripts on the slush pile for months; many are rejected unread. At **reverb** we promise to give an answer to any writer who follows our submission guidelines *within seven days*.
- **Working in partnership** – we view writers as talent to be nurtured rather than a commodity to be exploited. We pay high royalty rates and the lion's share of rights sales always goes to the writer.
- **Developing new talent** – we have dedicated a section of the readreverb.com site to information and support for new writers.

reverbforreaders

Without readers there would be no publishing, so we have set up **reverb**review to create interest in all writers, not just the ones that we publish. **reverb**review is a regular email newsletter that contains book reviews, author profiles, news and a regular column by **reverb** author Ed Lark. **readreverb.com** contains an archive of **reverb**reviews, features and news stories from the world of books.

reverbforretailers

Independent booksellers are the backbone of the trade, but more often than not get treated like the poor cousin by large publishing companies. At **reverb** we are dedicated to supporting the independent trade through offers, marketing material and author visits.

Printed in the United Kingdom by
Lightning Source UK Ltd., Milton Keynes
139067UK00001B/20/A